THE RULES

Becca Jameson

Copyright © 2015 Becca Jameson

Cover Art by Aimee Benson

All rights reserved.

ISBN-13: 978-1505785715

Acknowledgements

I'd like to thank my beta reader extraordinaire, Kellie, for all her help in the middle of the night making sure I didn't have any plot holes in this story. I'd also like to thank my editor, Aimee, for all her hard work fixing my craziness under a very tight deadline. Love you both!

Part One: His Rules

Chapter One

His gaze penetrated me from behind the moment I settled myself on the bar stool. It defied all logic, but I was very familiar with Mr. Alexander's stare by now.

He was approaching me, another bit of unreasonable knowledge I couldn't explain.

Cheyenne and Meagan sat across from me at the high-top table, completely oblivious to my plight. They'd arrived before me and were already sipping cosmos.

What I wanted to do was flee the room, get back in my car, drive away from Sky, and pretend I'd never decided to darken the doors of this particular exclusive nightclub. But that wasn't what I did. First of all, I was frozen to the seat, my legs crossed and squeezed together, my hands in fists in my lap. Stressful situations always drew that stance from me.

Second of all, I was intrigued.

I watched Cheyenne's face closely, knowing she would be the first to spot my boss and thus inform me through her facial expressions when he was on me. Meagan wasn't as quick. And she was currently chatting away about some crazy woman from her office who made her life miserable. I'd heard all that before. In fact, Meagan had been complaining to Cheyenne before I arrived. She hadn't paused except to nod at me and continue, flipping her long brown curls over her shoulder. Her deep brown eyes danced with the excitement of her tale.

Cheyenne leaned on one hand, her elbow poised on top of the table in a way that looked incredibly sexy. Cheyenne always looked sexy. She would look sexy wearing a trash bag after a week camping without shower facilities. That was Cheyenne. Her gorgeous blonde bob always looked like she'd had it cut and styled that very afternoon. And tonight was no exception. Everyone I knew envied her natural blonde hair and the gorgeous blue eyes that went with it. Meagan and I had met her the first week of college, and the three of us had been inseparable since then.

I kept my gaze on Cheyenne and didn't miss the second her brows lifted and her eyes drifted above my head. She didn't move a single other muscle, not even her face, just as I'd expected. What surprised me was Meagan. Suddenly, she stopped midsentence. That couldn't be good.

I felt Mr. Alexander's gaze. I even sensed his approach. I expected him to be coincidentally heading past my table to the bar, but there was the obscure possibility he would recognize me and greet me. I only had moments to consider the options.

What I did *not* expect was for a warm hand to land on my lower back—right in the oval cutout of my dress exposing my bare skin.

I sucked in a deep breath and tried not to flinch at this

unexpected contact.

And then my boss of two weeks leaned into my space. His lips were only inches from my ear when he spoke. "Ms. Kensington."

I turned toward him, completely flustered, only to find his attention now focused on my best friends.

"Ladies." He nodded at them. "Would you mind if I borrowed Amelia for a moment?"

At this, Cheyenne sat up straight, her chin lifting off her palm, her eyes wide, her mouth open. It took her about two seconds to recover, and then she smiled demurely. "Of course."

Meagan didn't say a word. For a woman who could talk as much as my oldest friend in the world, the second a sexy man approached, she was always at a loss. Her face flushed instantly, and she blinked at my boss as though he were a ghost.

They would both be taken aback since no one had called me Amelia in years. Only my mother ever called me Amelia. I'd gone by Amy since childhood.

Mr. Alexander was the sexiest man I'd ever seen in my life. I'd noticed him the second I started working in his building and hadn't been able to keep from shaking in his presence in the two weeks I'd been there. Every single time I was near him, I developed a twitch in every muscle. It was absurd and ridiculous, and totally unavoidable.

The man was my idea of perfection—tall, thick dark brown hair in need of a trim, a build that indicated he took care of his body, and green eyes that bore into a person and made them forget to blink. This was the first time I'd been out with my posse since starting my new job at Alexander Technologies, so I had yet to inform them of my boss's attributes. That conversation had been on the docket for tonight. But judging from the reactions of my friends, I'd say I wasn't alone in my assessment that Mr. Alexander was indeed perfection on legs.

Mr. Alexander wrapped his fingers around my biceps and helped me down from the stool.

It took me a moment, considering my legs were crossed and wouldn't cooperate in untangling themselves, for me to stand. Plus, at five foot four, getting down from that stool required a small hop.

He didn't release me, however, and I managed not to fall on my face. When I glanced at him, I swear a small smirk spread across his lips as though my plight were somewhat humorous and he was well aware of my height disadvantage.

He was patient as he guided me away from my friends toward the bar. He didn't release my arm until we arrived, and then only to let his hand slide down to the small of my back once again. He managed to somehow control everything about my stance with that simple touch.

Granted, his fingers were long and spread wide, so they did keep me angled in the direction he desired as well as seeming to have the ability to actually hold me up should my knees decide to stop functioning properly. The tips of his fingers reached inside the open oval of my dress, both higher up my back and dipping low toward my ass. Another inch and his touch would be inappropriate.

Hell, another inch and I might have fainted, forget inappropriate.

Mr. Cade Alexander, owner and CEO of Alexander Technologies, had his hand splayed on my bare skin as he leaned against the bar with his opposite hip to speak to the bartender. What the hell universe had I fallen into?

My gaze landed on the bartender. For one thing, I would have melted into the floor if I looked at my boss and absorbed what I knew he was wearing from the glance I'd taken on the way toward the bar, the glance I'd snuck in when not worrying about tripping over my high heels and finding myself flat on the floor.

I'd only seen his profile, enough to make any woman's panties wet. He wore a suit. The man was always in a suit. I'd considered that he might even sleep in suits. His tie wasn't loosened like the majority of the evening's patrons. Although, on second thought, I was sure he'd changed clothes since I'd seen him earlier in the day. He'd been in a gray suit at work, a matching gray tie and shirt. Now, he was wearing a black suit with a shocking maroon shirt and black tie. I'd never seen him in anything colored as boldly as that shirt.

In addition, I would bet my last dollar he'd shaved again this evening. His face, at least what I'd seen of it, was perfectly smooth as it always was. So unless he was one of those rare individuals born with very little, slow-growing facial hair, I had to assume he'd re-groomed before arriving at Sky.

The bartender was very attentive. He was tall and slim with dark messy hair. His gaze never left Mr. Alexander's, and he leaned close to him, nodding as my boss gave him instructions I couldn't make out over the din of the bar.

My face flushed when the bartender glanced in my direction, but he was unaffected. Finally, he righted himself, turned around, and headed to grab several items from behind the bar. Strange. At no point did my boss ask me what I might like to drink, and yet he'd apparently ordered me something. In moments, the bartender returned and handed Mr. Alexander a glass of white wine and a tumbler of something dark on the rocks.

My boss turned toward me, nodded at his arm, and lifted his elbow out from his body. He held a drink in each hand and wanted me to grab his bicep for our next journey.

I knew the moment the redness climbing up my cheeks increased. It wasn't difficult to discern.

Mr. Alexander's arm was solid. He didn't have an ounce of fat anywhere on his body, and I gripped him as tightly as I dared while he escorted me to a table in the corner of the room.

I had the sense to twist my neck and glance back at my friends, both of whom were staring wide-eyed, their mouths hanging open, a giggle primed on the corners.

This was so far from funny, I would have slapped them both if I'd been closer.

The corner was darker than the rest of the bar, and Mr. Alexander set both glasses on the high round table before assisting me onto a stool. And by assist, I mean he held my hand at first, lifting it while I teetered forward, and then when that didn't seem good enough, fast enough, or perhaps likely enough to occur without incident, he set his hands on my waist and settled me on the stool, not releasing me until he was satisfied I was in no danger of falling.

I still hadn't spoken a word as he pulled the other stool around until it was almost too close to mine and set his own fine ass on it, his legs so much longer than mine it took no effort at all. He hooked one shoe over the bottom rung and then smiled at me before nodding toward the glass of wine and leaning it my direction. "It's a 2007 Carneros Chardonnay. I think you'll like it. I prefer the '08 myself, but they're out of it."

My eyebrows rose. He thought I would like it? How did my boss have any idea what I drank, let alone what kind of wine? As the case would have it, I knew very little about wine, nothing about Chardonnay, and not an inkling about whatever brand he'd rattled off. I did, however, presume it cost a fortune.

I was young. Twenty-four. So far, the only wine I had consumed had come from very cheap packaging, usually with a screw top instead of a cork. I'd been in college for the last six years on a thin budget. Wine hadn't factored into my monthly expenses at any point. And since I'd graduated, I'd delegated every resource to securing a better apartment and scrounging around for appropriate clothing to wear to an office full of the most stylish people I'd ever seen in my life. Again, not wine.

I picked up the glass and took a sip. To do otherwise would have been rude.

My eyes closed as I swallowed. He wasn't kidding. It was crisp, fruity, and delicious. I took another sip before I set the glass down. After all, if I was going to face off with the hunk of testosterone on the seat next to me, I needed fortification.

"Is there something you needed, sir?" I finally asked.

Mr. Alexander had done nothing but stare at me, and his brow was furrowed. I was close to developing a complex. Finally, he grabbed his tie with one hand and adjusted it. He took a sip of his own drink and then faced me, clearing his throat. "I've never seen you here before." He completely ignored my question.

I shook my head. "I've never been here before." This was true. At no point in my short adult life had I had the funds, the clothes, or the wherewithal to enter Sky. But the girls and I were celebrating. We had all received our master's degrees in the last few weeks and landed jobs. As a way to mark this monumental event in our lives, we'd decided to act like grownups tonight, splurge beyond our means, and hit the hottest nightclub in the Atlanta area.

I had not for one second expected to encounter anyone I knew. After all, my friend set included other young twenty-somethings also fresh out of school with a pile of debts and an emergent need for better housing and clothing. Such was the way with recent graduates.

A renewed flush crept up my neck and cheeks when it occurred to me that perhaps my boss didn't like the idea of my being in this club.

His gaze flicked to my lips, and I realized I was chewing on the lower one, a bad habit I'd always had when I was nervous. I'd never been as nervous as I was at that moment, and my lip was in imminent danger of bleeding if I didn't stop.

Mr. Alexander must have thought the same thing because he lifted his hand to my face, gently set his fingers on my cheek, and tugged my lip out from between my teeth with his thumb.

I nearly died.

"How old are you?" he asked.

"Um...Twenty-four, sir."

If I wasn't mistaken, he might have flinched subtly as he lowered his hand to his lap. "You just started working for my company a few weeks ago." He stated what I already knew. The question was, why did he know that? Alexander Technologies was large. There were several hundred employees on seven floors. Mr. Alexander certainly wouldn't have any input into the hiring of a lowly assistant from the first floor.

"Yes, sir."

"You're Moriah's new assistant, right? On the first floor?" He asked this question as if it were the lowest job known to man, and I was in turn barely worth the scum on the bottom of the sexiest, most expensive heels I owned—fifty dollars from the outlet mall. The most outrageous thing I currently wore.

"Yes, sir," I mumbled. Why on earth was he talking to me? Why had he cornered me in the room and bought me an expensive glass of wine? And why were my thighs jiggling, my panties soaking, and my nipples worrying me with their abrasion against my best bra?

"Where were you working before you started in my office?"

I swallowed the lump in my throat. "Nowhere. I was in school."

His eyes widened from their narrowed perusal to a shocked

look. He took another sip from his tumbler and angled himself to face me more directly. "You just now finished your degree?"

Part of me wanted to slap him for his audacity. But he did have a point. It was downright ludicrous that I'd taken this job in his building. "Well, no, sir. I just now finished my master's."

"Your master's? Are you shitting me? In what?"

"Business administration, sir." I cringed, worrying he might fire me for my stupidity alone. I'd wanted to work for his company for as long as I could remember. I didn't care what position I started at as long as I had a foot in the door. Alexander Technologies was a difficult nut to crack. I nearly had to beg the woman who interviewed me to give me a chance even though she was very leery, seeing as I was completely overqualified for the job. If I had to climb that company ladder from cleaning toilets, I would have. As it was, I felt fortunate to have landed a job that didn't require me to wear plastic gloves and carry a mop.

Mr. Alexander stared at me hard and long until I squirmed in my seat. "Sit still, Ms. Kensington. I'm not going to bite." He didn't smile, though his tone was less intimidating than it had been.

I tried to stop wiggling. I crossed my legs and anchored myself with one heel on the center rung of the stool.

Mr. Alexander peeked under the table and then chuckled. He rolled his eyes. For what reason, I had no idea. There was no way I was going to ask. I didn't even have the ability of speech at all. The man was confusing as all hell. And again I wondered what I was doing in this weird alternate universe I'd fallen into.

"Drink your wine, Amelia. It's better before it gets too

warm." He held my gaze while he lifted his tumbler to his lips again.

My hand shook as I reached for the glass, but I did as he instructed. It really was delicious, and in another world I might have enjoyed it. But not in this realm, the one where my freakishly rich, sexy, thirty-something boss had cornered me in a swanky night club and begun to question me.

"So let me get this straight. You just finished your MBA, and you took a job with my company at the bottom rung of the ladder."

"Yes, sir. I hope that's not a problem, sir. I work hard. I'm not afraid to pay my dues. You won't be disappointed."

"Oh, don't get me wrong. I'm far from disappointed. I'm just confused." He lifted his brows. Every time he did that, his hair covered his eyebrows. He seriously could have gone to a hairdresser about a week ago, but I was secretly glad he hadn't. It was the only part of him that was soft. Even though it was neatly combed, it was naturally wavy, and the way it curled slightly at his ears and around his neck made him almost human.

The nervy man stared at me some more while he enjoyed another sip of his drink. His gaze roamed over my face and down to my chest before returning to meet my eyes again.

A horrible thought occurred to me. Perhaps he considered Sky his stomping ground. It could be that he didn't appreciate his employees frequenting the location. "Would you like me to leave the bar, sir?"

He furrowed his brow once again. "Why would I want that?"

"Well, I thought maybe you preferred the anonymity of being here where people don't know you, or at least a place you can unwind without running into people that work for you."

He chuckled. "The anonymity? Ms. Kensington, I haven't enjoyed a moment of anonymity in ten years. And my employees are free to frequent whatever establishment they can afford."

Ouch. That stung. He suspected I couldn't afford Sky. And generally speaking, he would be right. I tucked my bottom lip between my teeth again and my hands under my thighs. It was the only way I could keep from shaking.

"Don't do that."

Do what? Seriously? Was this man telling me what I could and couldn't do with my own lip? I knew he was because his gaze was once again riveted to my mouth. I let go of my bruised flesh and pursed my lips instead. I had no idea what made me follow Mr. Alexander's instructions, and it annoyed me to high hell that every single thing he did made me clench my sex tighter. He could probably command me to strip naked and dance on top of this bar table, and I would readily comply. That's how mesmerizing he was.

"I didn't mean anything by that. I'm sorry if I offended you."

He's sorry? That was at least as shocking as his previous statement.

"So, you intend to work your way from the ground up at my company. Is that it, Ms. Kensington?"

"Yes, sir." That had been the plan. Until tonight. Suddenly I wasn't the least bit sure how I would ever go back in the building. It was much easier when he didn't know who I was or pay any attention to me. That's the way normal everyday women prefer unbelievably sexy men to remain—slightly out of reach. Speaking to them face-to-face makes us regular folk stammer and make fools of ourselves.

"You can't be making enough money to pay rent."

"I'm not, sir. But I'll prove myself fast." I had confidence, and I wasn't about to hide it from him.

"How were your grades?"

"Straight A's, sir. I work hard."

He found this amusing apparently. He chuckled again and shook his head. I liked it when he smiled. He had one dimple on each cheek that softened his face and made him look younger than he probably was. "Okay, then. I'll let you get back to your friends. Enjoy your evening, Ms. Kensington." He stood abruptly, leaving me speechless at this turn of events, and sauntered across the room in the direction he'd initially come from.

I twisted on my stool and watched his fine ass as it moved away, unable to jump down yet and certain when I did, I would fall on my face. Lucky for me, when I glanced at my friends, I found them both hopping off their own stools, grabbing their drinks in one hand and purses in the other, including my own clutch, which I'd left on the table. They hastily rushed toward me, pulled up a third stool, and settled in.

"Holy fuck," Cheyenne began. "What the hell just happened? Was that Cade Alexander?"

"It was," I muttered as I turned, finally taking my gaze off the spot where my boss had disappeared. "And I have no idea what the hell just happened."

Chapter Two

On Monday morning I arrived at work slightly more nervous than I had on my very first day two weeks ago. My encounter with the owner of the company two nights ago had me frazzled. Unfortunately, avoiding him wasn't an option. I was, as he so kindly pointed out, on the lowest rung of the ladder at this company, which essentially meant I was anybody and everybody's errand girl.

In the first two weeks, I had been everything from a file clerk to a mail carrier. I had fetched coffee for more people than I could count and typed e-mails for half the staff as well. Word had spread quickly that the new girl on the first floor wasn't simply a pretty face. It seemed I had a brain and everyone could count on me to do their bidding without fucking it up. Less hassle. I was aware of this. I prided myself on this very occurrence. It was all part of my climb-the-ladder plan.

My only real concern was becoming too valuable as a peon to promote. That idea hadn't escaped my mind.

So it wasn't a surprise when the first thing Moriah, my direct boss, asked me to do even before I shoved my purse in my desk drawer was to report to Mr. Alexander. I cringed. This was not how I intended things to go down. If the owner of the company had asked around about me, he would have heard I was a bit overqualified for the job, even without my input.

What I did *not* want was to become his personal lackey. I wanted to be taken seriously.

"Mr. Alexander?" I asked, feigning surprise, even though I wasn't altogether shocked. Pissed. But not shocked.

Moriah didn't give me more than a glance. Apparently she didn't find the request curious, at least not yet. "Yep. He needs someone to run a few errands for him, and I told him you were responsible." At that, she lifted her gaze and smiled. She even winked. "You can thank me later."

Moriah knew what my goals were. She'd been the first and last person to interview me. She wasn't stupid. I'd told her outright how badly I wanted to work for Alexander Technologies and what I was willing to humbly do to get where I wanted to be.

Moriah had also given me many challenging assignments since I'd started. I'd already wowed Margie on the fourth floor with my accounting skills on two occasions. It seemed my luck had taken a dive if I was now forced to become Mr. Alexander's errand girl.

"I'm not sure about thanking you," I mumbled.

"Why not? What better way to prove yourself than getting in the boss's face? Lucky break, girl. Show him what you're made of. I'd love to keep you down in the trenches with the rest of us. You've accomplished more work in the last two weeks than anyone we've ever hired down here, but I like you, and I want what's best for you.

And I know shuffling papers and filling coffee mugs is going to drive you stir crazy fast. So go. I promised Mr. Alexander he wouldn't be disappointed."

"What does he need me to do?" I asked, tucking my damn lip between my teeth and then immediately dropping it as though he were standing in the room right in front of me, pulling it out with his thumb. A chill ran down my spine at the memory of his warm solid fingers on my cheek, his thumb pressing on my lip.

Moriah shrugged. "No idea. Errands, he said. Could be anything from dry cleaning to taking a memo. All I know is this is the first time he's ever called me before eight a.m. and requested I send someone up to help him." She shrugged again. "Don't look a gift horse in the mouth." At that Moriah went back to typing, her gaze shifting to her computer and her fingers clicking away so fast on the keyboard I knew I was completely dismissed from this conversation.

I made my way to the elevators, my heels clicking on the ground so loudly it sounded like fireworks were going off in the lobby. Although it must have only been me who noticed this because not a single other person paid me a bit of attention. As I waited for the elevator to arrive, I clenched my hands in front of me. They were sweating. This was not my style. I had always considered myself to be extremely confident with my chin held high. And then I met Mr. Alexander.

That man turned me inside out every time I was near him. I'd been near him far too many times in the last few weeks, but after the incident on Friday, I was dreading this like a wisdom tooth removal. I hated that he made me nervous. Nobody made me nervous. I hated that he caused me to become mute, completely tongue-tied. I especially hated that he made my panties wet and my nipples hard. That was the worst part. It was foreign to me.

I stepped into the elevator, wondering if I'd made the right decision coming to work for Alexander Technologies. There were so many businesses in the immediate area that would have hired me and paid me way more money. And none of them would have sexy CEOs who awakened my sexuality in a way I had flat out denied for all of my twenty-four years.

It wasn't that I was a prude. I hadn't saved myself for some religious reason or out of some sense of puritanical resistance to norms. It simply happened. I was a bit too straight-laced in high school, causing most boys my age to steer clear of me. And then in college I got too busy to deal with men. Most of them were overgrown boys anyway. The only men who ever made me lift a brow were usually older, either new professors or the people who worked at the places I co-oped.

So, here I was at twenty-four and rather virginal. Or, totally virginal. I'd had boyfriends, but none that made me enjoy their tongue down my throat enough to let them get to third base. Frankly, I'd begun to wonder if I was actually a prude.

And then I met Mr. Alexander. I was not a prude. This was proven instantly upon stepping into his space the first time two weeks ago. I'd gotten hot, the kind of heat that started in my neck and raced down my breasts to take up residence between my legs—wobbly legs.

My second day at Alexander Technologies had brought me close to the boss for the first time. I knew he was in his thirties, but somehow I expected someone significantly older. My mind hadn't painted a picture of a young guy—fit, sexy, vibrant—the kind of man I normally drooled after from afar. I had gone to the seventh floor to drop off several envelopes. As I handed them to his secretary, Judy, he popped out of his office to speak with her.

My body froze, my gaze landing on him and taking him in from head to toe while I should have been walking back to the elevator. His dark messy hair begged someone to run their fingers through it. His green eyes, the short flash of them I'd seen, sucked me into their pools. I was screwed.

The second time I saw him, I'd been talking to Moriah in the lobby as he walked by. Again, I had no idea if he noticed me or not. He gave no indication. He simply headed out the door with another man, conversing the entire time.

Each time I encountered Mr. Alexander, I got better at breathing, but only marginally. By Friday night's encounter, I was of a new frame of mind. If that man wanted to fuck me first thing on a Monday morning, I would gladly acquiesce. At least in my imagination.

When the elevator reached the seventh floor with a ding, I jumped. No one had gotten on with me at any point, and I'd ridden to the top alone. I stepped out onto the plush carpet and headed for the desk in front of me. Judy McLaren. Since the first time I'd met her, she'd been nothing but kind, and I intended to keep that rapport with her.

She smiled at me. "Hey, Amy. Mr. Alexander left me a list of things he needs you to do. I hope you don't mind."

I was a bit taken aback. I had expected him to speak to me himself. The thought I was not going to face him this morning was both a relief and a disappointment.

Judy continued, "He was in a rush, but he said he spoke to Moriah, and she highly recommended you to handle his business today." She handed me the list, which was again not what I expected. It was in a sealed envelope.

"What sort of things does he need me to do?"

"I have no idea. The envelope was closed when he handed it to me. I wouldn't worry, though. He's a private person. That's not unusual. I hope you won't be insulted if he asked you to pick up some sort of spice from a particular grocery store forty miles from here and then alphabetize his condiments at his private residence. He's eclectic. I'd just go with it and see if you can get it all done by the end of the day. If not, no worries. There's always tomorrow. I'm sure he left a prioritized list. He always does." She rolled her eyes.

"I see."

Judy smiled. "He's a great guy. I love working for him. He doesn't get mad, even if I screw something up. He just explains it better and we move on. So don't stress. Have fun." With that, I was summarily dismissed from Judy the same way I had been dismissed from Moriah. Not one person thought it odd that the new girl was summoned by the owner to run his errands.

Clutching the envelope, I backed up a few steps and then turned around so I wouldn't fall on my ass. I wore my second favorite pair of heels that morning, silver sling backs that made my legs longer and went fantastic with my silver jewelry. Probably not the best choice for running errands.

As I stepped back into the elevator, I smoothed my free hand down my skirt. It was a pale peach color made of silky material that didn't reach my knees. I thought it skirted the edge of appropriate for the office, sexy but professional. The blouse I'd chosen to go with it was white. I knew it hinted at what lay beneath just from being white and silky. I'd carefully worn a skin-colored bra that wouldn't stand out as obvious beneath the blouse. Some other lacy bra might have been overkill, but this one felt perfect to me.

I carefully tore the envelope open as I rode back down to the first floor. If Mr. Alexander wasn't in the office, there was no telling where he was. He could be out of town for all I knew. He traveled often. I prayed I wouldn't be required to go to his home. That would be more than I could bear. Seeing his personal belongings would do nothing to help me sleep at night. Getting a more thorough lungful of his scent wouldn't help out, either.

I almost groaned out loud when I opened the trifold paper and Mr. Alexander's credit card fell out also. The note was addressed to me personally, which meant he knew I would be the person fulfilling today's tasks. That wasn't a good sign. I straightened my spine as I absorbed that fact. I could do this.

After all, I was a woman. I'd been to stores before. I knew where to buy things and more or less what aisles contained what in a grocery store. It was a little shocking to see this list of personal errands, even though Judy had warned me of the possibility. Still, weird. Didn't the man have a personal assistant to do these things for him?

I stopped by my office on the first floor to get my purse and let Moriah know I was leaving the building.

She lifted her gaze toward me and smiled. "No problem. If you don't make it back here, I'll know why. I'll see you tomorrow."

She'll know why?

Moriah narrowed her eyes. She pointed at the paper clutched in my hand. "The list? I assume it's long. I've never known Mr. Alexander to leave a short list." She giggled.

"Oh, right." I held up the page as though seeing it for the first time. "Yes. Guess I'll manage."

"I'm sure you'll do fine. See you later." Moriah waved as I turned to go.

My legs were shaky as I headed for my car. It was eight fifteen in the morning. I hadn't intended to leave the office until five, and here I was right back where I'd started the day. Downtown Atlanta traffic was awful. As expected. I probably would have been better off waiting a while to begin. But then again, I wanted to make sure I finished everything as quickly as possible. This weird turn of events had left me unnerved. I'd meant to climb the corporate ladder. I had not meant to run the personal errands of the CEO in order to do so.

It took me forty-five minutes to get to Buckhead and locate the store indicated first on the list. It took me another half an hour to collect his very specific requests. And I did all this with a knot in my stomach while I imagined the woman who was going to reap the rewards of this scavenger hunt later tonight. Because there could be no mistake. Mr. Alexander had a date.

I actually grew a bit perturbed as I went through the motions of collecting two bottles of expensive wine that cost over seventy-five dollars apiece, prawns, some sort of specific premade potatoes from the deli that made my stomach grumble when I saw them, and a brand of fresh green beans in a steaming bag.

The man even included a dessert, which he'd ordered from the bakery section beforehand. I didn't pay attention to what was in that box, afraid I might be tempted to open it and eat the entire thing myself if it was anything near as fancy as the rest of the meal.

If it was chocolate, there was no way I would have been able to resist.

The store provided me with a Styrofoam cooler and ice to keep everything cold. After carefully stashing the groceries in my car, making sure there was no way the wine bottles would break against each other during the drive, I moved on to the next task.

What the hell? My eyeballs jumped out of my head as I squeezed the paper in my hand, wrinkling it as though it were a wad of trash already.

I had intentionally not read ahead on this list. It seemed prudent to make my way down it from top to bottom. And now I glared at the second task, seething.

The man actually wanted me to pick up a parcel from a lingerie store. Was he fucking kidding? The shop was high-end. I knew the name. I even knew where it was located. I'd driven by it before, drooling at the items in the window. I had not, however, been inside. Nor could I ever hope to enter the place in my lifetime. If I ever chanced to earn enough money to purchase something from Justine's, it would be much better used to feed a third world country instead of draping across my skin.

I swung out onto the street, headed in that direction, my hands now gripping the steering wheel and my heart racing. The audacity of this asshole.

My boss, I reminded myself. A man who knew perfectly well who was running these errands. I wanted to kill Moriah for recommending me. An ironic turn of events since Moriah thought she'd done me a favor. Perhaps he sent random people to do his bidding every day of the week, but today I'd drawn the short straw. Any normal person who wasn't interested in getting in their boss's pants to see if his cock matched the rest of him in virility would probably not be as flustered as I currently was.

However, I wasn't any normal person. I was me. And I did not want to know what sort of lingerie Mr. Alexander bought his girlfriend. Not tonight. Not ever.

Ugh. My parents had raised me better than this. My mother would die if she knew I was running around Atlanta picking up lingerie for my boss. This was not why I went to college. I had more self-respect than this.

I worked my way through the streets of Buckhead until I arrived at Justine's. It was almost ten. I shook as I stepped into the store, feeling like Julia Roberts in *Pretty Woman*. If the ladies working in this shop didn't see right through me and know I was a fraud, it would be a miracle. In order to avoid being tossed out on my ass before I did my instructed duties, I held my head high and marched straight to the woman behind the desk, totally ignoring the cute girl working among the racks.

"Hi. I'm here to pick up a package for Mr. Cade Alexander."

The woman lit up. "Oh. Right." She smiled warmly, making me relax marginally and helping me drop the fear of being thrown out like yesterday's dirty laundry. "Give me one second. I'll grab that for you."

She winked as she turned to head to the back room. I lifted my brows and glanced around the shop. I felt awkward, as though gazing at all this finery would somehow taint the abundant silks and laces.

"Here we are," the sweet, sugary voice spoke again at my back.

I twisted to find her holding up a fancy bag, lifting it over the counter. "I hope it fits. Mr. Alexander has good taste." She looked me up and down quickly. "Should be perfect." She winked again and then giggled as she set the bag on the counter. "Have a fun night."

I almost died. I couldn't even lift my hand to take the bag. It took me several seconds to register what she thought. And when I finally caught on, my mouth dried and my throat swelled. Not to mention the renewed flush racing up my neck. I'd flushed so many times in the last few days, I was going to get a permanent rash.

"Oh, I—" I cut myself off. There wasn't one thing I could say to make this situation any better. In fact, I was certain I could only make it worse. The best option was to take the bag, smile, and get the hell out of Justine's. If that woman thought the lingerie in that bag was for me, so be it. Arguing with her would only make me look stranger, and I was already riding high on the idiot train for the day. No help needed.

I have no idea how I made it out the door and back to my car, but I sat there trying to catch my breath for several minutes before I lifted the list again. Perhaps it would have been better to peruse the entire thing first. But at this point, I was afraid for my heart and my sanity. One item at a time. That would be my motto. No matter how mortifying it got, I would live through this day.

No one ever needed to know how I spent this particular Monday. Not Cheyenne. Not Meagan. Not Moriah or Judy. I would take this humiliation to the grave with me.

The bag from Justine's sat on the passenger seat mocking me. I hadn't looked inside, but I did know it wouldn't do any good. I could tell by the shape that whatever was in the bag was also inside a box. Thank the Lord.

The trip to the florist for white roses wasn't bad. Everyone liked to put flowers on their table, right? And the next stop I chose to put out of my head. By then I was becoming numb. Who cared if Mr. Alexander wanted to buy his girlfriend jewelry? I walked right up to the counter, told the clerk I was there to pick up a package for Mr. Alexander and then waited, not glancing around at a single item in the store this time.

I was way over my head with this one. If I thought the lingerie store was out of my league, it was nothing compared to Smith and Klein's. This was beyond my dreams.

Thank God the employee didn't hand me a ring-sized box. If he had, I might have exploded. By then I was beginning to think Mr. Alexander was not only having a simple date that night, but that he was about to propose. Who sent a peon from the first floor to pick up everything needed for a proposal? Not any man in his right mind. And certainly not a man I would ever consider dating.

If I suspected my boyfriend had sent another woman to buy things for me, I would kick his ass to the curb before he opened the door. My respect for Mr. Cade Alexander had shifted from high, to medium, and then low in the last few hours.

As I slid back into the car, I would find a new low—something much lower than the jewelry was about to rock my world.

The last thing on the list.

I'd noticed there was only one more line. I'd been elated to think this was coming to an end. Ecstatic. The thought of grabbing a late lunch and going back to the office had actually made entering that jeweler almost palatable. And then I could drag myself through the rest of the day and get the hell out of Alexander Technologies.

I intended to go straight home, lick my wounds, and open the want ads. There were plenty of other companies hiring people with my qualifications. I didn't need to endure this sort of abuse. It was demeaning and made my blood boil. And if it happened this one time, it would happen again. Hell, I'd even done the job well. That meant my boss was likely to decide I was his fucking go-to girl, and before I knew it, I'd find myself standing inside his bedroom holding his robe and slippers while he fucked his girlfriend.

Nope. This was not the life I signed on for. And I wouldn't lower myself to this level.

Except I'd made a commitment, and I also wasn't the type of girl to turn tail and run when the going got tough. So, I had to finish this day, see this through. Today and the next two weeks in my notice when I gave it.

But this last item on the list was so far-fetched, I hesitated.

Gifts by Julia.

I was familiar with Gifts by Julia. Everyone was. The name of the store was simply a pseudonym for a high-end sex shop.

Again, I was not a prude, but I also hadn't ever been to a sex shop. Nor had I intended to enter one anytime soon. So, the thought of making this last stop made my stomach roil.

Cade Alexander was an asshole. It was confirmed. Whoever he was fucking later tonight in a luxurious candlelit dinner with roses and jewelry and lingerie and prawns and goddamn fuzzy handcuffs could have him. I had lost my interest.

I turned my mind off as I made my way through the outskirts of Atlanta until I arrived at my last destination. I held my head high, although glancing around to make sure no one saw me, and entered the store without allowing myself to consider the implications of this stop. I prayed like the other places I'd been, the clerk would hand me a bag and I would never be remotely privy to the contents.

Luckily there were no patrons at that particular hour, and the man working the counter looked up and did the hard work for me. "You here for Mr. Alexander?"

Shocked and relieved, I nodded my head.

The guy handed me a black bag with a grin. He waggled his eyebrows in a way that did not even make me flinch anymore. And when he said "enjoy" as I left the store without uttering a word, I did so without vomiting all over his floor.

Yep. Cade Alexander was a dick. A complete asshole of the largest variety known to man. And now I had to drive to his house and deposit the implements of his sickness inside. I would have to go to his kitchen and put several items in the refrigerator.

I would not, however, breathe while I was inside. I no longer had any interest in knowing what his world smelled like. I would not allow myself to glance anywhere unnecessary. My absurd infatuation with Cade Alexander was over. Done. Complete.

And after I gave my two weeks' notice, I would also kindly turn down any requests that came from the seventh floor. If Moriah or any other employee wanted to utilize my services for the next two weeks, so be it. But I wasn't about to face the owner of Alexander Technologies ever again.

Chapter Three

What I did not expect, because it never once the entire day occurred to me, was that Cade Alexander would actually be in his home when I arrived. Even more to my shock was the fact that he was the one to open the front door when I knocked.

I wasn't at all sure who was going to be home at the time, but I assumed some cleaning crew or a maid or a butler or even a dog sitter. Not Mr. Alexander himself.

I stood frozen in my spot outside his front door, my hands laden with his sick gatherings. The fact that I'd insisted on making only one trip from the car was utter insanity. And now I stood burdened by his wares, speechless and angrier than I could ever remember feeling.

Mr. Alexander smiled. The asshole actually smiled. "You're fast. I thought it would take you longer than that."

I made no comment while he flung the door wider, grabbed the cooler from my arms and several bags that were hanging from my fingers, and turned to pad deeper into his home. "Come on. Follow me."

I found my voice fast. "If it's all the same to you, sir, I'll just leave these things and be going. I still have a lot to do at work this afternoon." I leaned into his house far enough to deposit the rest of the assortment of bags, careful to set the ones containing seventy-five dollar bottles of wine gently on the hardwood floor.

"Amelia," he called from deeper inside. "Follow me."

I righted myself and peered into the house at nothing but his large foyer. Mr. Alexander had disappeared. The last thing I wanted to do was enter his home. Now or ever.

But he'd practically commanded it. And now he was nowhere to argue with. If I simply shut the front door and left, I would probably piss him off.

Not that I could possibly piss him off more than he had me.

I waited, hoping he would return when I didn't heed his demand to *follow*.

Burned into my brain was a new image now, one I could have done without. Cade Alexander owned more than suits and ties. The man had opened the door in low-hanging faded jeans that hugged his hips perfectly. Designer jeans, but still. And the T-shirt he had on was also made for his body. It pulled tight across his pecs in a way that made my mouth water in spite of my anger. Damn him. And the worst part—his feet were bare.

No. That wasn't the worst part. The worst part was his fucking awesome ass I'd had the privilege of watching as he left me in the doorway.

Now I did moan. Still he didn't return. He also didn't yell for me to heel like a puppy again. Something about the way he'd invited me in hadn't sounded at all like an invitation. It had sounded like a demand.

I suspected he was used to getting his way. Naturally, otherwise why would I have spent the morning and half the afternoon running all over town buying things for his lazy ass because he was too uppity to purchase his own shit for his own fucking girlfriend?

Taking a deep breath, and having absolutely no alternative option, I reluctantly entered Mr. Alexander's home and shut the door. I picked up the bags I'd carefully set on the floor and proceeded across the foyer.

When I stepped into my boss's kitchen, my heart stopped.

I was no gourmet cook, not even close. I hadn't had enough time in the last six years to properly learn to cook much of anything. But I did appreciate a fine kitchen when I saw one.

This kitchen was on a level I'd never contemplated except perhaps on reality TV shows. Everything was stainless steel or white. The granite counter was a swirl of grays and whites. Pots and pans hung from the ceiling above a center island at least eight people could comfortably sit around for a meal. The floor was gray tile that bumped up against white cabinets.

Hell, the refrigerator was so wide, I wondered what one man needed with that much cold space.

When Mr. Alexander opened the door to set the groceries inside, I discovered one man didn't actually need that space at all. It was almost empty. Which answered my next question. Did my boss live here alone? Apparently so because I couldn't think of anyone I knew who would live off as little food as he had in stock.

If I hadn't arrived with the fixings for tonight's dinner, I assume any occupant would have starved or ordered pizza.

"Sit, Amelia," Mr. Alexander ordered, nodding at one of the many stools spaced around three sides of his island. I stared at the chairs, wondering how they would ever be spaced so perfectly again after I moved one of them. The house looked more like a display home than someplace a person lived.

"I really should get back to the office, sir." *Please let me leave.*

I was concerned about breathing any more of his air than strictly necessary. Images burned themselves in my head faster than my brain could take the snapshots. Forget the kitchen and its accoutrements. The man currently bent over with his head inside the fridge was enough to keep me up late for more nights than I wanted to ponder.

His ass was the finest I'd ever drooled over. I shook my head to erase the image and looked away. I was supposed to be pissed.

Hell, I *was* pissed. Freakishly annoyed with this man.

When he turned around, I had not yet moved from my spot. In fact, I still held the final bags I'd carried into the kitchen.

Mr. Alexander smirked and shook his head. "You don't follow directions very well, do you, baby?"

Baby? Did he just call me *baby?*

I was not his baby. I was nobody's baby. I never intended to be.

Then why did the term of endearment and the way it slid off his tongue make me squeeze my legs together and bite my lower lip?

"Sir, I—"

"Amelia, you've been running around all day." He nodded at the bags as he approached me. When he took the rest of the items from my hands, his fingers grazed over mine, sending sparks up my arms and making me rub the goose bumps from them the moment he stood back. "Sit on the stool. I'll get you a drink."

A drink? Was he crazy? There was no way I wanted a drink of anything. That would take too long. I wanted to get out of there.

He turned to set the rest of the bags on the kitchen table several yards away and then lifted his gaze back to me. "*Sit.*" His command was more forceful that time.

Without hesitating, I stepped on the bottom rung of the center stool and lifted myself onto the seat. I squeezed my legs together and gripped my hands in my lap. What the hell was I supposed to do now?

A deep inhale was a mistake on my part. After my calculated effort to not inhale Mr. Alexander's space, I had lost the battle. I already had an inkling what he smelled like from Friday night. Now I was inundated with his scent and that of his squeaky clean house.

Lemon was the predominant clean smell. Mr. Alexander's personal choice in aftershave covered it, lingering in the air in a way that tantalized me. I hated being aware of that fact.

"Did you have any problems?"

"Excuse me, sir?"

"With the list. Did you encounter any difficulties?"

"Oh. No, sir. I found everything." I found way too many

things. *I now know way more about you than I ever wanted to know about another human being, especially my boss.*

I gritted my teeth to keep from screaming at him that he was an evil asshole. I wanted to get this done and get out of there.

Mr. Alexander headed for the kitchen cabinets and grabbed two wineglasses from the rack hanging beneath them. Totally awesome. I wanted to own something like that one day.

"You're pissed." His mouth curved up in a grin on one side.

"Uh..." *Shit.*

"Why are you mad, Amelia?"

"I'm not mad, sir," I lied. Well, actually it wasn't really a lie. The word to describe how I felt was significantly stronger than mad.

He chuckled. "Really now?"

"No. I'm fine. I really should get back to the office." I swiveled in my seat, but my boss pinned me with his gaze.

"Stay still. Stop fidgeting."

Fidgeting? In a second I was going to start launching things at him. Forget fidgeting. He was on my last freaking nerve.

I froze, however, mesmerized by the way he operated the most fantastic corkscrew I'd ever seen. Every muscle in his bare arm engaged in the activity as he leaned into the bottle, and then with a sharp pop, he had the wine open. Before I could utter another syllable, he'd poured two glasses and handed me one. "It's not as good as the Corton Charlemagne you picked up for me, but it's still a fine wine." He took a sip.

I stared at him and then at the glass sitting on the island in front of me. He'd lost his mind if he thought I was going to have a drink with him. It was barely two in the afternoon, and I hadn't eaten anything since breakfast.

Mr. Alexander leaned both elbows on the counter and met my stunned gaze. He smiled and held that look for what seemed like an eternity. "My God. You're precious."

My eyes widened and my mouth opened, but nothing came out.

He pointed at the wine in front of me. "Take a drink, baby. I'm hoping it will keep you from grabbing one of my pans and whacking me over the head." He pointed above my head.

Why hadn't I thought of that fine idea? I might need to take him up on the idea if he didn't let me go soon. "Sir, with all due respect, it's two in the afternoon. I have more work to do, and I have to drive. I can't drink wine before doing either."

"You're done for the day. I'll have Arthur take you home when the time comes."

Who the hell was Arthur? I shook my head as though dazed.

Mr. Alexander lifted his glass again and hummed as he took his next sip. He swirled the clear liquid around in the glass and then held it up to the light. "Delicious."

The side of the island my boss stood on had a stove top with six burners. Mr. Alexander grabbed a pan from over his head next and set it on the stove, flipping on the burner and adjusting it to whatever temperature he had in mind. "Wine, Amelia. You're going to need it." He raised his brows and nodded at my untouched glass.

"Mr. Alexander—"

"Cade," he interrupted. "Or I like the way you call me Sir." Now he grinned. "But Mr. Alexander is reserved for the boardroom or my father."

He liked the way I called him *sir*? What the hell?

"Okay, sir, I really should be going."

"Amelia." He looked exasperated. "Stop arguing with me for one minute and relax. Drink your wine while I cook."

Cook? Every single thing he said added to my shock and discomfort.

"You must be starving. As fast as you got here, I'm sure you never paused to eat lunch. I haven't eaten either. We'll eat together."

I needed to put an end to this. And fast.

Before I could utter another word, I noticed what my boss was doing, and my heart nearly beat out of my chest.

Cade Alexander pulled the potato dish from the refrigerator and stuck it in the oven. He set the prawns on the island next to the stove and plopped the bag of green beans in the microwave.

He was about to feed me the very meal I just picked up from the store? I'd dropped into a bad episode of the Twilight Zone.

"Sir. What are you doing?"

He grinned his huge smile at me, his dimples making my knees weak. "Making lunch." He tipped his head to one side as though what he was doing was the most obvious thing in the world.

"But I assumed this food was for later, sir." I could have smacked myself in the forehead for saying that, but it slipped out unbidden. I also grabbed the glass of wine from the counter and took a long drink from it. Who the fuck cared if I was driving? At that point I needed the fortification more than anything. I had no idea why I was still in my boss's kitchen letting him bully me into doing his bidding, which right now included sitting still and drinking wine.

I could do that.

I didn't want to do it.

But I could do it.

"But you're hungry now, right?" He lifted one eyebrow and smirked again. It seemed as though most of what he said included some sort of inside joke I was not privy to.

"I am, but—"

"Then now is when we shall eat."

Confusion over my assumed idea that he had a woman coming over tonight clouded my brain. Perhaps I was wrong about that. Either that or he was feeding me her food and she was going to go very hungry later. Because he sure didn't have another meal planned for the near future out of that fridge.

Nothing managed to explain the other items I picked up along the way, however.

As though Mr. Alexander read my mind, he dumped the prawns into the oil in his now-heated pan and turned to the kitchen table. A moment later he returned with the roses. He set them on the island, removed the packaging, and then arranged them all in a vase he pulled from below the counter. He turned to add water, giving me another excellent view of his ass and the wide expanse of his back, which flexed and pulled with every movement, until my mouth went dry and I had to look away to avoid drying my eyes out.

Mr. Alexander set the vase on the table and removed other items from the bags. He made a pile of them on the end of the table. The small long box from the jeweler, the larger square box from the lingerie store, and the medium-sized black wrapped box from the fetish shop. That last one made me shiver and look away.

I had for sure slipped into another dimension.

"You're nervous," he noted when he returned to flip the prawns. The entire kitchen smelled heavenly.

"Uh, yeah."

"And pissed."

I didn't comment.

"Good. I'd be worried if you weren't nervous and pissed."

He knew I was nervous and pissed, had made me that way on purpose, *and* he was pleased? All I had were more questions. No answers. I picked up the glass of wine and took another drink. Not a sip. A drink.

My crazy-as-hell boss didn't speak again while he finished cooking. He topped off my wineglass with another of his famous smirks at one point, and he flipped prawns, checked potatoes, and grabbed the bag of steamed green beans from the microwave to rest on the counter.

I couldn't grasp a single thought. Nothing in my brain worked. So I watched. Apparently that was what he wanted anyway. So I did it.

When all three parts of the meal were ready, Mr. Alexander filled two plates and set them on the table. He returned to the island to grab our glasses and carried them over. And then he returned for me. If he hadn't, there was a good chance I would have simply continued to stare at him in confusion.

The next thing I knew, I was whisked into the air and stood on my feet. He had a way of collecting me with his hands at my waist and manhandling me into whatever position he wanted. Now was no exception.

Taking my arm, he led me to the table, pulled out a chair, and pressed gently on my shoulders to encourage me to sit. He scooted the seat in and dropped a cloth napkin in my lap. "Eat," he commanded as he took his own seat on the adjacent side of the table.

Damn him and his demands. And damn this meal for smelling so good that I couldn't deny him the satisfaction of eating his food. I was starving, and it looked like a meal I would have ordered at the finest five-star restaurant in town.

If only I could get my fingers to work properly and my throat to swallow.

Mr. Alexander took a bite. "Mmm. That's good. You should try it." He smiled at me again.

I swear my panties dampened. I had been fighting my physical reaction to him since I'd arrived, but sitting this close to him, having consumed most of a glass of wine on an empty stomach, there was no way to avoid his allure. It was magnetic. I wondered if all women felt it or just me.

When my boss of two weeks twisted in my direction, speared a prawn off my plate with his fork and held it up to my lips, I almost melted. I opened my mouth and let the delicate meat slide inside. And then I moaned. It was as good as it smelled and looked. The spices were perfect. The buttery flavor around the outside made my mouth water for more.

Mr. Alexander turned my fork and held it out for me to take. "There. Now, eat."

I did as he said, tasting the potatoes next, knowing they would be heavenly, which they were. And then a green bean, steamed to perfection and seasoned just as well. Before I knew it, I'd enjoyed every morsel on my plate and was reaching for my wine again.

Mr. Alexander had finished already. He sat back now, leaning against the back of his chair, watching me, his wineglass in one hand, his other hand resting on the edge of the table. "You enjoy your food," he commented.

I nodded. "Thank you. You're a fantastic cook."

"Thank you, Amelia. I'm glad you finally relaxed enough to eat it."

Every time he called me Amelia, warmth crept up my body. Nobody called me Amelia. But I had neglected informing Mr. Alexander of this, essentially because he was my boss and who cared what he called me?

He leaned forward and topped off our wine again. There was very little left in the bottle, which meant I had too much. Not that I was drunk. I was perfectly fine after a full meal and what amounted to two glasses of wine. But my cheeks were warm, and I was still supposed to be angry with this asshole for sending me all over Atlanta doing his dirty work. A job he should have done for his own woman, not sent the girl from the first floor scurrying around to accomplish.

I sat up straighter and tried to school my face. *I need to get out of here*, I thought for the millionth time. What the hell was I still doing in my boss's house?

"You're still pissed." He grinned that half grin again.

I started to speak and decided against it. Honesty was usually my best policy, but it seemed prudent to leave that one alone, especially in the face of the fact that I was both pissed and horny at the same time.

My boss leaned forward and turned to face me better. "What do you know about me, Amelia?"

My eyes widened. "Uh. What do you mean?"

"I'm sure you've heard rumors. Tell me about them."

I shook my head. I wasn't one to stand around listening to gossip in general. Specific gossip about the owner of the company never. Besides, I had been living in my own dream world for the past two weeks, preferring to continue to think Mr. Alexander was the sexiest, kindest, most wonderful man alive rather than listen to the giggles of the other women in the office.

His looks and quiet efficiency, which was all I really knew

about him until Friday night, had fueled two weeks' worth of fantastic dreams. Didn't matter a bit if everything I'd daydreamed about was untrue. That was the beauty of dreams.

He lifted a brow. "Nothing?"

"I'm not into gossip, sir." I wiped my mouth on my napkin to ensure I didn't have any lingering food on my face and set it on the table next to my plate.

He stared at me. "For some reason, I believe you." And then he tipped his head back and looked at the ceiling.

I waited patiently for him to ponder the paint job.

His head dipped back down just as fast. "Do you know what a Dom is, Amelia?"

"A Dom?"

"Yes."

I gripped my thighs with both hands in my lap, seriously contemplating picking up the bottle of wine and guzzling the rest of it. I held his gaze. Or rather, he held mine.

I swallowed.

He waited.

"You mean like BDSM, sir?" I wished I could have sucked that question back into my mouth before it was all out there.

"Yes."

Shit.

He stood then, pulled my chair out, and took my arm to help me stand also. It was nearly impossible, seeing as my head swam with questions.

My boss led me to the giant leather couch several yards from the table. The room was an open plan, although I hadn't taken any time to peruse the furnishings of the living space. Moments later, I sat on the sofa with my back rigid, my legs together, and my feet planted on the ground. I wished I had the rest of that glass of wine.

Mr. Alexander sat next to me. He sat sideways, however, one leg bent at the knee so he faced me. He took my hand and held it in both of his. He stared at it for a long time with his head dipped down to examine every aspect of the back of my hand as though it were fascinating.

His touch was like an electric shock. After what he'd said to me, which made not one bit of sense in my dense mind yet, he still managed to make me crave things I'd never had the urge to pursue before.

I wished I hadn't chosen that particular white blouse that morning. And the full peach skirt seemed far too short. In fact, the way I'd plopped down on the couch had left half my ass touching the cool leather. And there was no way in hell I was going to fix it now.

Finally he squeezed my hand and lifted his gaze. "You don't know the first thing about D/s do you, Amelia?"

I shook my head. That was the truth. I'd heard of it. Who hadn't? I'd read novels occasionally in my spare time. Again, who hadn't? They were titillating. But real life? Was the man who was my boss and the owner of a Fortune 500 company trying to tell me he was a Dom? And why would I need to know this?

He exhaled slowly, and then he released my hand and stood. He paced the room. I watched him, wishing I could fall through a crack in the Earth and come out on the other side. I did get a better view of this space, though. Clearly he was a fan of white, gray, and black because the living room matched the kitchen in its decor. The leather sofa was white. The floor was tiled in the same gray as the kitchen, with an enormous, delicious plush white rug in the middle between the huge sectional and the wall of built-in cabinets. The wood was painted white, and there was a flat-screen television in the middle section with rows of DVDs and CDs surrounding it. Flanking both of those were shelves of books. A ton of books.

But I needed to concentrate on my boss right then, so I yanked my gaze back to find him staring at me, running his fingers through his hair, both hands.

I was in so much trouble.

Especially because he looked even hotter when he lowered his arms, leaving his hair a mess on top.

"Look, Amelia. I have to be honest here. I'm attracted to you."

And there it was. I didn't say a word. I seriously doubted I heard him correctly. He ignored my non-response and continued.

"I mean *really* attracted to you. I have been since the first time you walked by my office. My cock instantly got hard, as it has every time I've seen you since. And baby, my cock doesn't get hard for just anybody. It's been a long fucking time since I've felt this kind of draw to a woman."

Holy shit. I couldn't believe what he was saying. I wanted to tell him to stop, but I couldn't breathe. And besides, all kinds of unwanted things happened to my body. My belly plunged, a tight ball forming in the center that knotted a little more with each word he spoke. My sex soaked my panties, and no matter how hard I squeezed my legs together, I couldn't ease what could only be described as need.

My sexy boss continued to speak, pacing again. "I thought I could control this thing. I thought I could ignore it. I tried paying no attention to you. I then tried paying attention to you. I had hoped when I approached you on Friday night I would find out you had bad manners or a chipped tooth, or an ugly laugh or something that would turn me off."

I had trouble following his rant. I tried to keep up. I did. But holy *fuck*.

"I had to jack off twice Friday night, and still you wouldn't get out of my bed," he accused, as though I'd done something wrong. His bed? I had never been near this man's bed. Not once. This was the first time I'd been in his house for heaven's sake.

"So I had this plan." He stopped pacing, nailing me with his gaze. "I was sure if I sent you all over Atlanta this morning to collect that pile of stuff, you'd either freak the fuck out and tell me to go to hell, or not even flinch and leave without a blink."

"I considered it, sir," I managed to mutter.

"Which one?"

I stared at him.

"Which one, Amelia? Telling me to go to hell or shrugging it off?"

"Hell, sir," I whispered.

This freaking pleased him. I couldn't believe it.

He smiled, and then his face straightened, and he turned to face the wall of bookshelves, giving me another view of his fine ass in the process.

I closed my eyes, trying to straighten out my head while at the same time ignoring his butt. When I opened them, the man was facing me again. And he was closer. "Amelia."

"Yes, sir?"

He rolled his eyes. "Cade."

I nodded. No way was I going to start calling him Cade.

"Unless you plan to stick a capital letter on the way you say *Sir*, call me Cade."

I had no idea what he meant by that.

"You're the greenest twenty-four-year-old woman alive. What rock did you climb out from under?"

I was sure that was an insult, so I said nothing.

"I'm sorry." He cringed. "That was uncalled for."

Huh. The man could apologize, *and* he felt remorse. Interesting.

"Who did you think all those packages were for?" he asked, pointing at the table.

"I have no idea, sir." I let that last word slip out unbidden, beginning to feel the impact of my choice.

"I realize that. But you must have had an idea. What was

it?"

I licked my dry lips to no avail. "Your girlfriend, sir?"

"Cade."

"Cade."

"Thank you. I don't have a girlfriend, baby." His voice was softer.

"Oh."

He paused.

"What was the point of the wild goose chase then, Cade?"

God that smile. "To piss you off, baby."

"You intentionally sent me running around the city all morning to make me mad at you?" I glanced at the boxes. "Is there even anything in those boxes?" I hated that I'd asked that question the second it came out of my mouth.

"Fuck, yes. There are things in them."

"What things?" Again, what was the matter with me?

Cade cocked his head. "You aren't ready to find out yet."

"Oh." I sat up straighter. Good answer. I didn't ever want to know what was in those boxes. Did I? Suddenly the fine line blurred, and I wasn't seeing as clearly.

"Suffice to say, they're all yours. And I'll give you each of them when I feel you're ready to receive them."

That was insane seeing as I intended to resign from this job first thing tomorrow morning and never see him again.

He must have read my thoughts once more because he

approached me and sat on the coffee table this time. He didn't touch me. But he was less than a foot away when he leaned his elbows on his knees and met my gaze. "Baby, you're a submissive."

I shook my head in denial. I would know if I were submissive.

"I know you don't realize it yet, but you are. And that solidified knowledge is making me so fucking hot I can hardly contain myself."

At that point, with his body so close to mine and his breath mingling with mine and his enormous expanse of fine chest stretching his shirt out in front of me...I didn't want him to contain himself. For once I wanted to live on the edge. Be reckless. Who cared? I never had to see him again anyway. Forget two weeks' notice. I'd resign this afternoon, just after giving this god of sex my virginity. I didn't care about the repercussions. I just wanted him to touch me.

Surely he would understand why I never showed up for work again.

"Sir—"

He cut me off by leaping from the coffee table and hauling me to my feet.

I'd forgotten he asked me not to call him sir. It triggered something in him, a wild abandon. I had trouble staying on my feet as he dragged me to the center of the rug and left me standing there, facing him while he resumed sitting on the coffee table, this time on the other side, still less than a foot away, still facing me.

"I want you to do something for me. Don't think about it.

Just do it. Don't hesitate."

"Okay." No idea why I consented to that.

"Take off your panties."

I hesitated. There was no way to avoid it. His request was as foreign to me as if he'd asked me to bark like a dog or flap my arms like a bird.

"Amelia, look at me."

I met his gaze.

"Take off your panties, baby." His voice was deep, hoarse, rough, penetrating, commanding. It pulled me like a magnet.

The wetness factor went up ten notches. I found myself doing as he instructed, reaching under my skirt and carefully sliding the beige lacy panties down my thighs, past my knees, and over each foot.

I was shaking as I righted myself. And that's not all I was doing. I was also dripping with arousal. Thank God I'd chosen the safer beige bra that morning, because otherwise there would be no way to conceal my nipples from his view. I wasn't entirely sure I was succeeding anyway. And I wasn't about to look.

Cade reached out a hand.

Instinctively I knew what he wanted, and I set my wet panties in his palm. My face flushed so hot I thought I would die. I couldn't stop myself from doing as he wanted.

"Good girl." He brought them to his face, mortifying me further.

I looked away as he inhaled my scent and then stuffed my

panties in his jeans pocket. "Submissive, baby. That's what I mean."

I nodded. I wasn't sure exactly what he meant, but I was beginning to catch on.

"Do you know how fucking sexy you are?"

I shook my head. Though obviously he thought I was the bomb.

"Amazing. Stunning. I'm going to take you places you've never known existed."

I had no idea where he intended to take me, but I gathered he wasn't talking about physical locations. He certainly had the money for vacations all over the world, but my instinct was sharp enough to know that wasn't what we were discussing. Not by a long shot.

"Are you wet, baby?" His voice remained lower than earlier, soft, gentle, soothing. Addicting.

I bit my lip.

"My baby is very wet, aren't you?"

That second question, like the first, didn't require a response.

"Show me."

I straightened my spine. It was one thing to take my panties off. Whatever he wanted me to do to "show" him was not registering.

"Press your fingers into your pussy, baby. Show me how wet you are for me."

I gulped. I was afraid I would faint if I didn't breathe more often. I stood there, not moving, my hands shaking again at my sides.

"Look at me, Amelia."

I lifted my gaze to meet his.

"I'm going to be as gentle as I can with you. I know this is all new to you. But you have to trust me, baby, to handle you as I see fit. Okay?"

I nodded. Fool that I was. Slutty fool with no brain cells left to count.

"Press two fingers into your pussy and show them to me."

I couldn't stop myself from obeying his command. I lifted my skirt only as much as was needed to get my hand close to my sex, and then I stroked two fingers through my folds and brought them back out.

Cade leaned forward and grabbed my wrist before I could decide what to do next. Still sitting on the coffee table, he brought my fingers to his mouth and sucked them between his lips. He moaned around them.

But more importantly, I moaned also. I'd never seen, experienced, heard, or read about anything that sexy in my life.

As he continued to lick and suck both fingers together and then each individually, the wetness he'd mentioned increased. I was afraid it would drip down my thighs. I leaned toward him, drawn like a magnet. "Sir…"

He released my fingers, but not my wrist. "Now you've got it. If you want to call me Sir, I want it to sound the way you just said it."

I had no idea what I had done differently, but I was ridiculously glad he was pleased. I pulled on my hand, but Cade held it firmly. He hauled me closer to his body until I stood right in front of him, his knees touching mine. It was a wonder I didn't fall, considering the height of my heels and the way I was wobbling all over the rug.

Cade finally released my wrist and grabbed both my thighs with his hands. He didn't set his fingers on top of my skirt, either. No. He smoothed them up from my knees and spread them on my bare skin. "Spread your legs wider, baby."

I stepped out, presumably hypnotized by this Dom.

"Good girl." His hands trailed up and down my outer thighs. "So obedient." His thumbs dipped so close to my core, I wobbled. "Set your hands on my shoulders, baby."

I grabbed his T-shirt with both hands, glad for anything to keep me balanced. My head swam with lust, and my body had no blood supply to keep upright because all of it was currently gathered between my legs.

Cade met my gaze, tipping his head back. "Eyes on me, baby. I'm going to make you come, and I want you to stand very still while I do it. Understood?"

A new surge of arousal rushed from my lower lips, this time leaking onto my thighs unavoidably. I had no voice. There was no way I could tell Mr. Alexander, Cade, that the extent of my sexual experience with men involved romance novels and the occasional tingling between my legs that accompanied a hot scene. Orgasms weren't in my repertoire. And he was crazy if he thought he could pull off such a stunt with me standing in his living room.

In fact, my nerves were on high alert just thinking about disappointing him. He'd been so pleased up until now.

Cade grinned, perhaps knowingly, as he let his thumbs reach around my legs until they separated my lower lips.

The second the cool air in the room hit my exposed labia, my legs shook.

"Stand still, baby. Just watch my eyes and feel. Use your legs to hold you up."

Not a chance in hell.

Cade released one of my thighs and reached between my legs. He nudged them farther apart, forcing me to step out again. His fingers danced at my wet lips, and then he stroked one finger through my folds.

I moaned. I couldn't stop the noise from escaping my lips. "Cade..." My eyes rolled shut. Every nerve ending I never knew existed came to life around my sex.

"Oh, baby. That's so fucking hot. So wet for me." He dipped his finger in farther, gathering my wetness and spreading it around my lower lips.

When he dipped his finger inside me, my legs started shaking. I found myself doubting my thought that he couldn't make me come.

"God, baby. So fucking tight. I've never felt a pussy this tight." His other hand gripped my thigh firmer. I wasn't sure if it was to steady me, or to control himself. In any case, the finger thrust into my channel and back out several times, and then without warning he brought it up to circle the bundle of nerves above my sex.

"My girl has a needy little clit, doesn't she?"

God, I so hoped I wasn't supposed to respond to that.

"Eyes back on mine, baby."

I opened my eyes, embarrassed while at the same time so swept away by these intense feelings I almost didn't care. I just wanted to experience whatever I was on the edge of experiencing. Damn the consequences.

"That's my girl. Keep your eyes on mine. I want to watch your face when you come for me for the first time."

My legs shook some more. My bra felt too tight. Nothing compared to the pressure building in my belly, though.

Cade's finger flicked rapidly over my clit. He rubbed it harder, faster, with more pressure.

I was so close to the edge of sanity that I rose up on my tiptoes.

A smile grew on Cade's face as he teased me. It felt fucking fantastic. And I needed more. Cade spoke two words at the same time his thumb pressed into my clit and held steady, "Come, baby."

I did. The elusive orgasm I'd heard so much about spread through my body and out my limbs. I moaned loudly. My clit pulsed at his thumb. It seemed as though my channel gripped in a rhythmic fashion at nothing, as though pleading with me for more.

I slumped against Cade, holding his shoulders firmly as the

orgasm subsided. My breaths were more like gasps, as though there wasn't enough oxygen in the room. I was so spent, my legs stopped functioning altogether.

Cade swept me into his arms, his hand still under my bare ass, and carried me through the room and down a dimly lit hall. He kicked a door open and proceeded into another room.

I leaned my head on his shoulder, unable to hold it up any longer.

Before I knew what was happening, I found myself lying on a bed, the covers pushed back. I would have protested if I had control over my voice box. But I was too sated to care about much else. My eyes drooped.

Cade reached for the buttons on the front of my blouse and undid them, slowly working his way down. I reached to stop him, but he set my hand gently aside and gave me a firm look. I watched him while he spread the silk of my white blouse to the sides and slid my arms free. Next he rolled me to one side and popped my bra, freeing me of that also.

The exposure unnerved me completely. The way he manhandled me should have made me furious. All I knew instead was the caring way he arranged me, wondering how I was going to be able to have sex now after the way that orgasm had left me replete. I assumed I would manage somehow.

Cade unzipped my skirt, and I was able to lift my hips enough for him to slide the material down my legs and over my feet. He bent to my shoes next, unbuckling the straps and slipping them off. Oddly, I felt more naked without my shoes than any other part of my clothing. I shivered beneath his gaze as he stared down at me.

No one had ever seen me naked. No one romantically, at least. I reached to cover my breasts in a sudden rush of embarrassment.

Cade grabbed my wrists and set them at my sides. He stroked his fingertips over my nipples until I arched into his touch and moaned. And then he quickly grabbed the comforter and tugged it over my body. He shocked me by tucking me in. My entire body was on fire. Every bit of the soft bedding rubbed against my skin, bringing it to life.

Cade leaned over and gently kissed my lips. It was the first time he'd kissed me, and it didn't escape my realization that he'd made me come before doing so. "Rest, baby. I wore you out."

Rest? He wanted me to nap?

He smiled. "I know you're still needy, but I've laid a lot on your plate today. I want you to rest."

"'K." I squirmed and then moaned again.

"Amelia."

"Yes, Sir."

He smiled. "Oh, God I do so love the way you say that." His face turned more serious. "Do not touch yourself. Understood?"

I nodded. The thought hadn't entered my mind until he said it. Now it seemed like the finest idea on the planet.

"Amelia." He moaned. "You're going to be the death of me. Do. Not. Touch. Yourself. That pussy is mine. Mine alone. You will *not* orgasm without my permission. Are we clear?"

I nodded, my breath caught in my lungs, perhaps permanently. I wasn't sure I even could resume breathing.

"Good girl. Rest." He kissed my forehead this time. And then he padded from the room, shutting off the light and leaving me in near darkness.

The air whooshed from my lungs. I didn't move a muscle for fear the abrasion of the sheets would make me break his rules.

His rules.

I'm in so much trouble. That was the last thought that filtered through my mind as I let myself do as I was told. Sleep.

Chapter Four

I woke up startled and confused, bolting to a sitting position as I glanced around the dimly lit room, trying to remember where I was.

When it hit me, so did a draft of cool air against my chest. I glanced down to see my naked breasts and then moaned in humiliation.

Cade Alexander.

Ugh.

The man had not only given me my first orgasm, but he then stripped me like a child and tucked me into bed. Another quick glance around the room assured me this was not his bed in his room. At least he'd spared me that dignity.

Also, judging from the light filtering in around the blinds, it wasn't night. I wasn't sure how long I'd been asleep, minutes or hours. But I was rested.

My purse was somewhere in or around the kitchen. My phone was in my purse. And my clothes... A glance around the room provided me with nothing. I eased out of the bed, hesitating a few seconds to make sure I had my feet solidly beneath me.

This had to be a guest room. It wasn't masculine enough to be Cade's. It was too small compared to the rest of his opulence. And the furnishings were sparse.

I tiptoed around the space, hyperaware of my nudity. Not a stitch of my clothing or my shoes could be found.

Fuck.

A quick trip to the adjoining bathroom also proved futile. My clothes were nowhere in sight.

Great. Now what?

I could hear faint music coming under the door.

I decided the best course of action would be to yank the sheet from the bed and make my way to the living room toga-style in search of Cade. I prayed no one else was in the house.

As soon as I padded into the great room, I saw him. He slouched down on the couch surrounded by papers, several of which were in his hands. He had a pen stuck above his ear. His laptop sat open to a spreadsheet on the coffee table.

I took several moments to ogle him from behind. It annoyed me how sexy he was. He wore the same T-shirt as earlier, and I suspected when I stepped in front of him I would have to bite back a rush of renewed arousal when I saw his jeans.

I padded closer.

Cade had eyes in the back of his head, of course. A sixth sense. He spun his head around to face me, his smile lighting up the room. "Hey, baby. How was your nap?" He set his papers aside. No, he did more than that. He gathered them all up from around him and stacked them on the coffee table next to the computer. "Come here."

I inched forward, but only to make it easier to speak to him. "Where are my clothes, Sir?"

He ignored me. "Amelia, come here." He reached out a hand.

I went to him like a puppet. When I rounded the couch, he grabbed my arm and pulled me closer. Before I knew it, he had his arm around me and hauled me into his lap. He plucked at the sheet tucked tight around my breasts. "That's cute. Ingenious."

My eyes widened as he made light of my situation. Nothing about his demeanor insinuated he was finished with me. That was when it occurred to me that although I'd had a fantastic orgasm at his hands earlier, he had not. There was little doubt in my mind he would want to have sex now. Of course he would. I wasn't even opposed to the idea. Afterward, I would never see him again. Who the hell cared if I slept with him before I left? I could certainly do worse in selecting someone to take my virginity. At least I knew it would be beautiful. The man was far from hard on the eyes.

I flushed. Contemplating having sex with Cade Alexander while sitting naked in his lap wearing only a sheet was enough to make me think I'd either died in a car accident earlier in the day, or I'd gone insane and was currently in a padded white room living in my own dream world.

"What's going on in that huge brain of yours, baby?" Cade tapped my temple.

"Did you want to have sex before I leave?" I sputtered those words out without thinking. But if it sped things up, it wasn't for naught. I really needed to get out of there, collect my brain cells from the front porch, and hightail it to my car.

Cade chuckled. "So blunt."

"Well, I just thought…"

"I know, baby. And you're so precious, like a bright light in the darkness."

Whatever that meant.

He turned me to face him more fully on his lap. "Look at me, baby."

His words, like all his words, bore a hole in my resolve. The way he said *baby* brought renewed wetness to the area between my legs. The last thing I wanted was to make a wet spot on his sheet.

I met his gaze.

Cade lifted one hand and stroked a finger down my face until he settled it under my chin. "I'm not going to fuck you today, Amelia."

Oh. This was a shock.

"You aren't ready."

How the hell did he know if I was ready or not?

"There are things you need to learn and understand before I claim that sweet, hot pussy of yours."

His words were crude. My ears heated, and I squirmed to escape his embrace to no avail.

Cade held me firmly around the waist with one hand, his

other still under my chin. "Eyes on me, Amelia. I have rules. There are many. But one of the most important ones is I expect you to look me in the eye when I'm talking to you."

I lifted my gaze from my lap to his face again. This did nothing to ease the heat suffusing my face. My cheeks burned with my ears.

He has rules?

"Good girl. Now, I want you to understand a few things." He turned to glance at the table and then looked back at me. "Those packages you picked up are all for you."

If it was possible, I flushed a deeper red. I didn't drop his gaze. To do so would mean looking in the direction of the table, and I didn't need the reminder of my humiliating day gathering gifts for his... They were for me?

"Now she's catching on." He smiled. I loved it when he smiled. "You'll earn those gifts. I'll give them to you one at a time when I think you're ready for them. I won't fuck you until you've opened the last one."

I nodded. Was this a game? Did he intend for me to do charades or something for the remainder of the evening? Or go on a scavenger hunt to prove my worth?

More heat. More of his intense staring. "It will take you at least a week to earn all three boxes."

That answered that question. He meant it when he said we weren't going to have sex tonight. Just as well. I might have lost my virginity doing so, but I would have lost a part of my soul also.

Cade released my chin to trail his fingertip down my neck and across my collarbone. He used that one finger to tug at the front of my toga between my breasts until it slipped.

I reached with both hands to hold the sheet, and therefore a small chunk of my dignity, whatever morsel remained.

"Rule number two," Cade began as he released my waist to grab my wrists and pull them behind me. He held them at the small of my back, tucking them in one hand. And then he resumed loosening the sheet at my chest. "When you're with me, I'll insist you be naked most of the time. Your body is divine. I want to see it, touch it, smell it, or anything else I can think of at my leisure."

He had to be kidding.

"I'll make some exceptions when we're in public, but when you're in my home, I expect you to remain naked." As he spoke, he managed to free my chest and tug the toga away enough to expose my lap.

I squirmed. Words wouldn't come to me.

Cade held my wrists firmer. "Sit still, baby." He spoke as he circled one of my nipples with his finger and then flicked the tip.

A squeak escaped my lips. The traitorous nipple immediately stood at attention.

Cade switched to the other one, stroking it until it matched its twin. "So gorgeous. Do you realize how sexy you are?" He lifted his gaze to meet mine.

I didn't move.

Cade chuckled. "You have no idea." His finger trailed down

my belly, making it dip as he touched my skin.

Goose bumps rose all over my flesh as he reached lower and then tugged at my pubic hair. His gaze came back to mine. "I want you to shave this off, baby."

Shave? Was he insane?

"If that seems insurmountable for you, I'll do it myself."

Now he'd reached an entirely new level.

And so had the burning in my cheeks. The image of Cade between my legs shaving my sex made me moan in a mixture of mortification and desire. I wasn't sure which sensation won.

"Which is it, baby?"

My eyes widened. My mouth fell open. Nothing came out.

"I'll let you decide later. If you shave it yourself, I'll know what you decided. If not, I'll assume you want me to do it for you."

As soon as I managed to escape this house and the hypnosis of Cade Alexander, there would be no "next time." This rule of his was moot.

"Another thing. You aren't to touch yourself without permission. I mentioned that earlier. I want to reiterate it." He gripped my chin again and held it steady, forcing my gaze to meet his. "That's a hard rule. I won't bend on it. Am I understood?"

"Yes, Sir."

He smiled. His hand trailed back down my body to cup my sex. "This pussy is mine. Your orgasms are mine to dole out when and how I see fit. You will *not* masturbate without my permission."

"Yes, Sir," I repeated, softer. My body stiffened. With his

fingers so close to my sex, I slipped deeper under his spell.

"Another rule. No panties. Ever. I abhor them. I like your pussy open and available to me at all times. Whether or not I take advantage is up to me, but the option is mine and mine alone. Your job is to be ready for whatever I decide."

I knew my expression was blank. There was no wrapping my head around his words.

I knew one thing for certain. He hadn't been kidding. He was a Dom. I'd never known another Dom, so I had no one to compare to, but I suspected Cade Alexander was used to getting his way, in all things.

"I think that's enough rules for today. If I pile on too many, you won't be able to comply, and I don't want to spend half the week correcting you. If I have to punish you ten times on the first day, then I haven't done my job."

Punish me.

I was in so deep... What a mess.

The knot in my belly that had formed hours ago hadn't abated. It needed release. The orgasm he'd given me while I stood in front of him and he fucked my channel with his fingers had only eased the ball of need temporarily. It was back in full swing now. And I wasn't pleased.

Cade cupped my breast and met my stare. He drew lazy circles around my nipple while he spoke. "I gave you a lot to consider. Please repeat the four rules I've given you."

I licked my lips. They were too dry. I couldn't have repeated his rules back if I wanted to. I was in a daze. And I was debased.

"I'll reiterate. You repeat after me." He paused. "You will remain naked in my presence any time I request it."

I swallowed. The thought of repeating those words made me feel so small I couldn't verbalize anything at all.

"Am I moving too fast for you, baby?"

This I could consent to, so I nodded.

Cade's response was to heave himself off the couch with me in his arms and carry me back through the house until he reached the room where I'd napped. He sat me on the mattress. "Don't move." He turned toward the window and opened the blinds. The room filled with the evening light. And then he was back. "Lie down, Amelia."

I was sitting on the edge of the bed, facing him, clutching the sheet around me.

Cade pressed gently on my shoulders and eased me onto the bed on my back. He tucked his hands under my arms and hauled me several inches toward the center and stuffed a pillow under my head. Next, his hands came to mine where they gripped the sheet. He pried them open, again gently, and lifted my arms over my head. "Leave your hands there, baby."

The sheet was yanked away immediately, leaving me open and vulnerable. As if that wasn't enough, Cade grabbed my knees and pushed them up and out, leaving my sex completely spread to his view.

The humiliation I'd felt earlier didn't compare. I turned my head to one side, fighting not to cry.

"Eyes on me, Amelia." His voice was soft and deep. "Amelia, now." His tone got firmer.

I slowly let my gaze come back to center.

"Baby, I know this is confusing, and you don't understand what's happening, so I'm going to make it clearer. You're a submissive, Amelia." He paused, apparently letting that soak into my addled brain.

I shook my head finally. "That's crazy."

"No it's not. You just didn't realize it before now." He tapped my nipple and then pinched it sharply.

I arched into his hand.

Cade trailed his fingers down my body toward my core.

When I tried to close my legs, he grabbed both thighs and held them wider.

I moaned involuntarily, and Cade slipped a finger into my channel with no warning. "Eyes on me."

I jerked my attention back to his face in time to watch him lick his finger clean of my moisture. "Baby, you're so wet for me."

This was indisputable.

His finger dipped back inside me, and then he brought it to my mouth.

I died three deaths as he spread my arousal on my lips. "Taste yourself, Amelia. Suck my finger into your mouth, baby."

I did, amazed by the salty sweetness that was my arousal.

"Good girl. Are you starting to understand what I'm saying?"

Not even close.

He rolled his eyes, but smiled. At least he wasn't angry. "If you weren't so submissive, you wouldn't be able to lie here spread open for me, so wet with need, your nipples jutting out, begging for attention. You're a natural, baby." He leaned in as he said this last part. "And you're mine."

At that moment, I couldn't argue his point. I was totally his. My entire body was on fire. My sex gripped at nothing, pleading for any sort of contact Cade would provide.

"So, let's get back to my rules. I have rules for a reason, Amelia. Most important is discipline. I'll train you to submit to me in the manner I enjoy. You will be rewarded beyond measure in a manner I can assure you'll enjoy. Is that clear?"

I nodded, though I had no idea why. I grasped onto the word enjoy and went with it.

"So, you will remain naked any time I demand it."

I nodded.

"Repeat my rule, baby." His hands landed on my spread thighs, caressing the skin between them.

"I'll remain naked with you, Sir," I whispered.

"You will not masturbate without my permission."

I swallowed. That one was easy since I hadn't masturbated previously without his permission. "I won't touch myself when I'm not with you, Sir."

"Good girl. You will keep your pussy shaved smooth at all times. I'll let you decide in the morning whether you want to take on that task yourself or have me do it."

I didn't see how I was ever going to shave myself down there. And I flinched every time he referred to my sex as my pussy, often in a manner that left me wetter than before.

"Amelia, concentrate. Repeat what I said."

"I'll shave my, um, hair, Sir."

"Good girl. Do you remember my last rule for today?"

"No panties, Sir."

He smiled. His hands roamed my thighs, getting closer to my center with each pass. My legs shook. Even my arms shook where I gripped my hands together above my head.

"Baby, you're so fucking sexy. I promise you won't regret this. Give me a chance, and I'll show you a world you've never even dreamed about."

I didn't doubt his capability in that department. I also needed to get out of there. Go home. Think. Make lists of pros and cons. I realized this was a foregone conclusion for Cade, but for me it was a major life decision.

At no point in my life had I contemplated submitting to another human being. I had never considered myself that weak.

Cade leaned in and nibbled a path up my thigh, making me suck in a breath. He lifted his face before he reached my center. "Tomorrow morning, come to work as usual, but I'll be talking to Moriah about making sure you climb up from the lowest rung." He smirked and then muttered, "She has a fucking master's in business admin, and she's bringing my people coffee." He rolled his eyes.

"Sir, *no*." I lowered my hands and lifted myself onto my elbows.

"No, what?"

"Well, first of all, there's no way in hell I'm going to date you and work for you at the same time. If you were thinking about seeing me again after today—" I cut myself off. "Hell, after the way I've let you manhandle me all afternoon, I can't go back to the office anyway, so this discussion is moot, but still, I would never want you to do anything to get me promoted. I intend to earn my way up in whatever company I land. I'll turn in my resignation tomorrow."

"Of course you won't." His brows furrowed. He shook his head. "Did I mention wanting you to quit your job?"

"No, but—"

"You aren't quitting your job, Amelia. End of discussion. If you still want to quit after you've opened that last package on the kitchen table, I'll be happy to oblige. But not now, not when I've just gotten you. I want you in my office. I want to know where you are at all times." His hands gripped my legs and pressed them open wider. "I want this pussy naked and available, and I want to know that it's in my building. We clear?"

We were so totally *not* clear. "Cade," I shook my head while I spoke, "this is ridiculous. I would never dally with someone I worked with under any circumstances. And in this case, it's too late. The damage is done. I can't go back there. I'll find another job."

Cade grinned. "Dally?"

I rolled my eyes. Of all the things I said, he wanted to make fun of my word choice. I squirmed, fighting to scoot out of his reach.

He held me tighter. "Don't move away from me, Amelia. We're having a discussion."

Exasperated, I lifted both hands and threw them in the air, causing myself to land flat on my naked back again. I spoke to the ceiling. "Nothing about this day has remotely resembled a discussion, Cade. You clearly run a dictatorship. If this is how you treat all your women, no wonder you don't have a girlfriend." I regretted those last words the second they left my lips.

In less than a second, Cade Alexander was on top of me. He straddled my torso, planted his knees on both sides of my body, and grabbed my hands to lift them back over my head. "Ms. Kensington."

I flinched at his use of my formal name all of the sudden. And even though he was totally manhandling me, his body hovering over me, his face inches from mine as he forced me to meet his gaze, my damn nipples were hard.

"Let me set a few things straight. First of all, I'm a Dom. I don't do girlfriends. I haven't had a girlfriend in years."

I winced.

"Second of all, just so you know, submissives do not generally make their own choices. Doms do not generally lay out a selection of options and let their sub choose. Now, I realize this is foreign to you. And if I thought for a second you couldn't handle this, we wouldn't be in this position. I tested you this morning. I knew already you were perfect for me. Hell, I knew it the moment you first walked by my office two weeks ago, your thick wavy hair bobbing behind you, your long graceful fingers separating papers expertly, a smile on your face that told me there was no other place in the world you'd rather be, that you'd hit the lottery when you landed yourself a job at my company."

I tried to soak in everything he said. I pulled my legs together and squeezed them tight against the growing arousal mounting as his gaze penetrated me and he let me in on just how long he'd been watching me.

"I knew, but I wanted to be sure. My knowledge was further confirmed when we shared that drink Friday night. There you were in *my* bar dressed in your sexiest black dress, wearing those fuck-me shoes, and perched on a stool looking like the world was your oyster."

His bar? Of course. Did he own the entire city?

He leaned in, the inches closing as I held my breath.

"I knew you were submissive when I led you away from your friends without a word from you and plied you with my favorite Chardonnay."

Yep, my sex could get wetter. He wanted me. Bad.

"And then this afternoon." He let his eyes close for a second and inhaled a long, slow breath before he continued, "Baby, the look on your face when you got here was priceless. You were fit to kill."

"I thought—"

"I know what you thought, and that was exactly what I wanted you to think. If you had shown up devoid of emotion and simply dropped off my purchases, then I would have been worried." He grinned.

"Baby," he lowered his voice to a whisper, "you're mine."

I opened my mouth to protest, but he released one of my wrists and set two fingers on my lips.

"Don't say anything right now. Just think about everything I've told you. I'll get Arthur to take you home. I want you to search deep inside yourself this evening and take a good look. Think hard about how it makes you feel when you do my bidding. Let go of the anger and place your attention on the tight ball of need in your belly, the one that threatens to explode every time I give you a command."

I held my breath.

"Even now," he whispered, "even while you're fighting a war inside your mind, your pussy is dripping wet. Is it not?"

I didn't move.

"Baby, is your pussy wet?"

"Yes, Sir," I mumbled.

"That's my girl. And that's what I want you to focus on. We can have all the discussions you need while I train you, but remember, the end result is always your pleasure, and mine. Submitting to me will open your eyes to a world of satisfaction you can't imagine. That's my promise to you." He released my wrist and eased off my body until he stood on the floor.

I hated that I wanted to beg him to fuck me. That's how aroused I was.

Cade tapped my pussy. "This is mine, Amelia. I know you're horny right now and probably want to pull my hair out, but don't act on that. Not tonight. Keep your greedy fingers to yourself and concentrate on what I've told you. Report to work as usual in the morning and do your job. Judy goes to lunch at noon every day for one hour. I want you to come to my office five minutes after twelve. Are we clear?"

I nodded. He had me under a deep hypnosis. There was no escape. And as he'd suggested, I wasn't at all sure I wanted to escape.

Cade reached for his phone. "I'll have Arthur pick you up."

"Sir, that's not necessary. I have my car here, and I'll need it in the morning to get to work."

He hesitated a moment and then nodded. "Okay, but please drive safely. It's late. From now on, when you come to my house, Arthur or I will pick you up." He set the phone aside and kissed my forehead.

My belly dipped. He was overbearing. There was no doubt about that, but his overprotective side was kind of endearing.

Chapter Five

I woke up gasping for air, my eyes instantly wide, my hand between my legs. The first thing I did was yank my fingers away from my pussy and stare at them in disbelief. Never. That's how often I'd awoken stroking my clit.

Instantly, my mind wandered to Cade's rule about touching myself. Not that I could be blamed for this one. I'd been asleep.

I glanced at the clock—fifteen minutes before my alarm would go off. I curled onto my side and snuggled under the covers. I was wide awake but had no desire to climb out of my bed yet.

I'd slept hard. Thank God. As soon as I'd stepped in the house the night before, I'd taken a long bath and pondered the day's events. When my thoughts became a hodgepodge of no new resolutions on my part, I'd dried off and climbed into bed. Again I'd lain there, staring at the ceiling and worrying my bottom lip until it was swollen.

This morning I had a decision to make. Go to work and face this new world I'd fallen into, or hide under the covers and pretend my stint at Alexander Technologies never happened.

The thought of never seeing Cade again was more than I

could stomach. The thought of *seeing* Cade again was also more than I could stomach.

The man was intense. His rules were intense. His expressions were intense. I had no idea if I could even begin to live up to his specifications.

But if I didn't try, I would spend the rest of my life wondering "what if?"

Yep. I had to get out of this bed and get in the shower. I would need the extra time to attempt to shave. There was no way I was going to take the risk of stepping into Cade's business without doing so. I would put nothing past him. The chances he would check to make sure I'd done as he'd demanded between now and five o'clock were high.

I slid from my warm cocoon and headed for the bathroom. I stripped off my tank top and panties and dropped them in the hamper. Cade had instructed me not to wear panties at any time. I'd struggled with the idea for about two minutes last night before deciding there was no way I was going to sleep naked. I couldn't do it. Not yet.

Shaving was a task that proved far more difficult than I anticipated. It was impossible to see everything between my legs, and I needed a third hand to hold my folds apart. Not to mention I became aroused every time I touched my pussy anywhere. And when had I begun to think of my sex as my pussy?

That infuriating man and his words.

I managed, barely, and dressed in a skirt that reached almost to my knees, the longest one I owned. If I wasn't going to wear panties, at least I needed the added protection. My blouse was also more conservative than usual. It was a deep royal blue and therefore hid my bra completely. This didn't mean I wore one of my less attractive, more functional bras. I didn't want to take that chance, either. I donned my favorite black lace bra and buttoned my blouse one more button than normal.

By the time I stepped into the office, I was a ball of nerves. I worried someone would be able to tell by looking at me that I'd spent the evening with the boss, letting him have his way with me.

Moriah looked up from her desk and smiled. She was just settling in herself. It was ten till eight. "Hey Amy, how'd it go yesterday?" She cringed. "Was it bad? I told you it might take you all day. I'm surprised you aren't still out satisfying that man's whims."

I shrugged. I'd rehearsed this conversation in my head on the way to work. "It was fine. Not too bad. And I eventually got it all done. Thank God." I rolled my eyes as though I were so totally over the incident.

"Well, lucky you. And the best news is I haven't received a commandment from the seventh floor demanding your service again today." She held out a piece of paper. "Margie needs you on four this morning. She's overloaded. She was beside herself when I said she could borrow you for the morning. If you finish, just check back in with me after lunch."

I took the page she handed me and nodded. "Will do." Every attempt to behave like it were any other day was difficult. My mind constantly returned to yesterday. The visions of me lying naked and exposed to Mr. Alexander's view would not abate. It was difficult to concentrate. It all seemed like a dream. People didn't really live out experiences like the one I'd been through yesterday.

I stuffed my purse in my drawer and headed to the fourth floor with my printout from Margie. I spent the entire morning working diligently on a spreadsheet she needed straightened out. Apparently she'd had a temp who seriously botched the entire spreadsheet.

Margie was shocked and relieved when I handed her the finished product at five after twelve. "You did the entire thing?" She stared at the numbers on the printout I'd made for her.

"Yes. Isn't that what you needed?"

"Yeah, but it took Shelly three weeks to create this mess. It took you three hours to fix it." She smiled at me and set it aside. "Bless you. I'm going to sleep much better tonight. And I'm going to call Moriah and tell her your talents are once again wasted on the first floor."

"Thanks, Margie. I appreciate the compliments."

"No problem." She waved me off. "Go to lunch."

I headed for the elevator, my knees shaking and my hands fisted at my sides as I waited for the elevator to arrive. As soon as I entered and reached to push the button, my finger shook and I lost my nerve. I stood there for long moments, my hand hovering in the air. And then I hit *one*. I needed to get out of the building. Suddenly the air was stifling. I couldn't breathe.

Moriah wasn't in the office. Thank God. I grabbed my purse and made a beeline for the outside. I needed oxygen. I needed to clear my head.

I did not need lunch.

My stomach roiled at the idea.

Instead I walked. I strapped my purse over my arm and ambled through the streets of downtown Atlanta, gazing up at the buildings, trying to think.

It was hot. Hell, it was June. Of course it was hot.

I didn't care.

I couldn't do this. It wasn't me. It didn't matter that every time I thought about Cade my insides bunched up with need. It didn't matter that visions of him hovering over my naked body last night made my mouth so dry I couldn't lick my lips. Nor did it matter that I wanted to throw myself at him and toss caution to the wind just to know what it would feel like to have a man inside me with the intensity I knew I would see in his eyes.

That wasn't me.

I wasn't that girl.

I was straight-laced. A good girl.

My parents were so proud of me, they bragged to all their friends about my education and my job. Granted, they had to fib a little to make my job interesting, but they trusted me when I'd made this decision. From two hours away in small-town Georgia, they had no way of knowing about my day-to-day experiences. I could paint any lovely picture I wanted about my job at Alexander Technologies. And I did.

My breath hitched when I considered telling them I'd

resigned after only two weeks with the company of my dreams. How would I explain that to my parents?

Yeah, Mom, Dad...my boss...well, he's kinda into BDSM and he wanted me to strip for him and do his bidding.

Ugh.

I kept walking. My cell phone rang, but I ignored it. Text messages came in too. I could hear the beeping in my purse, and it unnerved me. My girlfriends didn't usually call me during the day.

Cade.

It was hot, but the thought of him hunting me down on the streets of Atlanta made me shiver.

The man owned the company. If he wanted to get his hands on my cell phone number, all he had to do was ask someone in human resources.

I stared up at a tall building by my side, covering my eyes with my hand to keep the glare down. The mirrored walls made the sun even brighter. How did they keep the outside of a building so pristine? For a moment it almost looked surreal, as though out of a cartoon. The edges too perfect. The glass too shiny. The reflection too intense.

I dropped my face, feeling that perfection and taking it with me. Two weeks ago, I'd been that building. All the cards had lined up in my favor. I'd jumped up and down when I received the news that I would be working for Alexander Technologies. I'd gotten my hair cut and styled to perfection. I'd bought new clothes I couldn't afford that hung in my closet in perfect rows, my shoes beneath them. I'd even had my nails done so that everything about me screamed "professional and ready to work."

Yesterday morning, that world had somehow shattered. I wasn't sure if I could ever pick up the tiny pieces.

I turned away from the glass building, imagining the mirrored walls collapsing onto the ground in a billion tiny shards that would puncture me as they fell.

My steps were heavy as I returned to the office. I needed to turn in my resignation and leave. The worst part was ruining my reputation. Without giving notice, I wouldn't be able to use them as a reference. Hell, I wouldn't be able to use them anyway. Not now. Not now that I'd been naked with the owner and let him stroke inside me with his fingers.

Like some sort of slut.

How the hell I was ever going to explain this incident and get another job, I had no idea. How I was going to tell my parents, I had no idea. I didn't even have a clue how I was going to tell Cheyenne and Meagan about my crash and burn.

I re-entered the building, resolved to turn in my resignation.

The second I entered the office, Moriah looked up. She smiled at me. "Hey. Hope you had a good lunch. Mr. Alexander needs you. He said, and I quote, 'Could I possibly borrow the services of the new girl who helped me yesterday? She was efficient and professional. I need some research done this afternoon.'" Moriah beamed. "Girl, it was nice knowing you in the trenches. Obviously you won't be around on the first floor for long. I'm gonna have to hire someone else before I've even had you a month."

I stood there frozen, my mouth hanging open. "He said all

that?"

"Yep. And I've never heard him go out of his way to praise someone like that. Get on up there, Amy. Accept your good fortune and run with it."

I hesitated. This was not how I saw my afternoon going. Besides, I'd completely disregarded my boss during lunch when he'd specifically commanded me to be in his office at five after noon.

My hands shook, a recurring problem with me lately, as I contemplated my choices.

"You okay?" Moriah asked.

I hadn't moved.

"Just shocked." *To say the least*.

"Well, get unshocked." She smiled again. "Go." She pointed to the door.

I swung around, taking a deep breath, and made my way to the lobby. To say I was nervous was an understatement. Petrified to face Cade was more like it.

I rode to the top without breathing.

Judy greeted me when I stepped off the elevator. "Oh good, you're here. Mr. Alexander is scurrying around like a madman."

That made me cringe. *I'll bet he is*.

"He has some giant document he needs a brief on, and he needs you to read it this afternoon and give him the cliff notes. He doesn't have time to do it himself." Judy gave me a sorrowful look, her eyes slanted. "I hope it isn't boring as hell."

I took a deep breath. I had no idea what to expect when I

entered Cade's office. Would he be angry? I didn't know him well enough to know how he reacted to being told *no*. And my not showing for lunch was exactly that.

I eased past Judy, my legs feeling like lead. I clutched my purse at my side, realizing I had never stashed it downstairs.

Surely Cade didn't have a document for me to read, or any other thing for that matter. He was just hot under the collar at being stood up. I hoped he wouldn't make a scene that Judy would overhear. I was humiliated enough. I didn't need him to make it worse. If anyone ever found out I had taken my clothes off at his house, I would be disgraced.

When I stepped into his office through the open door, Cade was standing behind his desk, his mouse moving rapidly under his fingertips, his face angled at the monitor. "Come in," he commanded without looking up. His tone gave away nothing. He could have said those two words to anyone. He didn't look angry. He didn't look anything except busy. He released the mouse and then shuffled a few papers.

He lifted his face and smiled. "Ah, Ms. Kensington. Thank God. I could really use your help this afternoon. I have this lengthy document I need someone to read and give me the summation. I'm swamped and dining tonight with this client. If I don't sound like I've read through their material, I'll make a fool of myself." He sauntered my way as he spoke.

Was he serious? At no point in the last ten minutes since I'd entered the building had it occurred to me that his request had been legitimate. I'd expected him to shut the door and give me a ribbing.

And my only prayer had been that he do so quietly enough that Judy didn't hear.

He stopped his advance several feet from me and swept out his hand to indicate the laptop sitting on the conference table across the room. "I have a workspace all set up for you."

I glanced at the long mahogany table, the top perfectly buffed to a shine that almost matched the mirrored walls of the building I'd seen in the street. In fact everything about this office mirrored that perfection. Every chair was in its place, perfectly pushed against the table as though the cleaning crew actually measured the distance between them to ensure they were precisely arranged.

With the exception of a few papers on Cade's desk, not one item was out of place.

Perfection.

Not what I was feeling that day.

"Um, Mr. Alexander," I began. I had no idea how to continue. I didn't have a thought in mind.

Cade turned and strolled across the carpet toward the spot he'd indicated.

A blank notepad sat next to the computer, a pen on top of it.

I followed him. He had a magnetism that made it difficult, or impossible, to tell him *no*.

My resolve scampered from the room.

Cade took my purse from my hands as I reached his side.

He took two quick strides to his desk and stored it in a bottom drawer. I wondered why he had an empty drawer in his desk.

He clapped his hands together one time and rubbed them. "Okay then. The piece I need you to read is open on the desktop. Please be thorough. I'll expect concise notes that I can read easily. And I'll want you to give me about a fifteen minute presentation of your understanding at five o'clock. If you can't finish it by then, will you be able to stay a bit later?"

I nodded, my head moving of its own accord. This was ludicrous. All of it. I had no words.

"Good. Get to work then. I'll be here most of the afternoon myself, putting out today's fires. I may have to take a few calls. Hope that won't disrupt you." He turned away from me and headed back to his desk where he pulled out his chair and plopped down heavily to resume whatever he'd been doing.

The mouse moved at warp speed across the glossy surface of his desk, a mahogany that matched the conference table and the two cabinets in the room, each of which sat centered on the two walls that didn't have windows running the length of them.

I stared at Mr. Alexander for several moments, perhaps longer, wondering if today were even Tuesday and if I'd conjured up Monday entirely in my dreams. He acted like he'd hardly met me before. Except there was no way waking or sleeping I could have dreamed up yesterday. My brain didn't have the resources to provide such fodder. At no point in my life had I been exposed to enough BDSM entertainment to have imagined entering my boss's home, stripping naked, and letting him fondle me to orgasm.

Nope.

That wasn't me.

It had to have been someone else.

And here I was, standing rigid, staring at Cade, who had to know I hadn't moved, and yet didn't comment or look up.

That was the only indication I had at all that yesterday had not been an apparition. It was the only evidence he was even acknowledging the elephant in the room. His silence and ability to ignore me spoke volumes.

I somehow managed to command my feet to shuffle forward and rounded the corner of the conference table to take a seat. I had no idea why. I closed my eyes and took a deep breath in and out, trying to convince myself this was outrageous and to back up, grow a spine, and tell Mr. Alexander to go to hell.

A small piece of me must have disagreed because I couldn't bring myself to act on the inclination. Instead I picked up the mouse and wiggled it to get the screen to come to life.

Chapter Six

To say I was shocked was an understatement. My pointer froze above the mouse. My entire body froze. I couldn't even lift my face to glance at my boss. My neck stiffened. And the flush that raced up my cheeks burned.

Downloaded to the desktop was a book titled *The Rules*.

It didn't take a rocket scientist to ascertain what it was about. The cover alone made my skin pebble with goose bumps—a set of stainless steel handcuffs on glossy silk material. Nothing else.

I glanced at the pad of paper beside my free hand and winced. Was I supposed to take notes and read this, really? I couldn't look at Cade. I didn't want to see if he was watching me with a smirk or ignoring me entirely. Neither option would make me happy.

I clicked past the cover to the acknowledgements and then the table of contents. The chapter headings alone made me nervous. I squeezed my thighs together, pulling my ankles in to touch each other as I read the titles of each chapter. Words swam in front of me: obedience, training, submission, domination, punishment. I swallowed hard. I'd read romance novels. Most of the women I knew enjoyed a good kinky story. But this wasn't fiction. It was real, as real as the man sitting across the room, who clearly wanted to make a point.

I wished I'd worn panties. My thighs were wet before I opened to the first chapter. My newly naked pussy pulsed with the extra blood flow. My nipples ached, and I squeezed the sides of my chest with my biceps to alleviate the pressure of my bra.

Was I submissive? Maybe most women were a little bit submissive. Perhaps almost all of us would be titillated by reading about being dominated. But my reaction seemed over the top. Of course that could have been partly due to the fact that the man who wanted to dominate me sat in the same room.

Sheer curiosity caused me to open the first chapter and read. At no point did I glance away from the screen. At first I was embarrassed. For a long time I completely forgot about the pad of paper. And then I suddenly jerked and grabbed the pen with shaky fingers to summarize what I'd read in the first two chapters.

As the hours ticked by, I tuned out the rest of the world and kept reading.

I knew two things unnerved me—I'd never been so informed, and I'd never been so aroused.

I hated Mr. Alexander for a while, and then I switched to wishing he would please come to me and fuck me on the table. I wasn't sure I didn't hate him for being so astute about me.

Everything in the book made the ball of need in my belly grow. I had to stop myself from rocking my body in the chair more than once. I did anything I could to put pressure on my pussy without reaching directly between my legs and doing it with my hand. And there I was again, thinking *pussy* in my head. How could this man have done this to me in twenty-four hours' time?

The first time I let my gaze roam from the computer to the room at large was when Judy came in to say she was leaving.

I met her gaze and smiled, unable to speak. I'd entered another dimension. I wasn't on this planet anymore.

Judy hesitated a moment, a forlorn look on her face as though she was truly sorry to have gotten me into whatever mess I was in, and out of a bond of sisterhood, hated leaving me there to finish after business hours.

I forced a smile and nodded.

Luckily she left. If I'd needed to speak out loud, I wasn't at all sure my voice would have sounded like my own. Probably just a loud squeak.

Back to the task, I kept reading. I had two chapters left. Even though it was after five, I had been instructed to finish, so I did. When I was done, I clicked on the last page and straightened my spine. My fingers hurt from gripping the mouse, and my body was stiff from sitting there so rigidly. I needed to pee.

I took a deep breath and lifted my gaze. Cade sat on the edge of his desk, his legs crossed at the ankles, his hands loosely holding the sides of the mahogany on each side of his hips. I met his gaze. He stared at me intently. I couldn't decide what mood he was in. His face was blank.

Finally, he spoke. "Use the bathroom, baby. Freshen up." He nodded to the unopened door next to the entrance to the room. I'd had no idea there was a restroom in his office.

I pulled myself to standing slowly, stretching my legs and becoming uncomfortably aware of my bladder. He was sharp. With my head bowed, I passed him and headed straight for the bathroom.

The first thing I did was pee, and then I looked at myself in the mirror while I washed my hands. Who the hell was I? I'd come to the office this morning as one person and finished the day as another.

No. That wasn't entirely true. I knew without a doubt this day was far from over. I would be yet another human being before I went to bed that night.

I took a deep breath, smoothed my skirt, and exited the room. The door to the office was shut. Cade had moved to the conference table. The opposite end from where I had worked was covered with food. My stomach growled. I hadn't eaten lunch.

I wondered if he was truly meeting a client for dinner or if the entire thing had been a fabrication to get me to read *The Rules*.

It would appear he wasn't going anywhere, and I saw no evidence to suggest he had a client coming to the office. The room, which had been full of light during the day, was now closed off from the world with dark blinds on the windows.

Cade spoke, his words too soft for my ears. I lifted my gaze and discovered he was on the phone.

He spotted me, however, and motioned me closer. His expression didn't change. He was deep in conversation.

I padded across the room and stopped a few feet from the

table. Awkward didn't begin to describe how I felt. This was my boss, the owner of the company. I was in his executive office on the top floor. I didn't belong here. And I certainly didn't belong here without panties. I stepped my legs together.

I'd been there for hours, but the addition of a caller on the phone made me feel like we weren't alone.

I breathed heavier.

He circled me and came up behind me, still listening to the caller. Every few seconds he would respond with a *yes* or a *no* or some sort of *uh-huh*. His breath landed on my neck as he swept my hair out of the way. He kissed me behind my ear, his tongue delicately swiping the bottom of my earlobe.

I fisted my hands at my sides, well aware that Cade had me eating out of his hand.

After he inhaled long and slow against my neck, he wrapped an arm around my waist and led me across the room. When we arrived at his desk, he angled me exactly where he wanted me to stand. And then he surprised me by plopping down in his office chair. He met my gaze, his piercing into mine until I shivered. He undressed me with his eyes. His gaze ran up and down my body while he continued to speak with the caller.

Finally, he ended the conversation, but cut the other person off. "Okay then, Ben. Please just handle this. If you have to take them to task, so be it. Make sure we're on schedule and the quality is up to standards. If you need to spend more money than we budgeted, do it. I'll talk to you again tomorrow." Cade ended his call and set his phone on the desk without looking away from me.

We stared at each other for long moments, and then he smiled. "You're nervous."

"Yes, Sir."

His eyes closed slowly and then re-opened. "Do you know what it does to me when you call me Sir in that tone?"

"No...Sir."

He chuckled. "Of course not. How did you sleep last night?"

I swallowed. He made no mention of me not showing up at noon or the many hours I'd spent learning about his world. His rules. He skipped that as though it never happened and spoke to me about last night. I nodded.

"Words, baby."

"Fine, Sir."

"Good. I'm sure you were exhausted." He watched my face for a moment and then spoke again. "How far did you have to dig this morning to come up with an outfit that revealed so little skin?"

I flushed. I did that a lot around him. And since his brazen pronouncements were the cause, I didn't feel remotely apologetic. I also didn't respond.

"You know how I feel about clothes."

My eyes went wide. Surely he wouldn't ask me to strip here in his office.

"What did you decide about shaving, baby?" He leaned back farther and crossed one foot over his other knee. He looked so relaxed, and I felt the exact opposite.

"I did it, Sir."

"Good girl. I hope there's nothing but bare skin under that skirt now."

"Yes, Sir." I swallowed, waiting for the inevitable, and aroused by it at the same time.

The way Cade lounged in his chair was not something I'd seen him do at work prior to this moment. It was incongruent with the starched-to-perfection suit he wore.

I grew fidgety.

"Show me, baby. Take off your clothes."

I glanced around. I'd known he might request such a thing, but it still felt awkward. There were windows on two sides of his office. My gaze landed on the blinds.

"No one can see in." He sat up straighter. "And I'm not a fan of hesitation. Remove everything."

Moving as though I weren't myself at all, I took off my clothes. I stood naked before him. Shivering. Embarrassed. My nipples straining toward him. My pussy wet.

Cade stared at me for several moments. The only sign I had that he was ruffled at all was the pen he rolled between his fingers as he watched me squirm. "I'm going to show you how to stand, and I expect you to remember it and repeat it every time we're playing." He stood, pulling himself up as though he was tired or heavy. He circled behind me and set his hands on my shoulders to pull them back. "You'll stand tall in this position. Pull your hands behind your back and grab one wrist with the other hand."

I did so. My chest jutted out.

"Good girl. Shoulders back, arms clasped. Always. Got it?"

"Yes, Sir."

"Now spread your legs farther."

I stepped out.

"More, Amelia."

I flinched when he called me by my given name. I realized he called me baby when I was endearing and Amelia when I was exhibiting a behavior he didn't care for. "My friends call me Amy." I don't know why I chose to blurt that out, but I did.

"Good for them. I call you Amelia." He rounded me, blowing off my suggestion. He lifted my chin. "Most Doms like their subs to dip their faces and keep their gazes to the floor. You'd have learned that from the material you just read. That's not my style. I like your eyes on me. I know what you're feeling with more accuracy when I can see into your eyes."

I nodded.

"Did you take good notes this afternoon?"

I nodded again.

"Words, baby."

"Yes, Sir." I was pretty certain I would die if he truly intended for me to summarize what I'd spent the last several hours reading.

Cade chuckled. "I'll let you take those pages home in case you need to remind yourself of anything you learned."

Cade walked away then, heading for the long conference table. "Come here, baby."

When I turned around, I found he'd spread sandwiches and drinks on the end.

As I reached Cade's side, he grabbed my waist and lifted me onto the table.

I clutched his biceps during the flight, a squeal of shock escaping my lips. "Cade."

He ignored me, setting me down about a foot from the edge. "Lie back, baby."

I slowly lowered my body to the cold surface, shivering more than I had been.

"Hands above your head." He waited for me to comply, and then he grasped my knees and pushed them up and wide, the same position he'd put me in last night in his guest room. "My second favorite position. I like you on your back, your tits high on your chest, your pussy open for me."

I moaned and rolled my head to one side. His words made more moisture gather between my lower lips.

Cade set my heels on the table and pushed my knees farther. "Keep them wide. I need to taste you before we have dinner. If you remain still, I'll let you come. If I have to hold you open myself, I won't."

I inhaled sharply.

Cade's mouth descended without warning, not on my lips, but on my sex. He sucked my clit into his mouth, and I nearly shot off the table.

"So responsive, baby. Do you know how much that turns me on? Are you always like this? Or is it me?"

I tipped my chin down to see his face. "I don't know, Sir."

"Mmm." He didn't question me further. Instead he pressed my thighs open and licked a line between my lower lips. He moaned against my pussy, making me moan with him. In seconds my arousal went from twenty to fifty on a scale of one to ten. I had never been at one. I gripped my hands into a ball together and gritted my teeth as Cade licked and sucked and even stuck his tongue inside my channel.

I'd come the day before around Cade's fingers. Now I was seconds from coming against his face.

Cade sucked my clit between his lips and grazed it with his teeth. And that was it. I went over the edge, a scream escaping my mouth so fast I couldn't stop it. The pulsing of my clit against Cade's lips went on for so long, I couldn't see straight. When it ended, he kissed my pussy and released my legs.

I left them open, unable to close them. And besides, I hadn't been given permission. I was now Jell-O on the conference table.

"My girl's a screamer. We might have to do something about that if you don't want the whole office to know when you orgasm, baby."

Heat climbed up my face. I froze for a moment before it occurred to me there was likely no one else on the floor at that time, probably the entire building. But I would need to heed his advice if we were going to keep doing this.

Cade had more plans for me, however, and they didn't involve me lounging around naked on his conference table. He pulled me to sitting before I had muscle control and lifted me off the table to set me on the floor next to him. "Kneel beside me, baby. Legs wide, arms behind your back. Same position I taught you to stand, only on your knees."

I lowered myself at his side, glad for the rug beneath my knees, leery about the way he bossed me around. I was unable to deny his effect on me. After the day I'd spent doing his required reading, I was putty. And he knew this.

He lifted my chin. "That was beautiful. I love watching you come. I'm going to want to see you do it often." His thumb landed on my lower lip and stroked along the edge. "I won't give you that release every time, though, baby. Sometimes I'll leave you right on the edge, especially if you displease me." He released me and gave me a pointed look before he pulled the sandwiches closer.

There was no doubt what he meant. I'd displeased him this afternoon when I hadn't shown up.

My mouth watered. I was hungry, especially after that orgasm.

Cade brought a bottle of water to my lips and wrapped his hand behind my neck to tip my head back. He let me drink my fill and then set it on the table. "I like you at my feet, baby. A lot. Sometimes I'll let you sit at the table and eat. Other times, like today, I'll want you on your knees beside me. I'll feed you myself."

It didn't escape me that to him this relationship was a foregone conclusion. He'd told me last night I was his. He'd spent the entire afternoon staking his claim in a way that could not be denied.

Cade held a sandwich to my lips, and I opened for him to take a bite. At first my mouth was uncooperative. My teeth refused to chew. But soon my taste buds awoke, and I savored the bite, eventually swallowing.

Cade didn't speak while we ate. He enjoyed his dinner, and fed me as much as I wanted. Every time I opened my mouth for him, I slipped further under his spell. His hand curled behind my neck as he fed me, so gentle, caring. He tipped my head back when he offered me a drink. He brushed crumbs from my mouth. All the while, I remained kneeling at his side, my legs spread, moisture accumulating between them even though I'd come before we ate.

I wanted to stop this madness, stand and grab my clothes and run from the room, run from this city, run from my life. But I couldn't do it. I wanted Cade's attention even more.

I was horny and intrigued. And I knew deep down he was right. I was submissive. I craved his touch. I craved his cock. I silently prayed he took it out soon and slid inside me. Wasn't that the goal?

When we were done, I tipped my face to the floor and waited for him to address me. My actions were a direct result of the book I'd just read. If Cade had insisted I learn every detail of that book, he meant for me to put it to application. So I did.

Cade cleaned off the table and padded across the room. When he returned, he swiveled his chair to face me directly and resumed his seat. A pop made me flinch, and I lifted my face enough to see him pouring two glasses of white wine. "You may be at ease, baby." He held one glass out to me.

I sat back on my ankles, another thing I'd read that day, and took the offered glass.

Cade swirled it. "It's a 2009 Hanzell Chardonnay, one of my favorites. I think you'll be pleased."

I took a sip. My taste buds exploded around the flavor. It was divine.

Cade took several sips and set his glass on the table. He leaned forward, his elbows on his knees. "Look at me, baby."

I lifted my face.

"That's my favorite book on the subject. The most comprehensive and the closest I've come to finding something that fits how I perceive D/s."

"Okay, Sir."

He smiled and stroked a finger along my jawline before releasing me. "You make me so damn hard, baby."

I swallowed.

"Do you understand me better now?"

"I do, Sir."

He narrowed his gaze. "I'm not going to address your blatant disobedience today, except to point out that I don't want it to happen again. Are we clear?"

I licked my lips. I was clear. I just wasn't sure I liked it. Well, actually, the real problem was I did like it. I liked every bit of the way he spoke to me. I liked that he chose to take my choices out of my hands. I liked that he intended for me to obey him and would handle me as he saw fit if I didn't. I loved every single aspect of this. My body hummed with need. I could have gone my entire life without feeling a tenth of what Cade Alexander made me feel in two days.

But I was also a smart girl. Was this a smart choice? Giving up my free will to a man?

"I see your hesitation. I know you have questions. I want you to be assured I'll address every single one of those in due time." He leaned in closer, his face inches from mine as he continued, "You're mine, baby. I know you're struggling with that knowledge. That's to be expected."

I blinked at him.

He sat back and ran his hands through his hair until its messy disarray stood out in sharp contrast to his suit and tie. He reached for his tie and tugged until it came loose. Perhaps he was having as much trouble breathing as I was.

"We're going to explore this thing," he finally said. "Thoroughly. Not half-assed." He paused.

I watched his chest rise and fall as he breathed.

"Are you wet, baby?"

"Yes, Sir," I whispered.

"Have you ever in your life been that wet?"

"No, Sir." I shook my head. It was the truth.

"You just came hard. Was it enough?"

I shook my head.

"What do you want right now?"

I inhaled sharply. My lips parted. I had never used such language.

"Say it, Amelia." His impatient voice came out.

"Your cock, Sir." The harsher words of BDSM had seeped into me while I read.

"Good girl. That's the point. That's why we're here, baby. Your submission to me makes you so hot you can't stand it. Correct?"

"Yes, Sir." I gripped my wineglass with both hands, trying not to drop it.

"Take a drink, baby."

I sipped. He watched.

"Do me a favor. Give me the benefit of the doubt here. You know you're aroused by the idea of submission. I'm cocky enough to assume I'm a factor in that arousal." He lifted his eyebrows and gave a short grin. "What's to lose? You give this a try. If it doesn't work, we go our separate ways. If it does, we have the best sex in the world for the rest of our lives."

Those last words jarred me. Was he seriously thinking this could last? And what about the problem of me leaving my self-respect on the floor to get stomped on?

"Amelia." One word. He wanted me to consent.

"Okay, Sir." I couldn't believe I agreed. And I couldn't possibly say *no*.

"I don't expect you to follow that book to a *T*. There are

aspects I choose to handle differently, starting with eye contact, which I've already told you I prefer.

"I'll guarantee you several things. I won't injure you in any way. That isn't to say that I won't spank you. But I won't lay a hand on you in anger, and I'll never leave a mark that lasts longer than a few hours."

I nodded. How was I, a grown woman, kneeling naked in front of a fully clothed man, accepting the fact that he intended to spank me?

"You'll have a safe word. Red for now. You'll use it when you're in pain, emotionally or physically. Understood?"

"Yes, Sir." At least there was that.

"Many aspects of the book are up for negotiation. Many are not. For example, what we're doing right now is playing. How much of our time is spent in that role is negotiable. We'll explore it together and come up with an arrangement that suits us both. If the situation changes, we renegotiate.

"On the flip side, as I said before, your obedience to me is not negotiable when we're playing. The reason for this is I need you to trust me to know your limits and make the best choices. If you can't trust me, we have nothing. I realize this is a huge thing to ask since you don't know me yet, but I'm asking you to trust me and go all in."

"Okay, Sir." Could I do that? Again, could I not?

"Is there anything you can think of that needs immediate address?"

"Yes, Sir." I did. About two hundred things, but I would start with the most urgent. This job. "I worked hard to get this job. I don't want you to favor me at work. I don't want you to draw attention to the fact that you're...seeing me. I don't want anyone in this building to know about us."

"Fair enough."

"And I want you to let me quit."

"What?" He stiffened, his eyes going wide.

"I can't work for you and date you, or whatever this is. It's insane. I can't think around you."

He smiled. "I like that you can't think around me. Glad I'm not alone. But no, you can't quit."

"Cade—"

"No, Amelia. Anything else?"

I stared at him, my mouth hanging open.

Cade narrowed his gaze. "No, Amelia. Absolutely not. I want to know where you are. You may not quit. End of discussion. I will, however, keep this private. That I'll promise you."

"Mr. Alexander—"

"Do not call me that again, Amelia."

"Why? You get to call me Amelia when I specifically told you my friends call me Amy. Besides, I'm well aware that you call me by my given name when you're pissed at me."

He grinned. "Observant."

"Very." I stood, set my wineglass on the table, and looked

around for my clothes. They weren't in sight. When had he moved them? I crossed my arms over my chest and tapped a foot. "I need to get home, *Mr. Alexander*. I have a lot to think about."

"You'll get home plenty early, baby, but not yet. We aren't done here." He stood, reached for my arms, and tugged them from my chest. "Don't ever cover yourself in front of me. I love your body. I want to see all of it."

"You're very bossy." That sounded absurd even to me.

Cade laughed, tipping his head back. "You just now figured that out?" When he finished, he sobered and stepped closer. He cupped my breasts in both hands and stroked his thumbs over my nipples. "Exquisite."

I arched into him, reaching to grasp his forearms.

"And so fucking responsive."

My vision glazed over.

"Do you know what my favorite thing in the world is, baby?"

I shook my head, concentrating on his fingers and the way they played me. He gently pinched and rolled my nipples until they ached.

"The look on your face when you're so aroused it hurts."

I lifted on tiptoes.

"I saw that look for the first time Friday night before I'd ever touched you. I knew I wanted you immediately. You haven't disappointed me since."

"It's only been a few days."

He chuckled. "Is that a challenge?"

I had no idea. "More of an observation."

Cade pinched harder.

I moaned. His grip was too tight. It hurt. But not enough. Wetness flooded between my legs. "Are we going to have sex now, Sir?"

"Nope. I told you I wouldn't fuck you until you earned all three boxes on my kitchen table. I meant it."

My shoulders slumped. I pushed on his arms, trying to dislodge him. "If you aren't going to finish this, please let me go."

Cade held my nipples tighter. He smirked. "Oh, baby, you have so much to learn. Taking you to the edge is going to be my favorite pastime." He released me as he spoke and immediately grabbed my hips to set me back on the table. He kicked two chairs out of the way, making them roll a few feet from us.

He gripped my face in both hands and met my gaze. "You owe me. I haven't forgotten."

I swallowed. "Owe you what, Sir?"

"A punishment."

I stiffened. "For what, Sir?"

"For not showing up at lunch." He leaned in closer. "I won't tolerate disobedience in any way. When I tell you to do something, you'll do it. To make sure you have that clear in your head, I will punish you."

"How?" My voice was faint this time.

"Lie back again, Amelia."

Oh, *shit*. We were back to Amelia. I did as he said, lowering my back onto the cold surface of the table.

Cade immediately spread my legs and tapped my clit, making me buck upward and moan.

He thrust two fingers into my warmth and drew out the wetness to circle my now needy nub. I wondered how this was a punishment.

Cade swiped his fingers over my clit and then speared me with them again. He repeated this several times until I was panting and gripping the top of the table with my flattened hands. Just as I reached the edge of sanity, his hands disappeared.

I gasped. "Cade," I cried.

"What, baby?"

"Please. Oh God. Why are you stopping?"

"Punishment, baby."

My body sank. A whimper escaped my lips. My pussy froze. If it could have screamed, it would have. *No. No no no no no.*

Cade gripped my thighs as my breathing finally slowed and pushed them wider. "You did a decent job shaving, baby. Take more care tomorrow until you get everything."

I couldn't speak. His mundane request barely registered.

I lay like that forever. Finally, I was able to breathe easier. The need hadn't abated, but the urgency receded.

And then without warning, Cade thrust his fingers into me again. He fucked my pussy as deep as he could reach and then removed his hand to pinch my clit.

Shock. And then—oh, so fucking close. And then nothing.

I moaned. "Cade. Oh, God. Cade. Don't. I can't..."

"You can, baby. And you look so fucking sexy on the edge. I'm going to love training you to please me."

His words reached deep inside me. I wanted to please him so badly. I didn't know if it was because he was a Dom—my Dom—or if it was because I needed release. Either way, I would do anything.

"Let me suck you, Sir." I lifted my head, my legs shaking. I'd never given a blow job in my life. But I wanted to. Suddenly, it seemed important. Maybe he would stop torturing me if I sucked his dick. How hard could it be?

I wanted to see him. I wanted to taste him.

Cade smiled and shook his head. "That'll never work, baby. Don't try it again unless you want to experience real denial."

I was stunned. "What will never work?"

"Distracting me." He held my gaze while he pressed his fingers inside me, slower this time. Deep. He held them there, stroking my front wall while my vision clouded and my legs shook.

"Please," I muttered as I let my head lie back on the table.

His thumb landed on my clit and pressed hard.

I held my breath, willing my body to tip over the edge.

Cade's hand disappeared. "And another thing," he started, "don't ever come without my permission. I saw you willing it to happen. Your orgasms are mine. I'll give them out when I see fit. You won't take them greedily. Are we clear?"

"Yes, Sir," I muttered softly, deflated. Exhausted. And so on fire.

"I think you learned your lesson." He leaned forward and kissed my pussy gently. "Love this pussy, baby. So fucking much it hurts. Can't wait to bury my cock in here." He tapped my lower lips, making me flinch and moan again.

He chuckled. "So damn sensitive. It's going to be so easy to punish you. It takes two seconds to bring you to the edge, and then I can walk away."

He released my legs and grabbed my hands, pulling me to sitting.

I was shaky. I didn't see how I was going to stand, let alone walk out of the office.

Cade met my gaze. "I'm not going to torture you at work anymore this week. I don't want you to worry every day that I might drag you into my office. I don't like the idea of you working on the first floor, but I'll respect your need to remain anonymous in the office, at least for the time being."

"Thank you, Sir." A truce, of sorts.

"I'll send Arthur to pick you up at home tomorrow night at seven. Be ready."

"Okay, Sir."

"Good." He smiled. "God, you're precious."

I flushed. Again. For the millionth time.

Chapter Seven

I slept like a rock, again. Dragged myself to work, again. Completely unsure about my decision to continue this farce—again.

Surprisingly, my day was perfectly normal. Mr. Alexander, as I preferred to think of him while in the office, didn't bother me a single time. I never saw him. I wasn't even sure he was in the building.

Moriah said he left rave reviews about my work from the day before. I didn't meet her gaze and praised God she didn't ask me about what I'd done. I hadn't considered inventing something before I arrived. She sent me to work on the fourth floor again. Margie said she was going to ask for me to be transferred to her department. Since she'd lost her temp, she needed the help. And my work was far superior to the temp's.

I was elated. All of this had come about in two weeks without any intervention from Cade.

I was still uneasy about working in his building, but I would do it for now and see how things went.

I got home at six twenty and ran through the apartment like

a crazy woman getting ready. I only had forty minutes. I showered, shaved—everything—and quickly blow-dried my hair. I had never been particularly fussy about my hair. It lay nicely without much effort, and people had always complimented me on it. A few minutes was all I needed to put on makeup.

When Arthur arrived, I was ready at the door, small purse in hand, sexy black dress hugging my body. Cade hadn't mentioned what I should wear, but I knew he abhorred panties and was a fan of my skirts. So I went with that and smiled as I opened the door.

"Ma'am." Arthur tipped his hat. "I'm Arthur."

I smiled at him. "Nice to meet you." It felt incredibly peculiar having a driver pick me up.

I closed and locked my door and followed him to a Mercedes Maybach. It was the most luxurious car I'd ever been in, and it impressed me that Cade had a driver *and* a limo at his service. The anonymity of the back seat kept me from having to engage in conversation. I was stressed and fidgety. I didn't need to make small talk on top of that.

When we arrived at Cade's, Arthur opened my door and waited in the circle drive while I walked to the front of the house. He didn't say anything, just tipped his hat again.

I wondered if he would take me home later, and assumed that would have to be the case. Did Cade ever drive anywhere himself?

Cade opened the front door before I could knock. "Hey, baby." He took my hand. Well... Really, he gripped my forearm and let his fingers slide down to my hand as he tugged me inside.

Already at that gesture I was putty again.

He surprised me by flattening me against the door as soon as he shut it and kissed me. And God almighty could he kiss. He'd kissed me before, but never like that. His mouth was immediately insistent. He slanted to one side, his hands on my biceps, and slipped his tongue between my parted lips to devour me.

I gave as good as I received, anxious to know his taste. Every sweep of his tongue was perfection. I melted into him. The only thing keeping me from pressing my body along his was the way he held onto my arms. Even that was heady. He held me firmly, an odd mixture of gentle pressure that didn't reach the gray area of force, but was enough for me to know he was in control, not me.

Yep. Putty.

My brain cells scrambled when he released my lips to set his forehead against mine and smile.

When he grabbed my hand again and pulled me deeper into the house, I was afraid I might fall over my own feet. I managed to make it to the kitchen where he lifted me onto a stool and situated me at the island.

Even without words he was demanding. His every move had intention. He liked everything where he wanted it, when he wanted it, and that included me.

Cade left me there to pad to the refrigerator. I took the opportunity to watch his ass again. I felt overdressed when it registered what he was wearing, and I squirmed. He spun back around, grinning and holding up one of the bottles of wine I'd purchased on Monday.

"I may have overdressed," I said.

"Nope." He grabbed the corkscrew and went to work. "I like you just like that. I'll even let you keep the dress on for a while since you went to the effort and it's damn sexy."

And just like that, my pussy dampened.

Cade popped the cork and grabbed two glasses, which he filled, handing one to me. "See what you think."

I took a sip. It was even better than the last bottle he'd plied me with. And I knew what it cost. I'd bought it myself with his credit card.

"Mmm," I mumbled around the lip of the glass. "I know very little about wine, but you always manage to impress." I smiled at him. This was the most normal we'd ever been. I liked it. The tension you could always cut with a knife wasn't there, yet.

He circled the island and lifted me off the stool. "Couch." He nodded behind him as he tugged my hand again, walking backward.

I loved his space. It was clean and perfect, but inviting. As I sat on his couch, I felt the urge to lean into the soft leather cushions and relax. Relax wasn't in my vocabulary for the evening, though. Instead, I sat with my spine straight and my legs pressed together.

I glanced at him to see if he would reprimand me.

He chuckled. "You're so uptight."

"I never know what to expect with you."

He reached for a lock of my hair and twisted it around his fingers. "Let's straighten that out, shall we?"

I took another fortifying sip of wine. It really was delicious.

It occurred to me I hadn't eaten. If I wasn't careful, I would get light-headed fast. I wondered if he intended to feed me. I didn't mean that literally, although the thought made me shiver.

"Sometimes when we're together, we'll just be normal people."

I lifted both brows at him. We had never yet been normal.

He laughed. I loved it when he laughed. I loved those dimples on his cheeks and the way his eyes scrunched up when he relaxed. He was so fine to look at normally, but when he laughed, he was a work of art.

"Okay, I take total blame for not addressing much of anything with you before I stripped you and took control. That was rude. I apologize."

Cade Alexander apologized? Huh.

"We can't always be in the role. We'd be exhausted. Sometimes we need to just kick back and be normal."

"You can do that?" I teased.

He laughed again and grabbed me around the neck to pull my face in. He laid a long, delicious kiss on me that fed me the flavor of the wine from his mouth. And then he released me. "I can, baby. I'll be a perfect gentleman for the next two hours. Promise."

And then what?

The doorbell rang, startling me.

Cade didn't flinch. He jumped up and padded to the door, bare feet, red T-shirt stretching across his back.

I couldn't see the entrance from my seat, so I was shocked when he came back into my line of view carrying a pizza. "Dinner." He lifted it in the air to indicate the obvious.

"Cade Alexander eats pizza?" I asked. This was so much more the real me. Feisty. Joking.

Cade set the box on the coffee table and shocked me by bending to pull my shoes off. When he rose, he met my gaze. "I can be a regular guy. I love pizza. Now relax. Get comfortable. You look like you're about to face an interrogation for a crime you know you committed."

I slid back on the couch, lifted my legs, and tucked them under me.

"Good." Cade opened the pizza box and grabbed a slice. "I didn't know what you'd like, so I got supreme. Figured that way I could surely please you, and you could pick off what you don't eat." He handed me the first slice on a napkin.

It smelled fantastic, and I was starving.

I took a bite and then moaned at the flavor.

"I do have one rule, though."

My eyes shot to his.

"If you insist on moaning while you eat, I'll insist on stripping you naked and having my way with you." He looked at me pointedly. He wasn't kidding.

I managed to swallow that bite, but half of me wished he would do as he said. It would be difficult not to tempt him. So far, in my experience, being naked with him had not been a hardship.

I watched as Cade took his own slice and devoured it in about three bites. "Eat, baby." He nodded at my hands.

I lifted my pizza to my mouth and took another bite. After I swallowed, I spoke. "Supreme is my favorite, by the way."

"Excellent. See? We have something in common."

I rolled my eyes.

When we finished eating, Cade cleared away the mess, refilled our glasses, and leaned back against the couch. "Tell me about yourself."

"Not much to tell. You know most of it. I'm from LaGrange, about two hours south of here. I'm an only child. I had a normal childhood, went to college, then grad school, and here I am."

"How many boyfriends have you had?"

"Not many. Been too busy."

He let that line of questioning go. Thank God.

"You?"

"I'm from the suburbs north of here. Three sisters—Kirsten, Callie, and Katrina. All older." He scrunched up his face. "They all think they're my mother, even today. Six nieces and nephews, two apiece. My parents still live in the same house I grew up in."

How normal.

"How many girlfriends have you had?"

He laughed. "Touché."

"That's what I thought. Good answer."

He leaned forward. "None that made me feel the way you did in about two seconds last Friday." He reached for my head, wrapped his hand around my neck, and dragged me closer.

I lost my balance and put out both hands to brace myself against his lap as he kissed me a third time. And just as quick, he let go, and I bounced back, putting that small distance between us again. My face flamed at his announcement. *None that made me feel the way you did in about two seconds last Friday.* I would never forget that as long as I lived.

A phone rang, and Cade leaned back to pull his cell from his jeans pocket. He looked at me. "Sorry, baby. I need to take this."

"Okay."

Surprisingly he didn't move. He leaned into the couch farther and lifted the cell to his ear. "Give me good news, Riley." He listened for a few seconds. "Uh-huh... Okay... Well, stay on it... Thanks for the update." He didn't say goodbye. He just ended the call and turned back to me. "Sorry."

"No problem."

"I work all hours. You should know. Some of my people are on the west coast. Some are in other countries."

"Right. Of course." I couldn't imagine the stress. Although Cade did not seem stressed. When he worked, he worked, even if that work was a two-minute phone call. When he was done, he was done. Every bit of his attention reverted back to me.

He watched my face for a few minutes, seeming to think about something. "I have to go away this weekend."

"Okay."

"Come with me?"

I was shocked. Go with him? Away for the weekend?

"A friend of mine is getting married. It's his engagement party. I'd intended to go alone. But now, I have you." He reached for my hair again. "Say yes."

"Yes." I let that slip out without thinking. Probably too impulsive, but there it was.

And it was worth it to see his face beam. "Good. Great. I'll pick you up at about seven Friday night. We'll be back Sunday night. Does that work for you?"

"I think so." I nodded. I couldn't think of anything pressing I had to do. I needed to remember to let Cheyenne know. She'd mentioned shopping on Saturday. Plus, no one should go away for the weekend with a man they barely knew without telling someone. "What should I bring?"

"Nothing." He grinned huge.

"I mean clothes, dork. What kind of party is it? How formal?"

"Did you just call me a dork?" He leaped into my space in an instant, mirth dancing in his eyes as his body leaned forward inch by inch until I had to flatten myself against the arm of the couch at my back.

He didn't stop. He kept coming until his entire frame covered me, his hard body pressing into mine. With his lips inches from my own, he spoke again. "Listen, you minx. I meant exactly what I said. If you have some special makeup you need or some hair thingies, fine. I'll cover the rest."

I stared at him. "You'll cover the rest?" I finally repeated.

"That's what I said."

"You're going to buy me clothes?"

"Yep." He trailed a finger down my cheek and then my neck until it rested on my throat above the collar of my dress.

"You don't know my sizes."

"I'm good." His gaze wandered to the spot where his finger lay. "You won't need much. I don't intend to let you leave the hotel for much more than the party."

I swallowed. Was I ready for this?

I'd never in my life been away for a weekend with a man. And I'd been dating this one for about three days, if I could even consider what we were doing dating.

What we had going tonight was nice. Very nice. I liked it. A lot. And from the look in Cade's eyes, it was about to get nicer.

Cade stroked his finger lower over my dress, between my breasts, watching as he went. He kept going, lifting his body off mine as he leaned to one side to let his finger continue, dipping into the hollow of my belly where it sunk and then down one leg to my thigh. He brushed his pointer over the skin of my inner thigh under the hem of my dress, shifting his gaze to mine.

I willed him to reach farther. Touch me. Anything.

"Are you wet for me, baby?" His voice was lower, gravelly.

I nodded. I always was, but it intensified every time he flat out asked me.

"Good. See, I can do normal." He smiled, his finger still drawing leisurely circles on my thigh.

I spread my legs wider for him.

Cade suddenly released me and sat up, hauling me to sitting also. He kissed my forehead. "You're so fucking tempting."

I was?

"I'm not going to play with you tonight. I don't think I can without fucking you. And you aren't ready for that."

I wasn't? I couldn't keep up. I opened my mouth to question him, but he stopped me with a finger. "Don't. Just trust me."

I nodded.

"Arthur's going to drive you home. I need to make a few calls. I want to make sure I'm totally free for forty-eight hours to enjoy you this weekend."

I liked that idea. Especially after the sweet way he'd managed to spend the evening with me without stripping me both literally and figuratively.

"I'm not going to see you tomorrow, but I'll be there at seven on Friday. Be ready."

"Okay."

He shook his head and then kissed me again, slower, sweeter, longer. Not with the same urgency as before, but just as amazing.

Chapter Eight

I was running through my apartment grabbing things to stick in my bag when I heard the knock at my door. I wasn't ready. I dashed from my bedroom to the front of my apartment and opened the door, breathing heavily.

Cade stood there, casually leaning against the frame, grinning. "Hey, baby." His usual greeting made my knees almost buckle. His gaze roamed up and down my body as his face fell and his brow furrowed. He righted himself and stepped inside, pushing me back with a hand to my chest until he could shut the door. "What are you wearing?"

I glanced down, wondering what his beef was. I thought I looked fine. Comfy jeans. Tank top. Flip flops. "What?" Lord the man was intense.

He shook his head. "No way. Change." He pointed behind me toward the hall.

"Cade. What the hell?" Now I was nervous. "Aren't we just driving to Nashville tonight? That will take like four hours. It'll be almost midnight before we get there. Who cares what I'm wearing? This is comfortable." I plucked at my shirt, miffed with him. How dare he judge my clothes?

I straightened my spine. "Look, I'm not made of money. I don't own a shitload of fancy clothes like you do. This is me. Take it or leave it. If you're going to be an asshole about it, go without me." I stepped back.

Cade followed, taking two strides, grabbing me around the waist and lifting me off the ground to spin me around. He pinned me against the door before I knew what was happening. His hands wormed their way under my tank top until they were splayed on my bare skin.

I tried to wiggle free of his clutch, anger still eating at me, when he lifted his face. Laughter lined the edges of his eyes. He was fighting it. He'd tucked his top lip between his teeth. His hands roamed higher until he cupped my breasts through my bra.

"Cade. Let me go." I pushed against his chest, but he didn't budge. And I had no idea what he suddenly found funny, but I suspected I wasn't going to agree.

"You're so fucking sexy when you wig out, baby." He leaned in and kissed the side of my neck, infuriating me further.

I pushed on his hands, trying to dislodge his grip around my breasts, pissed as hell that my nipples had immediately responded to his touch. "I'm not trying to be sexy. Just realistic."

"Baby..." He reached under my bra and pinched my nipples. I stopped squirming. "Look at me."

Damn him. I met his gaze.

"Love the outfit. Tight shirt. Sexy as hell." He released my nipples as he spoke and tugged my shirt over my head to toss it on the floor. "And this bra. Cute." He reached for the front clasp, popped it open, and wiggled it down my body to join my shirt.

Cool air hit my hardened nipples, and I gasped at his audacity. I shouldn't have been shocked.

His hands roamed down to my jeans where he popped the button and lowered the zipper. He spoke as he tugged them over my hips. "These also look fantastic on you, baby. Perfect for running around town when you aren't with me." He kneeled at my feet and tugged them free.

When he stood back up, his smile had faded. "Panties? Really?"

I flinched. "I can't go without under jeans."

"Why the hell not?"

"I would rub. It would…hurt."

Cade narrowed his gaze. He seemed to be thinking. "Okay, here's the deal, baby. When you're with me, skirts, dresses, anything I can reach under and touch your pussy. When you're with your girls or out running errands, you can wear the jeans. And because I'm so good at compromise, I'll even concede to the panties." He grinned big, melting my resolve to be angry.

"Now, as much as I wish we could stay here and I could admire your naked body all night, we have to get going." He cupped my breasts again as he finished speaking. "How about I help you find something more appropriate to wear between here and the car, and we get on the road."

Between here and the car?

"Cade..." I warned.

He ignored me and took my hand to pull me down the hall. When we hit the bedroom, he stopped and I ran into the back of him in the doorway. "Holy shit. Did a cyclone hit in here?"

I glanced around. "Did I mention I'm not as tidy as you?"

"Nope." He stepped over clothes and headed for my closet. "Why in God's name do you have everything you own on the floor?"

I shrugged to his back. "Couldn't decide what to pack. I was trying things on."

He paused at the entrance to my closet, toeing some shoes out of his way. He looked over his shoulder at me. "I told you not to pack a thing."

I put my hands on my hips, trying to ignore how ridiculous I felt. "Surely you were kidding. I can't go away for the weekend with nothing but a toothbrush, Cade."

"Why not?"

I rolled my eyes.

He glanced down. "Take off the damn panties, baby. I hate them."

I tipped my chin up defiantly. Yes, I was testing him. Yes, he was making me hotter by the second. And yes, I was a little pissed by his high-handed ways.

Cade's shoulders slumped. He stepped into my closet, shuffled through several things on hangers, selected something, and re-emerged.

I paid no attention to whatever he held. My gaze was on his face.

Cade tossed the hanger on the end of the bed and pranced toward me like a predator. "Amelia, you so do not want to play these games with me."

Oh, but I did. And I didn't miss his use of my given name. My spine stiffened. It took everything I had to keep from crossing my arms over my chest. I didn't want him to have the satisfaction.

Calm as can be, Cade strode over my discarded piles of clothes until he reached my side. I had no idea what his intentions were, but him leaning down to heave me up and throw me over his shoulder hadn't made the list.

I squealed. "Put me down. Jesus, Cade."

The next thing I knew, I was facedown on the rumpled bed I hadn't made in months, my panties yanked down to my knees, and Cade was on the bed beside me. The entire mattress dipped as he landed.

I fought to flip over. He held my lower back with one strong hand. His other palm landed on my ass. Hard.

It knocked the wind out of me and shocked me into submission, literally. I froze, unable to breathe.

Cade rubbed my ass where his hand had landed. And then he spanked me again. Several times. I lost count. It hurt. And my pussy ached to be fucked. I was so embarrassed by my response that I buried my face in the mess that was my comforter and stifled a moan.

This should not be arousing.

Cade palmed my ass again, squeezing it gently, molding my flesh in his huge hand. "That's my good girl. Five more, baby. Stay still."

I sucked in a breath and held it while he landed three more slaps, paused to rub the burn covering my entire ass and part of my thighs. And then the last two, a bit harder.

I didn't move a muscle. For one, I was afraid I would come, and I didn't want Cade to know that. For another thing, I'd never been so humiliated. I was a grown woman who'd been spanked by a man as though I were a naughty child.

Which in a sense wasn't far from the truth.

He might have gone easy on me for wearing the panties in the first place. But even I had to admit I'd crossed the line when I'd flat out refused to remove them. I'd known somewhere in my mind what might happen. I might have even willed it.

But that didn't take away from the shame.

Cade lay down alongside me and stroked my skin lightly, starting with my ass and moving up my back until he brushed my thick hair from my hidden face.

I turned in the other direction, trying not to cry. If I breathed or spoke, I wouldn't be able to hold back my emotions.

"Baby, look at me." He reached across and tucked my hair behind my ear, but it fell right back into its place in front of my face. The first time in my life I was super glad my hair was so thick and unruly.

Cade set his chin on my back and continued to soothe my heated skin.

Thank God. If he'd forced me to face him, I would have freaked out.

As it was, he didn't give me enough time, but it was something. Grabbing my shoulders, he turned me onto my side, facing him. I kept my eyes shut, my lip tucked between my teeth. A tear rolled down my face, pissing me off. I knew there would be others, and I wondered how Cade would react.

Cade wiped my tear away. "That's it. Get it out, baby. You'll feel so much better after."

He wanted me to cry? Jesus, I was in over my head. But the tears piled up, running down my face until I was engaged in the full-blown ugly cry that included my nose running and me choking back noisy sobs.

I lifted my hand to cover my face, but Cade pulled it away. He kissed my cheek. "That's my girl. I know that was tough. It'll get easier."

It'll get easier?

I didn't want it to get easier. I didn't want it to ever happen again.

I wanted to tell Cade to get the fuck out of my apartment and leave me alone to lick my wounds. I felt like an idiot.

"Baby, look at me," he repeated, gently stroking my arm now.

I kept my eyes closed, willing myself to stop sobbing. I sucked in deep breaths, making things worse.

I couldn't move my legs because they were tangled together by my stupid panties. And my ass stung like hell.

Cade eased me back onto my belly and climbed off my bed.

I listened without moving, wondering what the hell he was going to do next. I heard him step toward my bathroom, his feet landing at odd intervals among my clothing. I heard the water running. And then he was back. He gently pulled my panties down my legs and then climbed back up to my side. He turned me toward him again and wiped my face with a cool cloth.

I felt marginally better. My ass still stung, but at least I could breathe.

Surprisingly, he settled me back on my belly, and I heard the pop of something right before a cool substance landed on my butt. "It's just cream, baby. Found it in your bathroom. It'll take away the sting." He rubbed it into my ass for an eternity.

I began to relax while he worked, my body loosening and sinking into the mattress. I was almost dozing when he finally stopped and leaned in to whisper in my ear. "I know you're tired, baby, but we really have to hit the road. You can rest on the way." He brushed my hair out of my face, and I finally opened my eyes to peer at him.

He was so gentle. Actually, he'd been gentle through the entire scene. He hadn't gotten angry. His blows had been hard and accurate, but not out of anger. He was completely calm.

I stared at him. Could I still go with him for the weekend?

He lifted me like a rag doll and held me in his lap, rocking me back and forth for several minutes while he looked into my eyes. "Such a good girl. I'm so proud of you. What you're feeling is completely normal. You slipped into a sub-space. It leaves you exhausted."

I said nothing, blinking at him.

His hand smoothed down my body until he reached my sex. "Were you aroused, baby?" He eased me on to my back across the bed and nudged my legs apart.

I let him, completely limp and unable to stop him. I wanted him to touch me.

And when he did, I moaned. Loud.

"Oh, yes. Baby you're so wet." He lifted his fingers between us and sucked them into his mouth. And then he smiled. "Everything's going to be okay, baby." He climbed off the bed, pulled me to sitting, and reached across to grab something at my side. A second later, he eased the dress he'd chosen from my closet over my head.

I glanced down. It was a sundress, soft material, low cut. I hadn't worn it for a while. I thought it was too short, and the way it hung in the back made it difficult to wear a bra. But of course Cade had no intention of adding a bra, and he probably selected it intentionally for the length.

I rolled my eyes.

"There she is." He smiled at me and tugged me to my feet. He snapped his fingers. "Hang on." He picked his way across the room again and returned carrying a pair of sandals. When he kneeled at my feet and put them on me, I grabbed his shoulders, fighting the urge to cry again at the way he took such care.

When he stood, he took both my shoulders in his hands and faced me. "Let's go, baby."

I nodded, finding my voice and glancing around. "I still need to pack a few things."

"Still?" He chuckled and glanced at the ceiling. "She doesn't get it."

I shrugged free of his clutch and ducked under his arm. I went straight to the bathroom and grabbed my bag from the floor. I'd packed everything I would need as far as makeup and bathroom shit. When I turned around, I ran right into Cade. He set his finger under my chin and lifted my face. "You got everything you need from the bathroom?"

"Yep."

"Then let's go." He took my bag from my hand, grabbed my arm, and tugged me out of the room and back to the front, flipping off lights as we went. He even reached for my purse on the table next to the front door. And that was it. He was done. He opened the door and ushered me out.

We were leaving, and I was taking nothing with me for a weekend trip to Nashville. Not even one pair of panties or a bra. Just makeup, toiletries, and a toothbrush. Great.

Chapter Nine

I was surprised to find the limo out front, Arthur in the front seat waiting. As soon as we approached, he jumped from the Mercedes and rounded it to open the back door.

I cringed, wondering what he thought had taken us so long. I also knew my face was red and splotchy from crying.

And it didn't help one bit when I wondered if Arthur was used to picking up crying women with Cade.

Cade set a hand on my back and urged me to get in the car.

After I climbed in, he appeared beside me. The back was roomy and comfortable. I gritted my teeth against the sting of my ass hitting the seat, sending renewed heat to my cheeks.

The door closed, leaving us in silence.

"Lift your skirt, baby. The leather will feel good against your sore skin."

I lifted my butt to do his bidding and turned my gaze toward the far window so he couldn't see my face.

I would sooner cut off my right arm than cry again.

I was aware of Cade setting my belongings on the floor, and

then he wrapped his hand around my neck and pulled me down into his lap. His fingers threaded in my hair as I braced myself against his thigh.

"Sleep for a bit, baby. You'll feel better."

There was no doubt I would gladly close my eyes and block out the universe to avoid confronting him right then.

Cade smoothed his hand down my body until he reached the hem of my dress. He eased the material up over my hip, leaving my bare ass exposed to the cool air of the car. When he stopped moving, resting his fingers across my belly, I resumed breathing normally.

My mind raced.

"Sleep, baby," he repeated gently.

Completely overloaded, I let it go and drifted into bliss.

When I awoke, it was to the sound of Cade's voice. He was on the phone, clearly trying to keep his tone down. But I was alert quickly, my face snuggled into his thigh, my hands balled up against my chest.

I blushed when I remembered why my ass stung, and that it was exposed.

Cade must have realized I was awake because his hand moved farther up my waist until he cupped my breast, idly stroking my nipple.

My body came completely alive in less than a second. I had to fight hard to remain still and not moan. Damn it.

Cade continued to talk in hushed tones, his hand never

ceasing its actions. It was so casual, I found it hard to believe how aroused I was and how much moisture gathered between my legs.

When he ended the call, he leaned over me, brushed my hair from my face, and smiled. "Hey, baby. You rest well?"

I nodded, pushing myself off his lap. I needed to regroup. And I needed him to stop touching me.

The latter he didn't oblige me on. He did release my breast as I sat, but only to tug me close to his body and kiss my temple. "Let's talk."

My ass was sore, but it wasn't as bad as it had been before. I glanced around. It was pitch dark outside. "What time is it?"

"About ten. You were exhausted. It's understandable." He tipped my face back with a hand on my neck, somehow managing to control my position even from that angle. His gaze met mine, his brow furrowed. "You okay?"

"I think so."

"I know you defied me on purpose. I knew it would happen eventually. It's normal behavior in a new D/s relationship. But you know I had to act, right?"

I swallowed.

He nodded. "When you make an innocent mistake, I'll go easy on you. When you blatantly disobey me, I won't. I think that's clear."

I stared at him, my eyes watering. Finally I found my weak voice. "I'm embarrassed."

"Don't." He shook his head. "It's part of D/s, baby. You'll

mess up. I'll punish you. And," he leaned his face in closer, as if that were possible, "you liked it."

I took several shallow breaths, trying to wrap my mind around his words. Who liked being spanked like a child? *You did*. It wasn't as though I could deny it. I'd almost come as his hand made contact with my ass. It had been so erotic. Still, I didn't relish the idea of being humiliated like that again. "I didn't like it, Sir."

"You did, baby." His hand moved up into my hair, tipping my head back more. He kissed my lips gently. "And it was so sexy."

I stared at him, unwilling to argue this point and knowing I would lose in the end.

"And I'm going to tell you something else."

I blinked.

"I intend to spend large chunks of time this weekend playing with you. I don't want to spank you again too soon. So keep in mind if you defy me, you'll find yourself in a time out, naked with your nose pressed to the corner of the wall. Spanking is quick and effective. It stops the behavior on the spot. You won't soon wear panties in my presence again. But if you thought it was embarrassing, wait until you stand in a corner for a while." He lifted one eyebrow.

I gasped. *He wouldn't.*

But I knew he would.

I thought about his words and how they made me feel for a long time. He let me rest against him in silence while he held a small electronic device up and flipped through pages of information, seemingly able to read faster than the average human.

Time out? No way. The knot in my belly became a tight ball. How unbelievably humiliating would that be?

When the limo came to a stop, I was surprised how much time had passed. It was almost midnight. Cade didn't wait for Arthur. He exited the car himself and helped me out.

I smoothed my dress down, hoping it wasn't obvious I was naked underneath.

It took Cade only minutes to check us in, and then he took my hand and led me to the elevator. A short ride up and we stepped straight into a suite of rooms.

I was shocked, expecting a hallway, not a living space.

Cade didn't flinch. He walked in, plopped my bags and his briefcase on a plush chair, and turned to face me. He took me in his arms and tipped my head back. "You're exhausted."

He wasn't wrong. Even after my nap, I felt like I hadn't slept in weeks.

Cade kissed my forehead, took my hand, and led me to a room off the main area. "Use the bathroom, baby."

I followed his instructions, padding to the adjoining bath while wondering if he would let me sleep or demand more from my body.

Like the rest of the suite, the bathroom was luxurious. It was larger than my bedroom at home, decorated in dark wood and tiles that were a swirl of maroons and browns. I used the toilet and then turned to the sink. I smiled. Everything I needed was at my fingertips, even though I hadn't brought my bag into the bathroom.

I washed my face and brushed my teeth. When I returned, Cade had pulled back the sheets and sat on the edge of the bed. I padded back to his side.

He immediately grabbed the hem of my short dress and pulled it over my head, forcing my arms up above me. His hands landed on my waist, and he placed a chaste kiss on each of my nipples.

He moaned as he lifted his gaze. "Your body is phenomenal. I'll worship it often. But not tonight." He stood and patted the mattress. "Climb up."

I followed his demand and lay on the softest sheets I'd ever touched. Cool silk that felt luxurious against my skin.

Cade covered me up and kissed my forehead. "Sleep, baby. I'll see you in the morning." He walked back across the room, shut off the light, and closed the door.

I was stunned for a moment. He wasn't going to sleep with me?

Apparently not. There must have been more than one bedroom in the suite.

Without dwelling any longer on the obvious, I closed my eyes, released a long breath, and let sleep suck me under.

Chapter Ten

Sunlight was streaming into the room when I opened my eyes. I quickly remembered where I was and smiled at the voice I could hear from the other room. Was Cade ever not on the phone?

I was rested. Amazing considering everything that had transpired last night. Instead of tossing and turning and worrying incessantly about spankings and time outs, I'd slept hard.

I slipped from between the sheets and padded to the adjoining bathroom, totally intending to take advantage of the shower I'd seen last night. It had jets coming from every direction, and I looked forward to my tension easing under the hot water.

The first thing I noticed when I entered the bathroom was the heated floor. No way the tile would be that warm against my bare feet otherwise. Lord. That was opulence.

I flipped on the shower, used the toilet, and then stepped beneath the flow of water, wondering if I would be interrupted or left to shower alone. I stood there forever, letting the warmth cascade over my body before reaching toward the dispensers on the wall and squeezing out shampoo. It smelled fantastic, and my scalp actually tingled as I rubbed it in. Whatever brand that was, I wanted some at home.

I took my time, soaping and rinsing and conditioning. When I finally shut off the water and stepped out, I felt like a new woman. The enormous fluffy towel felt wonderful against my skin.

When I turned toward the mirror, I grabbed the comb off the counter and worked through my thick hair. I brushed my teeth and stared at myself. I looked healthy and rested.

I was relieved to find a pale pink silk robe hanging on the back of the door. It wasn't much—and barely covered my assets—but it was better than stepping out into the main room naked. I slipped it on and tied the sash as I left the room. My feet were bare, but I didn't see any slippers, so I quietly opened the door to the bedroom and stepped out.

Cade had his back to me. He stood at a wall of windows facing the Nashville skyline, his phone to his ear. He wore nothing but a pair of navy flannel sleep pants that hung low on his hips and accentuated his narrow waist. No shirt. Bare feet. He must have sensed my presence because he turned around almost immediately and dismissed the caller. "Gotta go. I'll get back to you on that."

His smile was huge as he approached. I stood still, uncertain what he might have in mind. Every day with him was a surprise. When he arrived in front of me, he wrapped me in his arms and kissed my lips briefly. Then he buried his face in my wet hair. "Mmm. That smells good."

"I thought so too," I mumbled against his shoulder. "It was in the shower dispenser."

He'd showered also. His hair was damp. His bare chest was

so fine, I wanted to set my lips on it and nibble a path across his pecs.

Cade eased me back and met my gaze. "Wasn't sure what you liked to eat, so I ordered a variety of food." He wrapped his arm around my back and led me to the small table set up next to the kitchenette.

I wasn't usually super fond of breakfast, but this morning I was starving, and when Cade lifted the lids off various dishes, my mouth watered. It smelled so good.

He pulled out a chair for me, pushed me to the table, and then took a seat across from me. "Eat, baby. I already had my fill." He picked up a half-drunk cup of coffee and took a sip.

I loaded my plate with a little bit of everything and grabbed my fork. It didn't slip my notice that he let me sit at the table and feed myself. I wondered how often he would prefer me on my knees. While that had been the strangest meal ever, it had also made me hungry for more than food.

"I thought we'd tour the Ryman today. Have you ever been there?"

I shook my head. My mouth was full.

"I haven't either, believe it or not. Never had enough time. But I heard it's amazing."

I swallowed my bite. "Sounds good." *Especially if you give me something to wear besides this robe.*

"I'll let you eat then, and we'll get going." He stood, leaned over to kiss my forehead, and padded to another door I hadn't paid any attention to yet. It would have to be another bedroom.

I ate alone, not a bit sorry. I was hungry, and it was difficult to chew and swallow with Cade's eyes boring into me. When I finished, I returned to my bathroom, brushed my teeth again and went to work drying my hair. As I set the dryer aside and tamed my locks into place, I saw Cade leaning against the doorframe watching me.

His face was set. Not in anger, but in awe. A small smile lifted the sides of his mouth. He was dressed now, jeans, loafers, and a black designer T-shirt that was surely cut to fit him specifically.

And he held a box in his hands. Not just any box, but one of the ones I'd been sent to collect for him on Monday. Had that been just five days ago?

He lifted it with one hand. "Your first gift."

There had been three. And he'd told me he would sleep with me after I earned them all. I clenched the walls of my pussy at the thought—I was that much closer to having him inside me.

Cautiously, I took it from him and set it on the counter. Lord knew what was inside. It was delicately wrapped, and I recognized it as the one I'd retrieved from the lingerie shop. This made me both anxious and nervous. Obviously, whatever was inside was about to go on my body. During the day. For a trip to tour one of the coolest opry houses of all time.

My fingers shook as I pulled the end of the ribbon and then lifted the lid. I pushed tissue paper away, feeling Cade's eyes on my back, and reached inside to extract the contents. What I lifted out was a delicate sexy bra made of the finest lace I'd ever touched. It was pale pink, like the robe I wore, and the cups looked as though they would barely cover my nipples.

"There's more."

I reached back inside and came up with a matching garter belt in the same pale pink lace.

Cade sauntered closer and wrapped his arms around my middle from behind. He nudged my hair away from my shoulder with his chin and kissed me behind the ear. "Do you like them?"

"Of course," I whispered. They were too pretty to wear.

Cade drew his palms up my body and slipped my robe from my shoulders. At some point while I was fixing my hair, the sash must have come undone. He turned me to face him and took the delicate bra from my hand to help me put it on. It was weird having a man put a bra on me, but he did it expertly, plumping up my breasts when he finished.

I glanced down to see I had been right, the lace barely covered my nipples. It was more of a shelf. It was luxurious, however, like many things I'd experienced that morning, and my belly took a plunge at the way Cade eyed my chest, clearly pleased with the results. He dipped his face and kissed the top swell of each globe.

"You won't need the garter today. It's too hot for thigh highs, but I wanted you to have them. I'll enjoy them another time." He grinned and took my hand to lead me from the bathroom.

My toiletry bag was on my bed now, and next to it was another box. I hoped it contained more fabric than the first, or I would get arrested during our outing.

"Open it, baby."

I padded forward and lifted the lid off my next gift. It wasn't one of the packages I'd picked up, but a new one. Inside was a dress, not surprising. Also pale pink. It seemed to be a theme today.

"I thought that color would look fantastic against your skin." He grazed a hand down my arm and took the dress from my fingers. "Lift your arms, baby."

I did as he bade and let Cade lower the soft material over my head. He stepped back. "Perfect."

It was. I could have rummaged around in a store all day and not come up with anything that fit me better or made me feel as sexy. The bodice hugged my chest, the front cut low enough to show my cleavage, but not distastefully. The middle section was fitted around my belly. And then the bottom flowed out in a full skirt. The material was so fine that it hung loose around my hips and butt.

I felt decidedly naked beneath.

Cade pulled me into his chest and kissed my lips again. "Gorgeous. And you blush when you think too hard."

He was right. I always had. And lately it seemed bright red cheeks were my new permanent look.

"Trust me. It's long enough. No one will know what you aren't wearing beneath but me. And I would never share." He positioned me at arm's length with his hands on my biceps. "Trust me?"

I nodded. I did trust him. I had no idea why, but there it was. I had to trust him for this to work. So far, he hadn't let me down. Even yanking my panties off and spanking my bare ass hadn't been so bad in retrospect. In the back of my mind niggled the thought of intentionally acting out so he would do it again.

Cade led me from the room. A pair of delicate silver sandals sat next to the couch, and he urged me to sit, nodding at them. How did this man manage to pinpoint all of my sizes, including my shoes?

It occurred to me he could have easily gathered that information from my clothes while I'd napped in the nude at his house that first evening. At least that eliminated the possibility he was psychic.

Though with Cade Alexander, anything was possible.

When we stepped out into the bright warmth of the day, Arthur was waiting by the car. He smiled and tipped his hat as he opened the back door for us. I almost giggled picturing him standing there all night waiting in case we decided to go out. It was absurd. Of course Cade had alerted him in some way. After all, Cade never went a minute without clutching his state-of-the-art phone. It was more like a computer, and he clearly used it as such.

In fact, as I settled on the seat in the same spot I'd been in last night, Cade set the device on the console next to the door. "How's your tush, baby?" he asked while he toyed with a lock of my hair. "I should have rubbed some more lotion in." He lifted my chin, his eyes narrowed.

"It's fine." I swallowed. *Could we not talk about it?*

He paused and then released me, his face serious. "Don't keep things from me. Got it?"

"Okay." *What things?*

"If it's still sore, I want to know."

Oh, that.

"The intention is to leave your ass nice and pink, making it uncomfortable for a few hours to remind you of your disobedience. Any longer than that, and I've spanked you too hard."

"Okay." What more could I say? I didn't want to have a conversation about the state of my "disobedient ass" any longer. So, I changed the subject. "What time is the party tonight?"

He smiled and shook his head. "Nine. And don't think I didn't notice your attempt to evade my comments."

I flushed deeper. Damn him and his sense of all things.

Cade swiped a thumb across my cheek, sending goose bumps down my body. The inside of the limo was cool, almost too cool compared to the heat that would await us on the streets of Nashville in June.

I watched out the window as we drove. Nashville was smaller than Atlanta, a more old-world charm, historic, less industrialized. I had considered applying at another technology company in Nashville at one point—The Rockwood Group. In fact, we drove by it on the way through town. The building loomed tall and majestic, just like Alexander Technologies. I had decided to stay in Atlanta for the near future to be closer to my parents.

It only took about ten minutes to arrive at the Ryman Auditorium, and soon we were inside the majestic opry house. I tipped my head back to admire the entire view while Cade took my arm and led me to a gentleman off to the side.

The man smiled broadly as we approached. He was a middle-aged, round, balding man who had an air of excitement about his job. "Hi. I'm Simon. I'll be your tour guide today." He shook both of our hands as Cade introduced us.

"Great. If you'll follow me, we'll get started."

I glanced around. The entrance was filled with guests in line waiting to buy tickets. But not us. Of course. Cade Alexander would have planned ahead and paid in advance and arranged something more private. Naturally.

The tour was wonderful. Simon was a walking Nashville encyclopedia. He shared so much knowledge about the music industry, I would never begin to remember it all.

When we were done, Cade led me back outside into the bright sun. "Let's walk. There's a restaurant nearby. I'm starving." He led me down the street, his gait slow enough to accommodate my shorter stride like a true gentleman. He also kept a palm on my lower back any time he wasn't holding my hand.

The way he handled me warmed me inside. He really did have another side that wasn't bossy and demanding. And I liked this side of Cade Alexander. I liked the other side too. But meeting this Cade was a breath of fresh air.

Lunch was amazing. The temperature outside was perfect, so we chose a table on the patio. Cade told me funny stories about growing up with three older sisters, and I told him how lucky he was not to be the prime focus of his parents' attention for never-ending years. I loved my parents to pieces, and I joked about our relationship, but deep down I hoped I conveyed how much I appreciated everything they meant to me. Because that was what life was all about, and I wanted my own children to know the same love and respect I'd had growing up.

From Cade's tales, he'd been doted on by so many women in his life, he knew better than anyone what it meant to be loved.

We took our time strolling around downtown before heading back to the hotel. Arthur materialized out of nowhere and whisked us away.

Chapter Eleven

The moment we stepped back into the hotel suite, Cade's demeanor changed so fast I wobbled on my feet. As soon as the elevator closed, he advanced on me, pure predator. And there was no doubt who was the prey.

"I want to play," he stated.

"Okay." I backed up. I knew exactly what he meant. I was shocked we'd gone half the day without him mentioning the idea. I was equally relieved he made no motion to dominate me in public. I couldn't have handled that.

I was glad I wore flat sandals as I stepped backward into the living room. I might have tripped if I'd had on heels. My ass hit the back of the couch, leaving me no more room to escape. Not that I wanted to escape Cade Alexander, but instinct caused me to hesitate.

The man oozed masculinity normally. Now, it poured out of him. His gaze pierced me, pinning me to my spot. When he reached me, he framed my body with both hands on the back of the couch.

He didn't close his eyes as he kissed me sweetly, so I stared into his also. "Baby, you're amazing."

"You aren't so bad yourself."

He released the couch with one hand and reached under my skirt so fast, I gasped. In less than a second, his hand was at my sex, two fingers stroking through my folds. He moaned. "So wet for me. Always so wet. My sweet girl likes to play."

I did. The permanent tight ball in my belly grew tighter.

"Step out. Spread your legs for me, baby."

I managed that task with ease, opening myself up to his touch. He held my gaze while he stroked through my folds and then pushed two fingers inside me.

I moaned as I lifted up on my tiptoes, my legs already threatening to buckle.

Cade smiled. "Always so ready." And then his hand was gone, and he grabbed the hem of my dress and tugged it over my head.

I never saw where it went. The next thing I knew was his mouth at the upper swell of my breasts, nibbling, licking, sucking gently on my flesh. He chinned the lace of my bra down to expose my nipple and sucked it into his mouth, his hand circling around me at the small of my back. "So sweet," he muttered against my chest when he released me.

I breathed deeply as he stepped back, a whine escaping my lips. I steadied myself by gripping the couch on both sides of me. My entire body screamed for release.

"Let me make you feel good, baby."

I watched him through the haze covering my eyes.

"Trust me."

I nodded and licked my lips. As long as he finally fucked me, I didn't care.

Cade strolled across the room, tugging his shirt over his head as he went. He set it on the table and kicked off his shoes. He grabbed the second box from the table and turned to saunter back my way, his eyes promising everything.

When he reached my side, he held out the box. I released the edge of the couch with both hands and took it. This one made me more nervous than the first. It had come from the fetish shop. It wasn't very heavy, but still...

"Open it, baby."

I tugged one tail of the ribbon until it fell away. And then I lifted the lid off with shaking fingers. I didn't know what I was looking at. A pile of pink nylon circles of some sort.

Cade chuckled and took the box from my hands. He walked toward my bedroom. "Come, baby."

I followed.

"Take off your sandals and the bra," he said as I entered the room.

He already stood at the bed, the box on top.

I popped the bra easily and let it fall to the floor where I stood. I leaned down next to slip off my shoes. And then I stood naked before him, too far away for him to touch.

"Amelia, come here."

Uh oh. I padded to his side with some unease as Cade

removed the contents of the box.

"Relax, baby. They're just cuffs."

I could see that now. And I flinched when he ripped the Velcro of one circle, opening the cuff in front of me. He took my wrist and wrapped the pink nylon around it, sealing it with the Velcro. I didn't quite get the point, or perhaps I was kidding myself, but I let him repeat the process on my other wrist and then my ankles.

He lifted my chin as he stood. "Do you trust me, baby? I need you to trust me."

I nodded.

"I would never hurt you."

I nodded again. I believed that. He'd assured me often.

"And you have a safe word if I ever do anything that causes pain or anguish. What is it?"

"Red, Sir."

"Good girl." He swept away the comforter on the bed. I hadn't made it myself, but the cleaning staff had been through at some point while we were gone. He patted the bed. "Climb up. Lie on your back in the center. Spread your arms and legs."

I glanced down at my wrists and realization dawned. *Cuffs*. Like the kind one would use to secure someone.

I did as he demanded, crawling to the center and spreading my limbs.

Cade stroked a hand up one arm until I shivered. "Good girl." He grabbed my wrist and pulled it to the corner of the bed.

Something else from the box was in his hand. I didn't watch as he attached the new item to me and the headboard.

I tugged. It was secure. I wasn't escaping.

Cade circled the bed and repeated the action with my other wrist.

My heart beat faster at the restraint. "Did I do something wrong, Sir?"

He met my gaze and frowned. "No, baby. Why?"

I said nothing.

He glanced at my wrists and then smiled. "Oh, baby. No." He leaned forward and trailed his fingers across my breasts, carefully stroking over both nipples.

I arched into his touch.

"How wet are you now?"

I let out a breath and licked my lips. "Very."

"Then I wouldn't call this a punishment, right?"

I wasn't so sure about that. I had also gotten very wet when he spanked me. And besides, depending on what he intended to do, things could get really frustrating really fast.

He chuckled again.

There was no footboard. I watched as Cade removed a long rope from the box. He tied it to the loop on one ankle cuff and then bent down. I didn't know what he did, but when he stood again, he rounded the bed and stooped out of view once more.

I knew exactly what he'd done when he tugged my ankle

and tied the rope to its matching loop. He'd tossed the other end under the bed and now I was completely immobile with my legs spread wider than I would care to consider.

Cade climbed onto the bed and settled between my thighs.

I was suddenly far more naked than I'd ever been. I struggled against each cuff just enough to make my heart race.

"Stop squirming, baby. Relax." He stroked my inner thighs. "I know it's weird at first, but let yourself go. You'll enjoy it."

That may be, but at what cost? My self-esteem?

I tried to relax into the mattress, but it was difficult with his gaze roaming my body and his fingers following. Every nerve ending came alive as he danced the tips of his fingers over me, starting with zones that weren't even erogenous before today and moving in circles toward my nipples.

He watched my face as he pinched the tips. "Look at me, baby."

I did.

"You okay? Nothing's too tight?"

"I'm good, Sir."

"Scale of one to ten, how aroused are you?"

"Fifty." I wasn't kidding.

He chuckled and released my nipples to trail down to my pussy. "I love this bare skin." He teased the areas I had shaved. "I love knowing you're totally naked for me."

I flinched as he grazed my clit, a tiny noise escaping my mouth. I tugged my hands, forgetting they weren't going to budge.

Cade pressed two fingers inside me and scissored them until I couldn't stand it anymore. "Cade, please..."

"What do you need, baby?"

"I need you to take off your pants, Cade. Please."

"Why would I do that?" He chuckled.

I moaned. "Please, Cade. Stop teasing. I need you inside me."

"I know, baby. But not yet. I want you to experience restraint without sex this time."

Was he crazy? I gulped for oxygen at the prospect. I almost cried. I did whimper. And I hated he brought me to that level.

Cade leaned over my body until his face hovered over mine, inches separating us. "Eyes on me, baby. I want to watch your face when you come." He thrust his fingers harder, in and out, each time flattening his palm to my clit.

My breath hitched in my throat as I concentrated on the feelings. The need. The cravings.

I wanted his cock. Not his fingers. It was indeed as frustrating as I'd expected. I didn't even know what it would feel like to have his length inside me. I just knew I wanted it more than anything.

Cade knew that too. His smile told me everything.

He set his thumb on my clit and pressed it down while he fucked me with his fingers, adding a third. "Come for me, baby."

I shattered at his command. Every muscle in my body convulsed. I struggled against the restraints to no avail.

Cade didn't let up. As the orgasm subsided, he kept moving until I climbed back to the top so fast, it shocked me. In no time, I was right there again. I couldn't see him anymore. My eyes clouded over, and I gave up, closed them, and tipped my head back.

"Again, baby. Come for me."

I went right over the edge again. Cade did this to me. My pussy gripped his fingers as hard as possible. My clit pulsed in rapid succession. I felt like I was falling. Free-falling from a very high location. It took forever for me to hit the ground, and when I did, it was into a soft bed of warmth. Not jarring as I'd expected.

I opened my eyes as Cade removed his fingers. He licked them clean while he watched me. And then he leaned over me, braced on his elbows on both sides of my head, and kissed me hard.

I could taste myself on his lips, and I liked it. He'd done it before. It was sexy for some reason. I wondered what he would taste like. I suddenly wanted to know more than anything.

When he finally broke the kiss, I found the courage to ask for what I wanted. "Let me suck you."

He flinched, one corner of his mouth raising up. "Hell no. I would never survive that. You'd ruin my reputation before you even wrapped those sweet lips around my cock."

I was shocked. Also pleased at the same time. He wanted me bad enough that he knew he wouldn't have the restraint. I shrugged. "Who cares? I'll never tell. Please, Cade. It's only fair."

He chuckled deep and long that time. As he sat back, he pinched my nipples again, making me arch into his hands. "Fair? Did you read your assignment the other day?"

I flinched. Right. Of course.

He continued. "There's no 'fair' in D/s, baby. There's just me dominating you and you obeying my commands."

"Okay, Sir."

"Good." He lifted off me.

Immediately I felt the cool air hitting my skin. My pussy was soaked, and the air made me hyper aware of what it lacked.

Cade kissed my temple. "Gonna take a long shower, baby. You rest."

"Cade." I lifted my head as he walked away. "No you don't. Let me go."

He chuckled and turned to face me at the door. "I like knowing exactly where you are while I shower." And he left.

I wanted to throw something at him. And I still might. Later. When he let me go.

Chapter Twelve

Cade held my hand as he helped me from the back of the Mercedes. "I don't know how long we'll stay," he said over my head. "Do you mind waiting, Arthur?"

"Of course not, sir." Arthur rounded the Mercedes and shut the door as I stepped free. "Take your time. I'll park in the garage below the hotel."

"Thank you. You know how these things are. Sometimes I can stomach them. Sometimes not."

I wondered what he meant by that. These were his friends. Right?

Cade settled his hand on the small of my back as he led me to the front door. He leaned down and kissed my shoulder. "Have I mentioned how fucking sexy you are tonight?"

I giggled. He'd mentioned that a few hundred times. Yes.

In fact, the moment I stepped from the bedroom wearing this dress was a moment I would never forget as long as I lived.

Cade had presented it to me after his shower, hanging it on a hook on the bathroom door and setting dainty silver heels beneath it before releasing me from the bed.

Whatever anger I'd built up toward him while he'd showered dissipated immediately when he hooked that shimmering silver dress to the door. My eyes were glued to the luxury. "God, Cade. That's amazing." I hardly paid attention as he ripped the Velcro from my limbs and rubbed my wrists and ankles.

"Glad you like it. You're going to look like a million bucks in it." He hauled me to sitting and then squared off with me, breaking my view. "Shower. Hair. Makeup—not too much. Then the dress. Meet me in the living room. Half an hour."

"Got it." I saluted him.

"Are you sassing me, Amelia?" He narrowed his gaze, but laughter played with the corners of his eyes.

"No, Sir." I swallowed and pursed my lips. Things were going so well. The last thing I wanted was another spanking or a stint in the corner he'd threatened. "Sorry, Sir."

"Okay then. Just checking."

I stood and padded to the bathroom.

Precisely half an hour later, I'd stepped into the living room and met the most wonderful gaze of my life. I thought he might drop his tumbler the way he shook when he saw me. His eyes went wide and his mouth fell open. He didn't speak for long seconds. I had finally managed to leave Cade Alexander speechless.

He'd shocked me again when he presented me with gorgeous dangling silver earrings and a matching bracelet. I felt like a princess.

Now, as he led me into the hotel lobby where the party was being held, he stroked his palm up my bare back, skimming the sides of my breast with his thumb.

I squirmed. My nipples hardened.

Cade drew me closer to his side and set his lips on my ear. "Stop wiggling, baby."

I lifted my face. "Stop touching me so intimately, Sir." I smiled at him, but my sass was back out.

He stopped walking and narrowed his eyes. "That's twice, Amelia."

"We aren't currently 'playing', *Sir*." I emphasized the word *playing* and then stressed my exaggerated *Sir*.

"We're always playing to some extent, *Amelia*." He winked. "And you won't tempt me again, imp. I won't hesitate to find a secluded corner in which to punish you. Are we clear?"

I swallowed. I didn't think he was kidding that time. "Yes, Sir."

"Good girl." He splayed his hand wide again, intentionally brushing my breasts as we continued. My nipples rubbed against the soft material of the dress. I glanced down to see if it was obvious to anyone else how erect they were. The gown was amazing. I was still in awe. The halter-style front dipped just low enough to be decent. It shimmered when I walked, the silver glistening in every kind of light. It also hugged my body to perfection, the sides of my bare breasts skimming the edges of the luxurious fabric. The back was completely bare down to my ass, arguably a bit too low, though Cade insisted it was perfect and no one could see anything they had no business seeing.

The elegant material also lay fitted against my hips, a slit up the side reaching high on my thigh, making it possible for me to walk. The whole ensemble was made more fantastic by the dainty silver heels covered with Swarovski crystals. It had to have cost a fortune. I didn't even want to know.

We rode to the third floor in the elevator, my man as attentive as ever behind me, his arm wrapped around my waist, holding my back against his front. His palm lay flat on my belly. Another couple stepped in with us to ride from the second floor to the third, smiling as they took in our stance.

I felt like I'd won the lottery. I had, in a way.

When we reached the ballroom, I was shocked. I'd known it would be over the top based on the way we were dressed, but this was beyond anything I'd ever been to. Wall-to-wall, people covered the dimly lit room. If this was the engagement party, I couldn't imagine what the wedding reception would be like.

Cade led me into the party, his hand still at my back possessively. I liked it. I hadn't brought a purse. There was no need. I had everything I could want at my back. We wouldn't be eating other than hors d'oeuvres, so even lipstick wasn't necessary. Besides, I wasn't wearing any. Cade had sent me back into the bathroom to remove it before we'd left the hotel. After he'd kissed me in that dress, he'd had my pink all over his mouth. And since he claimed he intended to kiss me a hundred times during the evening, I was only permitted lip gloss. I'd easily complied with that request.

Servers walked by us with various drinks on trays, but Cade

ignored them and made a beeline for the bar. "Never know what's in those glasses. I'm particular about my drinks." At least that was his intention. We got stopped several times along the way.

At one point, a man with a beaming smile who looked the same age as Cade slapped him on the back. "Dude. You made it." I guessed him to be Riley. He looked at me and reached out to take my hand. "You must be Amelia."

I nodded. "Most people call me Amy." I rolled my eyes. "You must be Riley."

He let me go and turned back to Cade. "You're right, man. She's gorgeous." He gripped Cade's shoulder. "You could do worse."

Cade cleared his throat. "Riley. Stop while you're ahead."

Riley's eyes twinkled as he smiled. I had the impression he did that often. He was about six one, maybe an inch taller than Cade. His darker skin made it seem he'd just returned from the beach that morning. His dirty blond hair was the tiniest bit too long, making him look more human than most of the people in the room. But what really stood out were his eyes, a deep penetrating blue that seemed to soak in everything he saw.

"Gotta mingle, Cade. But find me again in a few, yeah?"

"Will do." Cade hurried us to the bar and ordered two glasses of whatever. It seemed like he knew every wine on the planet the way he rattled off names of various Chardonnays every time he ordered. I wondered how he knew what types they had at each location.

Cade led me back into the throng. He introduced me to various men as we meandered. Interestingly he did not introduce me to many women, only the ones on the arms of one of his buddies.

"Most of these guys are business associates," he informed me the next time we were alone.

I nodded. I felt much calmer after my glass of wine, less intimidated.

After a few more people greeted us, we headed back toward the bar. The bartender nodded at Cade and handed him two more glasses without a word. Cade handed me one and hauled me closer to kiss my neck. "I need to speak to some people, baby," Cade whispered close to my ear. "Will you be okay if I leave you here for a few minutes?"

"Of course." I leaned my back against the long bar and took another sip of my wine.

Cade met my gaze head on. "You sure?"

I nodded and smiled at him. "Go. I'm fine, Cade. I'm a big girl."

Seconds after he walked away, a tall, slender brunette who easily could have been a model and carried herself as though she were, squeezed in next to me and took a champagne flute from the waiter's hand. "It will never last, you know."

At first I paid no attention to her, but then I realized she was staring down at me. Even in my heels, I was only about five seven. She towered over me. Her face was hard.

"Excuse me?" I must have misunderstood her words.

She angled her head toward Cade, who stood across the

room with a group of men, his back to me. "Cade Alexander. Whatever little game you're playing with him, it'll never work."

My mouth opened, but I just blinked at her.

She gave a sharp laugh. "He's not your type." She let her gaze roam up and down my body, taking in the entire package. "It's obvious you aren't from money. I'll bet my last dollar Cade bought you this dress...and put it on you himself." She lowered her voice as she spoke.

I flushed the deepest shade of red, set my wine on the counter behind me, and turned to face the room, determined to ignore this bitch.

"Cade doesn't go for girls like you, honey. He's got tastes that run in a direction you could only dream of. Trust me. I would know."

I jerked my gaze to her, unable to stop myself. "Excuse me?" I repeated, regretting my reaction immediately.

The crazy bitch had her hair pulled back in a tight bun, so tight it stretched her eyes outward. Her makeup was overdone, and in my opinion, borderline slutty. She was right. I was nothing like her, and I was proud of that fact, even if it did cost me Cade Alexander in the long run. But that was none of her business.

She gave me another evil grin. "Use your teeth when you go down on him, honey. He likes the thrill of the bite." With that, she walked away, her head high, her perfect hips swaying under the long black gown that fit her so perfectly I had no doubt it had been tailor-made for her svelte body.

For long moments I watched that bitch disappear into the

crowded room, unable to move a muscle. A twitch formed in one of my eyes. I finally yanked my gaze to scan the area and found Cade in the same spot.

As soon as I could move my legs, I made my way out of the room and down the hall. I had no idea how I managed it, but I didn't cry all the way to the bathroom and into the last stall. Thank God the room was currently empty. I wasn't even sure why I was upset. Who the fuck cared what that bitch said to me. I was with Cade. She was clearly jealous.

But she'd also implied she'd slept with him. And that made my skin crawl.

I leaned against the door and tried to catch my breath. I needed to wrap my head around what had happened and pull my shit together. No way in hell was I going to let that bitch rattle me. Or at least, I wasn't going to let her know she'd done so.

I also had no intention of telling Cade. It wasn't his problem. This was my issue. And I would handle it with my head held high and a smile on my face.

I caught my breath and gathered my thoughts.

I remained very still when three other women entered the bathroom. I knew there were three of them because they were talking on top of each other as they came in giggling. Only one used the toilet. The other two stood at the mirror fixing their makeup.

I didn't move. I wasn't ready to face anyone. And I sure didn't want to make small talk. The only people at the party were rich. I had no way of knowing which ones were snobby bitches like the brunette with the tight bun, but I didn't want to chance it.

And I didn't have to, because suddenly my blood went cold.

"Can you believe that skanky whore Cade Alexander brought?" The voice was high-pitched and full of laughter.

The other two women giggled. One of them spoke. "I know. Who does that tramp think she's fooling? I'd be embarrassed."

I swallowed back the bile that rose in my throat, ignoring the tears running down my cheeks. I was not a slut, by any stretch of the imagination. Nor was I a whore. I hadn't even been with one man yet.

My hands shook as I covered my mouth to keep from emitting a sound.

The women continued to trash talk me as they left. Silence followed. Blessed silence. I was totally not welcome at this party. It was ridiculous to think I would ever be welcome by the people in Cade's world in any way.

Those women were the epitome of nasty, but that didn't mean they didn't have a point. I didn't fit in. I never would. And to pretend otherwise was insane.

I took a deep breath, tore off a piece of toilet paper, and wiped my eyes. When I exited the stall, I headed for the sink and glanced at the mirror. My reflection wasn't fit for anyone to see. And I sure didn't want anyone to find out they'd gotten the best of me. The damage was irreparable. I prayed no one was in the hall, eased the door open, and stepped out with a sigh of relief, my body turning to head in the other direction, away from the party.

I took two or three turns, my steps getting faster as I looked for a way out. When I finally saw an exit sign and pushed into a stairwell, I breathed a sigh of relief. Now I just needed to get out of the building, find Arthur, and figure out what to do about Cade.

As luck would have it, the stairwell emptied into the parking garage. A valet stood several yards away and approached me. "Can I help you, ma'am?" He didn't comment on the state of my face.

"I'm looking for Cade Alexander's driver. Would you possibly know where I might find him?"

"Of course, ma'am. Just a moment." He turned and walked back to his podium, made a quick call, and then nodded my direction. "Right this way."

I followed him, hoping the walk wasn't far. My legs threatened to collapse.

We rounded a corner in the garage, and I saw Arthur coming toward me. His face was scrunched in concern. "Ms. Kensington," he began as the valet left me in his care. "Is everything okay? I would have come to the front. What are you doing out here?" He glanced past me, probably looking for Cade.

And then the tears fell. Like a hose that had been bent under the accumulating pressure of the faucet for too long, my face opened up, and I couldn't hold back another second.

Arthur took my arm and led me to the car. He opened the door and ushered me inside. Surprisingly, he climbed in after me and reached for a box of tissues. He handed them to me and waited a beat before speaking. "Where's Cade?"

"Still inside." I shook my head. "He doesn't know I left."

Arthur's face was covered with concern. "I need to let him know you're out here, ma'am."

I met his gaze. I hadn't really paid close attention to him before. He wasn't as old as I'd assumed. Maybe fifty. He was handsome. Not gorgeous like Cade, but attractive in his own way. His hair was cut short and groomed perfectly, a tinge of gray starting to bleed into the edges. He didn't reach for his phone yet, even though he'd made it clear it needed to be done.

"I know. Just give me a second." I reached for another tissue and wiped my swollen eyes. I set my head back on the headrest. "I'm such an idiot."

Arthur took a breath, hesitated, and then spoke his mind. "I'm no expert, but I've worked for Mr. Alexander for many years. I can only imagine the caliber of the patrons inside that party."

He hit the nail on the head.

"Yeah."

"This had nothing to do with Cade."

I shook my head, tears falling again. Nothing and everything. I couldn't do this. I didn't fit in his world.

"Ms. Kensington?"

I opened my eyes and met his gaze.

"Cade's a good man. The best. He doesn't put up with anyone's shit. You need to talk to him and let him handle this. Trust me."

I nodded.

Arthur didn't say another word. He exited the limo and

shut me into the cocoon of the interior.

It took less than five minutes for the door to whip open again and Cade to fold himself inside. "Jesus, baby. What happened?"

I cried again. When would these tears let up?

He let me sob, not caring that I got his suit jacket wet, or his shirt, or his tie. And that made me cry harder. I grabbed his lapels and held on while the river flowed.

Finally I sat up straighter, and Cade handed me a pile of tissues. I chuckled half-heartedly as I wiped my face. "I'm such an idiot."

"You aren't." He squared my shoulders to face him.

I realized the car was moving and lifted my face. The glass partition between the seats had also been raised. Arthur was giving us privacy. "You don't have to leave just because I did. Go back inside."

He furrowed his brow. "What kind of asshole do you think I am?"

I smiled. "The rich kind," I joked.

He opened his mouth, shock making his eyes go wide. "Amelia. I'm not a jerk. I don't give a fuck about those people inside. I don't even know most of them. I came here because my best friend is getting married. If his guests can't extend common courtesy to my date, fuck them."

How did he know?

"Someone said shit to you, didn't they?"

I nodded, biting my lower lip before I released it. "It's done. Leave it alone."

"Are you crazy?"

I shrugged. "Are you?"

"What's that supposed to mean?"

I rolled my eyes. "What are you doing with me, Cade?"

"Enjoying a weekend away?"

I cleared my throat and rolled my eyes again. "No. I mean in general. I'm a twenty-four-year-old, middle-class girl from the first floor. I don't fit into your world, Cade."

Cade released me and ran his hands through his hair. "Seriously?" He was mad. "You think I care about that shit?"

The car pulled to a stop, but Arthur didn't leave his seat in the front. I could see him through the glass barrier and wondered how much he could hear.

Cade glared at me hard and then yanked the door open and climbed out. He reached back inside for my hand, and I followed him to avoid a scene on the front sidewalk of the most expensive hotel in downtown Nashville.

Neither of us spoke a word as we made our way to the elevators and then stepped inside.

Cade's fury was evident in the way his nostrils flared every time he breathed. He actually scared me for the first time. If he would spank me for wearing panties, what would he do for leaving his friend's party to cry in the limo?

When the door opened, Cade squeezed my hand tighter

and pulled me inside the suite.

I winced as the doors shut behind me, and he released me to stomp across the room. I stood rooted to my spot, waiting for who knew what while Cade headed straight for the bar. He poured himself a tumbler of something brown over ice, probably whatever he'd also been drinking the first night we'd spoken last Friday.

He surprised me by pouring a glass of wine next and carrying both drinks to the coffee table. "Come here, Amelia."

I moved. I admitted to myself I was nervous about his reaction, but I convinced myself he wouldn't hurt me. Nobody poured a woman a glass of wine so thoughtfully and then slapped her across the room. Right? It would be incongruent.

Cade handed me my wine as I sat on the edge of the couch, back straight, feet together. I held the glass, not having any desire to consume it. He slumped onto the couch next to me, not quite touching me. A long silence ensued, during which Cade consumed most of his drink. When he set the glass on the coffee table, he turned toward me.

"First of all, I don't give a fuck how much money you have or don't have. Period. Do not insinuate otherwise ever again. Are we clear?"

I nodded. *Oh shit.*

"Good. Second of all, some of those bitches with piles of money think they run the universe, and they're wrong. They can go straight to hell with their hoity attitudes. I don't need any of them, and I'd rather be alone than endure a moment of their fake faces and lies. Are we clear on that?"

I nodded again.

He took my chin and held it. "I like you for who you are, Amelia. Nothing else. I was attracted to you from the moment I saw you for the way you held yourself. Of course your looks were in play that first day also. That's human nature. When I saw that thick, brown wavy hair swaying down the hall, those fantastic legs extending beyond the bottom of your straight skirt, and those fuck-me heels you wore to work with your head held high, I swallowed my tongue.

"But then I got to know you, and I found out I liked what was inside even better. You're a gem, Amelia. A perfect diamond in the rough. And the fact that you also happen to have a truly submissive side that suits my personal tastes is icing on the cake. Are we clear on that point?"

I nodded again, swallowing back another tear. And then my mouth moved. I couldn't stop it. "How many women in that room have you slept with?"

Cade's eyes went huge. He dropped my chin. He watched my face. He didn't speak for so long, I wasn't sure he'd heard me. And then he bit out, "That bitch." His jaw twitched, and he stood and began to pace the room across from me. "Are you fucking kidding me?"

I had no idea how I revealed so much with that simple question. Apparently a lot.

Cade stomped around the room. He grabbed his tumbler from the coffee table and made his way to the bar. At the last second, he hesitated and launched it at the wall instead of pouring another drink. The glass shattered, and I glanced back and forth between him and the wall.

And then he stomped back to me. He took a deep breath and put his hands on his hips. I had to tip back to see his face. "There was only one woman in that room I've ever had my dick in. I'll regret that action until the day I die. It was thirteen years ago. We were drunk at a frat party, and she lured me into her nest. I've never told anyone that, especially not Riley."

He heaved for breaths. "Whatever venom she spewed came from her diamondback mouth, and you need to wipe her skanky ass from your mind. The only reason I've ever spoken to her again was for Riley's sake. I have no idea what he sees in her, but he's my best friend, and I've tried to smile and adjust my face for years whenever I've been around that bitch."

I gasped. "The woman I spoke to was his fiancée?"

"Tall, model, black hair pulled back in a tight bun that makes her face look like it got stretched to pull out her early wrinkles?"

I nodded.

"Yep. That's the one."

"Shit."

"Yeah. And now I have to tell my best friend since childhood that his fiancée is a complete fraud."

"Oh God." I stood. "You can't do that."

"Why the hell not? I can't not do it. I've been giving her the benefit of the doubt for years. I knew in my gut she was bad news, but she managed to keep herself from dribbling her shit in my lap for a long time. If she thinks she can treat my date like she did, she's wrong."

I opened my mouth.

He held up a hand. "I don't even want to know what she said. I've never hit a woman in anger, and I don't want to start tonight. If you mention a word she spewed, I'm liable to head back to that party and slap the grin off her fucking face."

I pursed my lips, deciding it would be best to keep our chat to myself after all.

"If that bitch implied she slept with me and that she was better than you, that's all I need to know. Is that what happened?"

"Yes."

He nodded. He tore his phone from his pocket and stared at it. And then he walked from the room and shut the door to his bedroom.

I sat back down on the couch, shaking at the amount of power I yielded. I both hated it and wanted to grin at the same time.

Cade Alexander was really into me. He wasn't messing around. And no bitch was going to ruin it. He would see to it.

I picked up my wine, wincing at the thought of what Cade was saying to Riley. I'd barely met his friend when we'd arrived—too distracted by my own man to pay much attention to another. There had been so many people at the party, I never saw him again in my short attempt to fit in with the wealthy.

I hoped Riley didn't blame me for his fiancée's actions.

I took a long sip of yet another delicious Chardonnay and tried to relax.

Chapter Thirteen

When Cade materialized from his bedroom, he was completely calm. His brow was still furrowed, but he didn't show any signs of imminent implosion. He'd removed his tie and unbuttoned the top few buttons on his shirt.

I stood and smoothed my hands down the front of my dress.

He didn't say a word about his talk with Riley, and I didn't want to bring it up either. Whatever happened between Cade and his friend was between them.

Cade met my gaze. "Why are you still wearing that dress, baby?"

I wasn't sure what he meant. "Uh, Sir?"

He chuckled. "It's sexy as hell. I'll give you that, but I'm over it." He rounded behind me and turned my back to his front. Then he released the clasp at the top behind my neck. The fabric shimmied to the floor to pool around my feet.

I leaned down to step away from the dress and pick it up. Cade might not have wanted it on me anymore, but I didn't want anything to happen to it.

Cade chuckled.

"What?"

"Suddenly you decide to clean up after yourself?"

I glanced at the dress. "That dress is amazing. It must have cost a fortune. I don't want to step on it."

He pulled me into his arms and kissed me. The kiss lingered, deepening. He held me tighter. I could feel his erection against my belly through his dress pants.

My nipples rubbed against the front of his shirt, stiffening. I wanted him badly. I said a silent prayer that he wouldn't make me wait any longer.

When he broke the kiss, his eyes were heavy. Sexy. He was aroused. He stepped back and unbuttoned the rest of his shirt, never losing my gaze. Slowly he removed the starched material until he stood bare-chested in front of me.

I had learned to love this man's chest. I stepped forward and set my palms flat on the smooth surface, leaning toward him. I still wore my heels, bracelet, and earrings, but nothing else. "Cade," I whispered. "Please." I wasn't too proud to beg.

He took my shoulders in his hands and stared at me. Then he shocked me by swinging me up to cradle me in his arms and marching from the room straight into his bedroom. *His* bedroom. Not mine.

Cade tossed me onto his bed.

I scampered back a few inches from the edge, my high heels digging into the mattress. I reached to remove them but halted when Cade spoke. "Don't, baby. I like them. I want to take you for the first time while you're wearing those sexy heels." He grinned and shrugged. "I'm a guy."

I relented. If his fantasy involved me wearing the most expensive silver heels I'd ever worn, so be it.

He removed his belt and then unbuttoned and unzipped his pants.

I held my breath. For as many times as he'd seen me naked and made me writhe beneath him, I had not yet seen his body below the hips.

When he lowered his dress pants, taking his underwear with them, I inhaled slowly. *Jesus. Shit.*

I wasn't a prude, I thought not for the first time. But God almighty, were they all like that one?

"You okay, baby?"

I lifted my gaze to his smirking face, realizing I had scooted away from him subconsciously. I stopped moving, but my legs were pressed tightly together. I looked at him over my knees. "Of course." I licked my lips. I understood the concept. And people said it always fit, but Cade's thick length was a far cry larger than even his three fingers together, and he'd thrust those into me several times.

Cade reached down to pick up his pants. He pulled a condom from the pocket and then draped the slacks over the end of the bed. Next, he tugged the comforter down. "Lift your ass, baby."

I wiggled several directions until he had the top few layers removed and I sat on the silk sheets.

Cade put one knee on the bed and then hesitated. He reached for his bobbing shaft and stroked it from the base to the tip while I watched, mesmerized.

"Baby, look at me."

I yanked my gaze to his, a bit embarrassed to have been caught staring.

His brow was furrowed. "How long has it been?"

I swallowed. "How long has what been?" I knew what he meant. I was stalling, and a bit sorry we were having this conversation. I'd hoped to avoid it altogether. I really didn't want Cade to treat me with kid gloves. That just flew out the window with his question, which I inadvertently caused with my weird reactions.

Cade climbed onto the bed. He grabbed my ankles and tugged until I fell flat onto my back. Then he straddled me, circled my wrists, and pulled my arms over my head. His face was inches from mine when he cleared his throat.

I met his gaze. I needed to at least own up to my lack of experience.

"Amelia?"

I couldn't find the words.

"Fuck me." He leaned in farther. I could see his eye start to twitch. I hoped he wasn't angry.

I waited.

He waited longer. And then his face dipped so that all I could see was the top of his head. "Oh my God. Why didn't you tell me?" He lifted his gaze.

I said nothing. I was slightly mortified. Not for the first time. He acted like I'd committed a crime. I squirmed in his clutches, trying to dislodge myself from his grip. I needed space.

He held me tighter. "No you don't. You don't get to drop that bomb on me at the eleventh hour without an explanation."

He was right. I owed him that much. Even if he chose not to have sex with me in the end, I wasn't being fair. "I'm sorry, Sir," I mumbled. "I should have told you. I... I just thought it would be easier."

"Easier for whom, Amelia?" His voice was gentle. His face was hard.

"Both of us?" I gathered more words. "I didn't want you to look at me like—" I swallowed and continued, my voice barely audible this time. "Like you are right now."

Cade flinched. "How am I looking at you?"

"Like you're disappointed."

His eyes widened.

I continued before he could respond. "Look, I'm sorry. I understand if you don't want to, um, you know. I have no experience at all. It was totally selfish of me to keep this from you."

I couldn't read his expression.

"Will you let me go? Please. Cade." I struggled against his grip on my wrists and squirmed my ass, trying to free myself.

"Stop moving, baby. I'm going to come on your stomach if you don't."

I froze.

He smiled. "And stop fretting so hard. You're going to hurt yourself."

What the hell?

"Don't get me wrong. I'm going to spank your ass until you can't sit down after I fuck you. But first I'm going to make love to you until the only thing you know is my face and my cock buried inside you. When I'm finished taking your virginity, an honor I'm humbled to have bestowed on me, I'm going to fuck you hard. When I'm finished with that, you'll never doubt you're mine again. Are we clear?"

I gasped. I couldn't begin to process all he'd said. He wanted me anyway?

He grinned again. "Baby, you're so fucking sexy when you blush. I hope I can keep sharp enough to bring that pink out on your cheeks for the rest of my life."

What?

I couldn't move. My heart pounded, and I squeezed my legs together against the need growing between them. "You—uh, you—"

He released one wrist only to tuck it under the first so he held them both with one hand. "Like I said, stop straining yourself. What did you expect? Did you really think I would turn you away for being a virgin?"

"Well, yes. The thought did cross my mind."

"And that's why you never told me?"

"That and the sheer mortification of the idea."

He chuckled, deep. His free hand landed on my face and cupped my jaw. "That's insane. You know that, don't you?" He shook his head. "Clearly not. Baby, there's no red-blooded man on this Earth who wouldn't cherish that gift. Not even the assholes."

I wasn't sure I believed him. "I have no experience. I bring nothing to this party."

"And that means I get to teach you everything from scratch and watch your face as I take you places you've never been with any man. Every single look in your eyes will belong to me. I'll never worry that inside your head you're comparing me to previous lovers. A wet dream come to life, baby."

When he put it that way... I forced a small smile. "Okay."

"Jesus. I'm glad I figured this out before I hurt you."

"I can take it, Sir."

"I'm sure you can, but you don't need to. At least not alone." He stretched out over my body, releasing my wrists, until he planted his forearms beside my head. "I'm completely humbled, baby. Thank you for this."

I nodded.

Cade rolled to one side and propped himself on one elbow. He stared down at my body and stroked his fingers over my skin. "Spread your legs, baby."

My leg closest to him was trapped against his. I pulled the other one away from my body and let my knee fall open. I couldn't plant my heels on the silk sheets without ripping a hole in them.

"Cade?"

"Yeah, baby."

"Please take off my shoes. I'm going to worry about the sheets if you don't."

He chuckled. "Okay. But I want to fuck you again later with them on." He reached for my foot and slipped the back down until I was free. Then he did the same with the other.

I planted my heel on the bed and gave him my full attention. Tentatively I reached for his cock. He let me. I stroked my hand from the base to the tip just as I'd seen him do.

Cade groaned. He gripped my wrist and pulled my hand away. "Sorry, baby. I thought I could let you touch me. Turns out I can't. Not right now. Later. When I'm not about to come before I get inside you."

"Okay." I warmed at the idea I had that effect on him.

His fingers might have been shaking as he reached between my legs. He was suddenly so sweet. I hadn't thought I wanted sweet from him, but now that I had it, I was glad. Just this once. Or maybe occasionally in the future too.

When he parted my folds and gathered my wetness, I lifted my hips off the bed. "Please, Cade. Don't drag this out. I need you. So bad it hurts." I wasn't kidding. The knot in my belly was surely worse than any discomfort I might feel from him filling me.

"Are you sure, baby?"

"Yes. God, Cade. Now."

He sat up, grabbed the condom he'd set on the bed, and

tore into it with his teeth.

I watched as he rolled it down his length.

And then he was between my legs, his tip nestled at my entrance.

I bucked, hoping to force the issue.

"Look at me, baby."

I did.

"I want you to keep your eyes on mine. Got it?"

I nodded.

"I want to watch every expression on your face. Do not lose eye contact."

I nodded again. This was important to him.

He gritted his teeth as he pressed forward slowly, as if this were more painful for him than for me. But I realized with relief he was doing his best to hold back his orgasm. It felt that good.

I smiled inside. Outside, I couldn't control my expressions at all. All my blood flowed to my sex. I wrapped my hands around his biceps and held him tight.

Cade pushed in farther.

The tightness was unexpected. I sucked in a breath.

Cade waited, watching my face. "More, baby?" he gritted out.

"Yes. Please. Just do it, Cade."

He didn't listen to me. He kept his slow entrance, stretching my insides. So much pressure.

I couldn't avoid lifting my ass, my feet digging into the bed beside his hips.

Cade groaned. "Stop, baby. Let me."

I fell back to the mattress, sweat beading on my forehead. The stress of the unknown alone was killing me.

The ball of need expanded to encompass my entire belly until it hurt. "Cade." One sharp syllable.

He must have heard my urgency because he thrust home.

I cried out, the instant pain sharp but brief. My eyes fluttered shut as I acclimated to his girth. Quick panting breaths.

"Eyes, baby."

I opened them again to meet his gaze. His hands were on my head, holding me gently, his thumbs stroking my temples. "You okay?"

"Better than. Move."

He smiled finally and then did just that. His hips pulled almost out and then thrust back in. He wasn't exactly gentle, but he was careful. I wasn't in the mood for gentle.

He missed nothing, his eyes roaming over my expressions from behind his furrowed brows. "Fuck, baby. So damn tight. I'm not going to last." He tucked his lips into his teeth and continued to stroke in and out of me, each thrust better than the last. The walls of my pussy were alive like never before. I wanted more. I never wanted this to end.

Cade jerked one hand down and wiggled it between our bodies. He pressed his thumb to my clit and rubbed.

I moaned louder at the pressure. I was going to explode. Not like I had all the other times he'd brought me to orgasm, but on an entirely different plane of pleasure. It scared me. I clutched at him, feeling out of control. I teetered toward a realm I knew nothing about. And I wasn't sure my heart could survive.

I screamed. "Cade." And then I slammed over the top, my orgasm milking Cade's cock as my body did what it was made to do. It went on for much longer than expected, my clit rhythmically throbbing against Cade's thumb as he continued to thrust into me, harder now. Faster.

My orgasm was just easing up when Cade suddenly thrust deep and held steady, his thickness buried deep. I felt his release as he came inside me, his cock pulsing in the same manner as my pussy had clenched around him.

He did this for several moments before he finally seemed to see me again. He slumped lower against me, squishing me. I didn't care. I didn't want him to pull out. Ever. I was okay with starving to death in this bed. Better than okay.

But Cade caught his breath, pulled out slowly, and flopped to one side of me on his back. He hauled me with him, dragging me like a rag doll onto his chest, his arm wrapped around my shoulders.

His chest heaved. "I think you killed me. See if I have a pulse."

"Won't do any good because I died before you did," I said against his chest. I couldn't lift my cheek.

Chapter Fourteen

At midnight, we were both leaning over the coffee table nibbling on the assortment of appetizers we'd ordered from room service.

We hadn't eaten much since our late lunch, and we were starving. When Cade finally leaned back against the couch and propped his feet on the table, I climbed over him to straddle his lap. He wore his flannel pajama pants. I wore the skimpy robe that was now completely open in the front. I ground myself on his cock, loving the feel of his hardness at my entrance, even through his pants.

Cade grabbed my arms and held me steady. "I've created a monster."

"You promised me hard and fast for the second round."

He chuckled. "I think you're forgetting a step, baby. I believe I said I was going to spank you and then fuck you. Big difference."

I shrugged. My pussy clenched.

"Baby, are you trying to goad me into punishing you?"

"Maybe." I let that word drag out.

He rolled his eyes. "What good is spanking you going to do if you like it?"

"I don't know, but I'm willing to find out." I was shocked by my new boldness.

Cade hesitated for one second, and then he moved fast, flipping me over his knee so that I landed hard against his thighs. Before I could catch my breath, he jerked the silk robe off my shoulders, but left my arms trapped inside the sleeves. He held the wadded ball of material at my lower back. I had no balance. My feet were in the air.

Cade molded his palm over my ass and squeezed hard. His touch was rough. He didn't give me much of a warmup before he landed the first spank.

I flinched on a moan. I really was a bit of a slut. Wetness spread between my legs. I needed more. Whatever he would give me.

Cade soothed the spot where his hand had landed for a few seconds and then swatted me again.

This time I arched into his touch, my voice caught in my throat.

"Oh, baby. You needed this. Didn't you?"

I didn't respond.

"It feels so good, baby." He spanked me again. Two more times, once on each cheek. Then he rubbed the spot. "Spread your thighs, baby."

I squirmed to do his bidding. It was hard without the use of my arms. I was totally off balance.

Cade shocked me by thrusting two fingers into my pussy.

I screamed. It felt so good.

He removed his fingers and groaned. "Last time I'll be able to punish you with a spanking. I can see that." His hand landed again, this time at the juncture between my thigh and my ass. That one hurt. He had my attention.

He did it again on the other thigh.

I squealed at the sting, but my pussy still craved his touch. I thought he would continue, and I wondered how hard he would be able to spank me. But he suddenly stopped. He flipped me over and cradled me in his arms while he stood.

My hands were still trapped at my lower back. I tried to untangle them, but he gave me a hard look. "Don't."

I stilled.

Cade carried me behind the couch, flipped me over, and deposited me over the back. I landed on my belly, my ass in the air, my arms tangled at my back. I was confused.

I heard the rustle of a condom wrapper and stiffened my body.

Cade stepped between my legs, pushing them apart. His fingers reached between my thighs and stroked through my soaking pussy. "Baby... So ready for me." He set one hand on my lower back to steady me and nudged his body between my legs. "You okay, baby?"

"Yes." I breathed heavily.

Cade thrust into me. Hard. Fast.

My pussy clenched at the renewed fullness. A twinge of discomfort was followed by pure bliss.

His hands were on my hips. He pulled out and plunged back in, holding himself to the hilt. He leaned forward and pulled back a lock of my hair. "Talk to me, baby."

"God, Cade. Keep going."

That was all he needed. He grabbed both my hips and fucked me. It felt amazing. I rose into the air, seemingly above my body at the number of sensations jamming every one of my synapses. I wasn't sure I breathed. Instead I rode the high, concentrating on nothing except the pressure inside me building and building as he thrust harder. I listened to the noises he made, knowing I caused them.

"Come for me, baby."

I obeyed instantly, my body convulsing beneath Cade's grip as though far more than my sex were involved in the orgasm.

Cade came right behind me. I knew the second he did by his rigid stance against me and the long groan he emitted.

When his pulsing finally stopped, he spoke. "Yep. You killed me. I've gone to heaven."

I slumped, letting my body relax against the sofa cushions. But Cade was quick to lift me. He tugged off my tangled robe, pulled out of my pussy, and cradled me in his arms to carry me to his bed.

I was so sated, I couldn't move. I didn't need to, either. Cade padded away to clean up, returning with a warm cloth, rolled me onto my back, and spread my legs to clean between them.

I watched in rapture at his gentle touch.

When he was satisfied, he rolled me to my belly and rubbed lotion into my sore skin. If I kept up my sassy attitude, I would never be able to sit again.

He left again, flipping off lights all over the place before returning.

"Don't get any ideas, gorgeous," he said as he lay next to me and pulled my body into his side. "That isn't happening again."

I pushed out my bottom lip to fake pout.

Cade chuckled deep. His body shook all over. "A monster, I tell you. Gah…" He reached toward the bottom of the bed, pulled up the comforter, and snuggled us into a cocoon. I had never been so comfortable. My ass burned. My pussy was sore. And I was perfectly content.

It seemed like only seconds went by before I opened my eyes to find Cade on one elbow staring at my profile. He was also caressing one side of my face with a finger. "You never moved all night. I was wondering if you were alive."

I smiled. "More than I've ever been."

Cade pushed the covers off my back and trailed his fingers down my spine to the dip above my ass. He drew circles on my butt next. "I hit you too hard."

"Nope. Just right."

His brow furrowed. "I'm gonna rub more lotion into this after I bathe you."

"You're going to bathe me?" That was the part I honed in on.

"Yep." He kissed my shoulder and kept caressing me, lower now, against my thighs. "I'm going to shave you too."

My breath hitched, and I spread my legs a bit, hoping he would take the hint.

"Not going there, baby. You need to recover."

"I'm good."

"Not going there. End of discussion."

I blew out a breath. "Then why are you still touching me?"

"Didn't say I wouldn't make you wish I were going to fuck you. Just that I wasn't going to."

I lifted my ass to buck him off. "Tease."

"Greedy imp."

I smiled. My life was so perfect. I never wanted to move.

But Cade had other ideas. He wiggled his hand under my body and flipped me to my back.

My ass burned, but the cool sheets soothed.

He stared for a long time at my front, up and down, lingering over my breasts, my belly, the spread of my thighs. "Luckiest man alive."

I bit my lip.

He finally met my gaze. "We have to get a move on. I'm

sorry, but I got some calls. I need to go into the office this afternoon."

"On a Sunday?"

"Yep."

"You do that often?"

"No. But sometimes it can't be helped." He lifted me to sitting and then stood. "I'm gonna start the shower. You meet me there."

"Yes, Sir."

He narrowed his gaze. "Two minutes, baby."

"Yes, Sir."

"Not going to spank you again for punishment."

"Yes, Sir," I repeated.

"You like the idea of time outs?"

I shook my head. Not even close. I sobered. Standing naked in a corner with my nose to the wall was not an inviting idea. I craved contact, even if it was negative like a spanking. Being ignored was not going to do it for me. I lifted myself off the bed fast and beat him to the bathroom, turning on the shower myself.

Cade chuckled as he stepped behind me and hooked me with one arm. He kissed my shoulder. "I have currency."

I shivered. "What does that mean?"

"Means I've found something that will actually work as a disciplinary measure. Something you truly find distasteful."

"Oh, Lord." I hoped he didn't need to use it.

Chapter Fifteen

By one o'clock we were back at Cade's house, and Arthur had set our bags inside the front door, far more of them than we'd left Atlanta with. Cade had provided me with another short sundress, which I now wore with no bra or panties. It was a little revealing, but we hadn't gone anywhere but the limo, so I'd relented when he pleaded with me about the bra.

When we'd entered the Mercedes, Cade had raised the shield between Arthur and the back section, yanked the dress off me, and proceeded to settle on his knees between my legs. I was moaning so loud before we pulled out of Nashville, there was no way my noises hadn't reached the front seat. When he finished, Cade licked his lips. "Couldn't resist the smooth skin."

I cringed. I didn't need the reminder of him shaving me. The shower had been completely awesome. He carefully washed my entire body from head to toe and even let me return the favor. But when we stepped out, he sat me on the counter, grabbed a razor, spread my legs, and proceeded to ensure I was as bare as he preferred.

After that, he'd dropped me on my wobbly legs and rushed

us out the door.

I was still needy and shaking when we got in the car, and thus glad for his decision to go down on me.

After I came twice against his insistent mouth, all the while gripping the edge of the seat with my fists, Cade finally came up for air. He licked his lips and moaned. "Never get enough of that, baby. Love the way you scream when you come."

"I do *not* scream."

He grinned big. "Oh, baby. That's precious." He kissed my naked belly and held me to his cheek.

I glanced toward the front of the car. "Do I?" she whispered.

He chuckled.

He pulled himself onto the seat beside me, and I switched with him, slipping to the ground and popping the button on his jeans. "It's only fair."

"Not going to argue with you."

I lowered the zipper, and Cade lifted his hips while I tugged his jeans down enough to let him free.

I touched him with my fingers first, watching the way he bobbed when I stroked his skin.

Cade sucked in a breath, and I lifted my face. "Another first. I might screw it up."

"Baby." His hands threaded into my hair. "You have no chance. Any time your mouth is anywhere near my cock, I'll be a happy man. Only one rule. No teeth. Otherwise, you can't fail."

I inhaled sharply and tried not to let my face reveal the intense desire for murder I felt toward that fucking bitch of a fiancée his best friend had. I didn't even know her name, and I wanted to kill her.

Luckily, Cade's eyes drifted closed at that moment, and I lowered my face to his cock. The last thing I wanted to do was ruin this for him by letting that bitch into the car.

As soon as I wrapped my lips around his length and heard him moan while his fingers dug into the sides of my head, I let that woman loose and enjoyed my first blow job. It was heady. Powerful. I brought Cade to orgasm fast, swallowing his come deep.

By the time I had finished and Cade pulled me into his lap, we were both chuckling. We'd only made it to the outskirts of Nashville. It was going to be a long drive.

Now that we were home, Cade was scurrying around trying to get back out the door.

"I'll go back to my place and clean up a bit while you work."

"You'll do no such thing." He paused and took my face in his hands. "You'll stay right here. Watch TV. Rest. Nose around if you want. Do not leave this house. I want to know you're here waiting for me when I finish up."

I nodded, swallowing the lump in my throat.

Cade released me and stuffed items into his briefcase. "Besides, you couldn't possibly get your apartment cleaned by the time I finish working." He gave me a pointed glance. "Gonna have to work on that, baby. I'm a neat freak."

I looked around. "I see that."

"Yeah, well, remember that time out idea?"

I curled up my nose. "You wouldn't."

"Hey, when kids don't clean their rooms, they get punished by their parents. Right?"

I didn't answer.

He kissed me on the lips again as he stuffed his phone in his pocket. "Act like a kid, get treated like one, baby." He wasn't kidding.

I didn't respond. I wondered how on earth I would ever be able to fill that goal of his. I was either going to have to get a lobotomy to alter my personality or spend a great deal of time enjoying the feel of the cold wall against my nipples. I cringed.

Cade didn't notice my plight. He pointed at the items scattered on the floor by the door instead. "Start with that mess." He smiled at me. And then he snapped his fingers. "Wait." He dropped his briefcase next to the door and rustled through the bags until he found what he wanted. He pulled the last box from the pile, the one last gift I had yet to open. The one from the jewelry store.

I stayed very still while he brought it to me. "I want you to have this."

He'd said I had to earn all three boxes before he made love to me. He'd broken that vow, but only by twelve hours.

"What is it?"

"Open it."

I tore open the wrapping paper on the oblong box and lifted

the lid. A necklace shined up at me. Silver. Gorgeous. A figure eight adorned the front.

"It's an infinity necklace. I'm sure you've seen them. Many people have them. But for me it symbolizes something more."

I lifted my gaze.

"I want you to wear it as a commitment to me. As my submissive. A symbol of what we have."

I fought a tear in the corner of my eye. That sounded so intense.

Cade smiled. "I know you don't quite get it, but this is huge for me. I've never made a permanent pact with any woman before. If you wear this for me, it tells me you're committed to serving me, in a manner of speaking. You put your trust in me as a Dominant to take care of your needs and see to your happiness."

The tear broke free.

Cade wiped it away with his thumb. "You aren't supposed to cry."

I sobbed out a response. "You can't tell me how to feel." I tried to smile through my emotion.

He pulled me to his chest and rocked my body, the necklace pressing between us in the box. When he released me, he reached into the box and pulled out the thin gold chain. "Some subs wear a collar. Sometimes they wear it everywhere they go. Sometimes they only wear it when they're at play or at a club. This is more subtle. No one will suspect what it means unless they happen to be in the community and know that we are also." He held it up. "Will you wear it?"

I nodded, fighting more tears.

Cade unclasped the lock and circled behind me to lift it over my head. I brushed my hair to one side and tried to rein in my emotions while he hooked it.

It was dainty, but the second it hit my skin I felt the weight of its meaning.

Cade's fingers stroked around to my throat and fondled the infinity symbol. He pulled my back into his front. "You're mine, baby." He kissed my neck.

When he circled to face me, I was a mess. "You need to get to work," I said. If he left now, I could break down in tears of joy without him wigging out.

He didn't heed my advice. He pulled me into his chest, my tears soaking his shirt. Now he would need to change. He kissed the top of my head and held me through my mini breakdown. When I finally sucked in a last sob, he held me out and met my gaze. "I better invest in tissue stock if I ever plan to marry you."

Oh. My. God. Was he serious? My legs threatened to buckle.

Cade just stood there smirking.

I punched his chest. "Don't do that, you idiot."

He buckled in a mock show of injury. "What did I do?" he teased.

"You can't say things like that."

"Why not?"

"Because we've only been...whatever we are...for like a week, that's why."

He chuckled. "I know when I have a good thing. There's no sense beating around the bush."

I rolled my eyes and changed the subject. "You need to change shirts." I plucked at his shirt where I'd soaked it with my tears.

He shook his head. "It'll dry."

I couldn't believe him. He might think I was a mess, but he was coming down a notch too. I was sure in another life he never would have walked out the door leaving that mess by the entrance. In this new life, Cade Alexander was going into the office with tears on his shirt and bags strewed around the foyer.

I smiled through my secret elation.

Cade kissed me soundly one last time and left me to contemplate my fate. Clean up all these bags or spend the evening naked in a corner.

I hastily went to work.

Chapter Sixteen

A half an hour after Cade left, I had everything put away. The various items he'd purchased for me sat in a pile on his kitchen table. I figured I would take them home whenever that occurred. I couldn't spend the night because I didn't have anything to wear to work the next day.

A sudden knock at the door made me flinch. Should I get it? I wasn't expecting anyone of course, but it could be Arthur or some other staff member. Cade hadn't mentioned such a thing, but he could have forgotten.

I padded to the front door, aware that my dress was only marginally appropriate for company.

When I opened the door, I found a woman standing there, a small child hugging her leg tightly. I glanced past her to see if Arthur had returned. His car wasn't there. He was probably waiting at the office for Cade. I certainly had no plans to leave the house.

The only vehicle I spotted was an older Honda Accord that must have belonged to this woman.

"Can I help you?" I asked politely.

"Who the fuck are you?"

I was taken aback. Apparently the child was too. She flinched and hid farther behind her mother. I knew this was her mother. They had the same long blonde hair, and I'd noticed the same features until the child of about four hid. Who talked that way in front of a kid?

"Um, excuse me?"

"You heard me. Who the fuck are you?"

I didn't know how to respond to that. The woman's gaze traveled up and down my body, making me feel self-conscious. She had the same hoity attitude as the women I'd met the previous night, though she didn't appear to fit into their world, judging by her state of dress and the age of her vehicle.

The woman's gaze landed on my neck and stayed there. She reached out a hand and grasped my necklace before I knew what she was about. "He give this to you?"

I struggled to free myself from her clutches.

She yanked. The necklace broke free. She tossed it to the ground behind her.

"Are you mute, bitch?"

I stepped back. I should have slammed the door. Maybe called the cops. But this crazy woman pushed her way into the house, lugging the child behind her by the arm as though the little girl were nothing more than an annoyance. I felt sorry for the kid.

"Start talking," she said as she roamed into the house farther, shaking the little girl off her leg and giving her a stern look. "Wait here. Don't move."

"What are you doing?" I finally found my voice. "If you're looking for Mr. Alexander, he isn't here. You'll have to come back later." *Please come back later.*

The woman laughed manically, tipping her head back like she was deranged. She set her purse on the island, having worked her way into the kitchen. She looked around and then pulled some papers out of her enormous bag. She held them up. "Not that I should have to explain myself to you, but I'm Cade's wife, bitch. And that's his daughter. So I suggest you get the fuck out of my house and don't look back."

I gasped. I didn't reach for the papers.

She held them in my face, forcing me to glace at the top one. It was indeed a marriage certificate. I took it from her and stared at the information. She wasn't lying. Olivia Grantham Alexander and Cade Michael Alexander had married six years ago. I flipped to the other page. And the little girl in the foyer was indeed Cade's child, born almost four years ago. My fingers shook as I held the papers out for her to take back. "I see."

"I hope you do." She stuffed them back in her purse. "I'm going to take Libby to get an ice cream. While I'm gone, you get the fuck gone too. Got it?"

I nodded.

The woman stomped past me. She held her head high again like the women I'd met last night. She even walked like she was from money, but this bitch had hit hard times.

She grabbed her daughter roughly by the arm and dragged her back out the door, slamming it behind them.

I jumped at the finality in the silence of Cade's kitchen.

I glanced around, unsure for a moment what to do. My head was swimming. I couldn't wrap my mind around anything. Too much information slammed into me at once.

Cade had a wife.

He also had a daughter.

I grabbed my head as it began to pound.

That woman was a bitch. I could see why he wasn't with her. I wasn't stupid enough to think she lived here with him. I wasn't even sure she'd ever been to the house before. They were surely estranged.

But that left a pile of damning facts I could not ignore.

The man had a *wife*. He'd failed to mention that detail. And she knew enough about his lifestyle to recognize the significance of the necklace he'd given me not one hour before.

My seemingly perfect world had shattered in two minutes.

He also had a kid. No matter what he thought about his wife, he needed to take care of his own daughter. And if that woman was as crazy as she seemed, he needed to be in court getting custody, like yesterday.

I stomped from the room, searching frantically all over the house. I opened every single door and looked around like a wild woman. I looked through his bedroom and in every hall, even his desk. Not one photo. The wife I could understand, but the man had not one single photo of his own child.

That was crazy.

How could he do that to an innocent kid? Even a stranger deserved better treatment. Hell, if I saw a kid being treated like that walking down the street, I would do everything in my power to extricate the poor soul from the situation.

This was Cade's own flesh and blood.

I slumped to the floor in his office, tucking my head between my knees and heaving for oxygen.

I wasn't going to be able to fix this or rationalize it. There was no way for Cade to fix it, either. Nothing he could say would make me see his side in this. He'd lied to me. By omission, but still. This was huge.

I pulled myself to standing and headed for the kitchen. I grabbed my purse and called a taxi. I waited by the front door, staring at my broken dreams on the kitchen table across the great room, fighting the tears that wanted to leak from my eyes.

I'd cried a river in the last day. I could keep these at bay until I got home. I had to. The cab driver would think I'd lost my mind otherwise.

I was taking absolutely nothing I hadn't come with. I wished I could even leave the clothes on my back, but there was nothing else for me to wear. The only things I held were my purse and my overnight bag filled with my makeup and toiletries.

The cab was fast. Thank God. I stepped onto the front porch, taking a deep breath, and closed the door behind me.

I stepped over the broken necklace on my way down the walkway, nearly jogging as I raced from my ten day break from sanity.

As the cab pulled away from the house, I looked out the window, a tear falling down my face unbidden. *Good-bye, Cade. Have a nice life.*

Part Two: Her Rules

Chapter Seventeen

Five months later...

The incessant beeping dragged me out of a deep sleep. When it registered as my alarm, I groaned and wiggled one arm out from under the covers to slap blindly at the top of my clock without turning my head or exposing any other skin.

I was snuggled and warm. I didn't need it to be day yet.

I took deep breaths, still burrowed under my covers. After a few minutes, I flipped to my back and unburied my head enough to stare at the ceiling.

I smiled as I remembered what my life consisted of. For the first time in months, it wasn't a forced smile, either. I finally felt a sense of contentment that had eluded me for so long, I'd hovered on the edge of a black hole.

Cheyenne and Meagan had been with me through it all. They had been the ones to pick up the pieces and glue me back together. I owed them my life, literally.

I finally had my dream job. I took a deep cleansing breath.

I'd only been a full-time employee with The Rockwood Group for two weeks, but already I knew it was the right decision.

I hadn't started at the bottom rung this time. I'd been smart. I'd held out for a position I was qualified for instead of jumping at the first opportunity that came along.

Five months.

The first week had been spent crying on Cheyenne's couch. That was all the time I'd given myself to mourn, telling myself I couldn't dedicate more days to missing Cade Alexander than I'd actually spent *with* him.

I'd gone straight to my apartment after leaving his house, cleared out everything that mattered to me, and headed for Cheyenne's, never looking back. I sent a brief e-mail to Moriah letting her know I would not be returning to work. That hurt. I'd never been so irresponsible. But I had no other option. I left no opportunity for Cade to find me.

Meagan had been the one to sell my furniture and turn in my keys. I'd broken my lease—a lease I'd only had for a month—but no other choice seemed viable. The financial hit was tough at first. But I managed to make my minimum payments on time and keep my chin above water, barely.

A week after I took up residence on Cheyenne's couch, I opened the want ads and started looking. Two days later, I switched from Atlanta to Nashville in my search. Leaving Atlanta seemed like the best call. And Nashville was the home of The Rockwood Group, a company that had long been one of my top contenders after graduation.

The Rockwood Group had no openings that were realistic choices. I researched temp agencies and decided that was the perfect route to get myself in the job market.

Instead of fretting over my abrupt departure from Alexander Technologies and how that information would look on a résumé, I left it out. Easy.

I went to Nashville on a Wednesday, ten days after leaving Cade, to interview with a top-notch temp agency. They hired me on the spot. No one questioned what I'd done since graduating a month ago. That short interlude could easily be explained away as a period of job hunting.

The relief over that decision alone had lifted my spirits. I spent the long weekend hauling my stuff from Atlanta to Nashville, securing a small one-bedroom apartment, and purchasing second-hand furniture. On Monday morning, two weeks from leaving my heart in Cade Alexander's house, I was dressed to kill and working my tail off.

My first assignment had been a two-month position with a mid-sized company that immediately adored me and found me invaluable. I loved them too, but knew that was not my final stop. My sights were high. My sights were still on The Rockwood Group.

My second assignment had been with a smaller business that needed a temporary office manager. I learned so much from them that I should have paid them for their time instead of the other way around.

The day I got the call that I would be placed with The Rockwood Group, a complete fluke, I nearly screamed into the phone. I even treated myself to a new suit that evening. My head was almost clear by then. The fog would slip in when I was alone on my couch in the evening or on the weekend. I tamped it down with ice cream and hot fudge sauce.

I worked my ass off for The Rockwood Group, making an impression in every department I touched. I worked long hours, skipped lunches, and made connections. That hard work paid off.

As of two weeks ago, they'd bought me out from under the temp agency, and I was now a full-time employee on the fourth floor as the manager of a half dozen other employees.

I smiled up at my ceiling once again and dragged myself out of bed—or off the mattress rather. I hadn't splurged for a frame yet.

Enough traipsing down memory lane. It was real. Every day when that alarm clock went off, I remembered it was real. I was on a path that led to good places. I had a starting salary that made me squeal in delight. Soon, I would be able to move from my dingy apartment to a larger, classier place in a better part of town. I had managed to pay off my credit card debt in the last few months, and for the first time ever, my only outstanding loan was six years of education.

The best part was I had a date tonight.

I'd met Brad Phelps at my previous temp job. He'd flirted with me while I'd worked there, but I'd made myself unapproachable. Dating co-workers was absolutely never going to happen to me again. But last weekend, I'd run into him at Starbucks, and we'd had coffee together.

He was kind, polite, attractive, educated—everything I

should have wanted in a man. I hadn't dated since I'd left Cade, and I knew I needed to put myself back out there. Brad made me laugh. He opened doors for me. He bought my coffee. And he asked me out.

He didn't cause a tight knot to form in my belly. He didn't make my nipples stand at attention. He didn't make me long to have his lips on my skin.

I shook these ridiculous thoughts aside. I needed to move on. And I would. What the hell was wrong with me?

I refused to be ruined by ten days with a man who lied to me, spanked me twice, and made me feel like I had no control over myself. Well, that last part was entirely my fault. Nobody was responsible for the way I felt. That had been on me.

I had a date tonight. It felt good, and I smiled again as I entered the shower.

In half an hour, I stood in my closet choosing an outfit. I wore a navy pencil skirt and the perfect nude pumps. I was on my third blouse, the first two rejected ones draped over the door knob. I finally had "the one" on and made my way to the kitchen.

My furniture made me cringe. Bare bones is how I'd lived for five months. I had purchased only the most necessary items, a second-hand table and chairs, a garage-sale couch, and a bedroom dresser that had seen better days. The two items I had not scrimped on were my mattress and my television. I needed both to maintain my sanity.

I would have four days off next week for Thanksgiving, and I intended to spend them apartment hunting and furniture shopping.

First, coffee.

Then I hit the road.

By seven thirty I was in my office, going over the day's events. Most of the employees would arrive at eight. I always felt one step ahead of myself if I beat everyone there. I had a team meeting at ten. My assistant, Lisa, would set up the conference room when she arrived.

By the time ten o'clock rolled around, I was ready to roll. My team of six arranged themselves around the conference table, coffee and bagels in hand, and I proceeded to scribble away on the giant white board at the head of the room as we brainstormed ideas for the latest cell phone app we were developing.

My back was to the entrance of the room, but I felt eyes boring into me. I finished what I was writing and turned around only to catch a glimpse of someone walking away. A man. Tall. Lithe. A flash of dark blond hair. Had I seen him before? I paused for a moment, an eerie sensation crawling up my spine. No one else seemed to have noticed. The door was wide open. Anyone could wander by. That wasn't unusual. Could have been the department head. Could have been a deliveryman, for all I knew.

Several of my employees twisted their necks to glance out the door, but only because they saw where my gaze landed, not because they'd experienced the same weird sensation.

I focused my attention back on the group and smiled. "Where were we?"

Unease ate at me irrationally for several hours after the

meeting. I returned to my office, so distracted I barely heard Lisa call my name. "Lillie?" When I didn't turn around, she spoke again, louder. "Ms. Kingston?"

I jerked her way. "Sorry. My head is elsewhere today." Combined with the fact I was not used to responding to either Lillie or Ms. Kingston. But Lisa didn't know that.

I was hiding. I would hide my entire life if I could get away with it. Amelia Kensington had easily become Lillie as a nickname, and somehow I'd managed to slip Kingston onto almost every form without anyone noticing that my real name had a few extra letters. I would do anything to keep Cade Alexander from finding me.

Lisa smiled and rolled her eyes. "I can imagine. You have about fifty projects going on at once, and you just started here. I'd be under my desk if I were you."

I smiled back.

"Anyway, Mr. Cross from development would like to meet with you in half an hour in the conference room. Will that work with your schedule?"

I glanced at my watch. Three o'clock. I had a stack of work to do before the end of the day, but no meetings. "Perfect. Tell him I'll be there."

"Okay. He said to bring the compilation of ideas from this morning."

"Got it."

Lisa left, and I scurried to organize that morning's notes, which ate up the entire half hour.

At three thirty I was already in the conference room setting up several proposals on the easel when Mr. Cross came in with two other men. He headed straight for me and reached out a hand. "Ms. Kingston."

I shook his hand and smiled genuinely. We'd met several times, but this was the first project we'd be working on together. "Please, call me Lillie."

"Lillie then." He took a seat, and I turned to the other two men who'd come in with him. And my eyes went wide.

"Brad." I shook his hand.

"You two know each other?" Mr. Cross asked.

Brad responded. "We worked together before Lillie jumped to the big office."

Mr. Cross laughed. "Ah, you temped at Stephen's Engineering before you came here, right?"

I nodded. "I didn't realize we were working with your firm on this project."

"Yep." Brad took a seat at the table. His smile was huge. Obviously this did not throw him off his game.

The man with him, another man I remembered from Stephen's, also greeted me and sat.

"Perfect. Show us what you've got, Lillie."

I turned to the easel and lifted a finger toward the upper right corner. Just as I was about to speak, another voice, belonging to no one in the room, crawled up my spine and tore a giant hole in everything I'd spent five months building for myself.

"Yes, *Lillie*, show us what you've got."

I hesitated for what was probably only a second but seemed like a pause in time that lasted an eternity, willing that voice to belong to anyone other than the very man I knew was currently in the doorframe. As long as I didn't turn around, perhaps the universe would shake itself up and scramble all the inhabitants so that voice changed and transferred itself to any individual alive other than Cade Alexander. Someone short and fat and ugly would be much better.

My panties were wet. My bra felt too tight.

My date for tonight sat right behind me, closer than Mr. Alexander. I'd been in Brad's presence more times than Cade's. More hours for sure. I'd had more meals with him. I'd laughed more often with him.

At no point had I gotten damp between my thighs with Brad. His voice did not climb up my spine and make me melt.

I wanted to slap Cade Alexander even before I faced reality and turned around.

He was pissed. He leaned against the doorframe, legs crossed at the ankles, hands in his pockets. His gaze was hard, penetrating. His words had been filled with anger.

But I was the only one who noticed. I was the only one in the room who knew him well enough to realize he was infuriated, and all that tension was directed at me.

In fact, I was the only one in the room who knew we'd ever met before.

Cade wandered into the room as though he owned the place. He pulled out a chair at the same time Mr. Cross jumped up from his seat and leaned over the table, holding out a hand. "Mr. Alexander. So good to see you. What brings you to our neck of the woods?"

Cade barely glanced at Mr. Cross. He took the man's hand with the bare minimum of courtesy and then plopped in his chair and leaned back. "Business. Don't mind me. Carry on. I'll just listen in, if you don't mind." His gaze was on me. No one else was even in the room.

But I *did* mind.

Besides, there was no way I could make a presentation to the three other men in the room with Cade staring at me.

Interestingly enough, I could have easily spoken in front of my other surprise visitor, Brad. But not Cade.

And that infuriated me. That he could weasel himself under my skin with so little effort made me want to scream.

"Lillie?"

I jerked my gaze to Mr. Cross and cleared my throat. "I'm sorry. Could we possibly do this another time?"

Mr. Cross flinched and furrowed his brow. "Not really." He glanced at Brad and the other man. "The men from Stephen's Engineering made themselves available for us this afternoon."

I nodded. "Right. Of course." I turned back to face the board. This was insane. I needed to pull myself together and pretend Cade wasn't in the room. I'd managed to pretend he wasn't on the planet for five months. I could ignore his physical presence for thirty minutes and present the results of my team's decisions.

But Cade wasn't interested in that idea. "Ms. *Kingston*. Please. Pretend I'm not here." He emphasized my abbreviated last name in the same way he'd annunciated my new nickname.

"Do you two know each other?" Brad asked. Ah, great. Leave it to Brad to be the astute one.

"No," I responded too quickly.

"We've crossed paths," Cade added, "though Lillie might not remember me. It was before she was in an accident that caused irreversible brain damage and significant permanent amnesia."

Mr. Cross gasped. Hell, so did Brad and his coworker. Mr. Cross's attention switched to me. "Lillie?"

Brad's attention was focused on Cade. He was a smart guy. He even stood. If there had been anything remotely funny about this situation, I would have laughed hysterically at Brad's stance, as if the man could take Cade in a fight. Cade was taller, broader, and spent at least an hour a day working out.

I jerked my attention to Cade. "Could we not do this here, please?" I stared at him, hard. Begging him to listen to me.

"What? I've come up with no other explanation. Do you have one?" Cade remained in his chair, appearing calm and relaxed to everyone else in the room. I was the only person who knew what lurked beneath the surface. I flinched, imagining his palm on my bare ass, spanking me for hours in atonement for a five-month disappearance. Or worse. How long would a person have to stand naked in a corner to make up for what he perceived as my misdemeanors?

Now I shivered. "Mr. Alexander..." I glared at him, hating him for the way he made my thighs tingle and my nipples tighten. I could taste him on my tongue from across the room. My panties were wet beneath my skirt. Yes, my panties. I wore them every day. And not sexy ones, either. Nope. I'd purchased normal everyday cotton bikini briefs. And my pubic hair was back to its original state.

Even standing in the same room as Cade, I felt defiant for the things he couldn't see.

Brad spoke next. He still stood, his chair pushed back against the wall. He glanced from me to Cade and back. And then he reached down to grab his briefcase from the floor. He gathered his notepad and several papers off the table and stuffed them into his leather bag.

His voice was calm when he spoke. "I think Ms. Kingston is right. We should reschedule." He didn't meet my gaze. Except for the way he stuffed the papers sideways into his bag, wrinkling them without a care, and then finally jamming them in far enough to yank the zipper closed, no one would have known from his voice how perturbed he was.

Brad left the room abruptly without looking over his shoulder.

His coworker and Mr. Cross stood next.

I glanced at Mr. Cross, whose eyes were wide, his mouth pursed in confusion. I was sure the man had completely misinterpreted nearly every unspoken vibe in the room. He would have assumed Brad was aggravated with The Rockwood Group as a whole for wasting his time, as opposed to me personally. After all, Mr. Cross had no way of knowing I'd arranged a date for that very evening with the man who'd just stomped from the room knowing full well his territory had just been trampled on.

Brad's coworker lifted his eyebrows and scurried after Brad.

Mr. Cross hesitated and then made his disappointment in me transparent in his sharp tone. "Ms. Kingston, please let me know when it would be convenient for *you* to meet with my people. I'd hate to disrupt anything." He gasped and then turned toward Cade. "Sorry, Mr. Alexander. I—"

Cade held up a hand. He'd yet to move from his relaxed stance in his chair. "No worries, sir. So nice to see you again. I'm sorry for the disruption."

Mr. Cross nodded and then fled the room, probably to stew over the fact that he'd dressed me down in front of a man he knew was a high roller in this industry.

I left my belongings where they were and marched from the room also, knowing Cade would follow me. There was no way in hell I was going to endure his abuse in the conference room in front of a wall of windows. As it was, two coworkers were already gathered in the hall, pretending to have a conversation when I walked past them.

I headed straight for my office, Cade on my heels. He was silent, but I felt him just the same. When I entered, I held the door as he passed by me, and then I leaned out to speak to my astonished secretary, whose eyes were huge, her mouth hanging open. "Hold my calls, Lisa." And I shut the door, almost too hard.

I spun around to find Cade wandering around my office as though he owned the place. Hell, he'd acted like he owned the entire building from the moment he'd entered the conference room. I wanted to strike him again. Just because he was some big business owner in Atlanta didn't give him the right to storm The Rockwood Group and act like he owned it also. What an asshole.

I was so infuriated, I didn't even like him at that moment, and that was a first.

No. That was a second.

I'd hated him pretty hard after meeting his *wife*.

Cade picked up several papers from my desk and skimmed them while I stared him down from across the room, arms crossed over my chest, foot tapping in nervous tension on the ground. "What the hell are you doing here, Cade?"

He lifted his gaze slowly. "I could ask you the same thing, *Lillie*."

"I work here."

"So do I."

That shocked me. I gasped. "You what?"

"Amelia, I own this company, same as Alexander Technologies."

"Since when?"

"Since I bought it."

"Which was when?"

Cade didn't respond to that question.

My cheeks went completely hot. How the hell could I not have known this? It wasn't possible.

He grinned. "Relax. You aren't negligent. I'm a purely silent partner. My best friend runs the place."

His best friend. I stumbled forward. "Riley?"

"Yep."

Now that I should have known. "Wait. The owner is David Moreno."

"Yes. David Riley Moreno. He's gone by Riley since we were kids. There were too many Davids in our class." He grinned again. It really made him happy to one-up me.

My skin crawled as I realized who had passed by my meeting that morning. I hadn't met with the owner of The Rockwood Group. He'd been out of town on business since I'd assumed my new position, and there'd been no call for me to have met him as a temp.

"He called you."

"He did." Cade crossed the room and stood in front of me, his hands stuffed in the pockets of his tailored suit.

"You should leave."

He chuckled. It wasn't in humor.

"I'll tender my resignation immediately." I stepped around him and headed for my desk, my dreams going up in smoke. How could I be so stupid?

Cade turned around and planted himself in the guest chair

at my desk while I busied myself gathering up the mess of papers on my desk in an attempt to stack them. I would never know where anything was now, but it didn't matter since I was about to quit the best job I'd ever had.

"You're still just as messy, I see."

"That's none of your business. Why are you still here?"

Several seconds of silence passed before Cade spoke again. "You owe me."

I straightened to my full height and inhaled sharply. "I owe *you?*"

"Yes." He leaned his elbows on my desk. "Sit down, Amelia."

Fury burned my skin. "I'd rather not, Mr. Alexander."

"Amelia. Sit. Down." He separated his words and spoke louder that time.

My ass hit the chair behind me, but my heart pounded and my brain protested.

"Now. Let's see if we can sort this out."

"There's nothing to sort." I kept my back rigid, my thighs pressed together. It took tremendous self-control to avoid shaking a knee up and down.

Cade narrowed his gaze. "I'm trying to figure out why you're so pissed, seeing as you're the one who walked out on me."

I opened my mouth to speak and then decided he didn't deserve an explanation. "I see."

He raised one eyebrow. "Isn't that what happened?"

I tapped my foot, unable to maintain my composure. "Sure."

Cade pursed his lips and inhaled deeply, clearly containing a high level of fury under the surface.

I didn't give one fuck. Let him be mad. I wasn't the lying, cheating bastard in this arrangement. He was.

He sat back finally, staring at me with those damn green eyes that seemed like eternal pools of the most gorgeous hot springs in the world. I'd never seen a natural body of water that color, but I imagined it would look like that.

"You've confounded me, Ms. Kensington."

"Really? So sorry," I sassed. "Are we done yet?"

"No we're not done." He straightened again. "Until you satisfactorily explain to me why you disappeared from the face of the Earth not one hour after tearfully accepting my collar, we're not done."

"It's going to be a long night for you then." I busied myself pretending to work by shaking my mouse and turning my gaze to my computer monitor.

He stood and leaned over the desk to get my attention. His hand reached out and grabbed my chin, forcing me to meet his gaze with enough pressure that I did so and not so much strength I would bruise. "You will look me in the eye and explain yourself, Amelia."

"I will not, Cade. I owe you nothing."

A frustrated growl escaped his lips as he released me and stood to his full height. "Do you know how worried I was?"

I doubted it lasted very long. After all, he had another fucking *family* to deal with. Even if his wife was a bitch, he still would have had to handle her, and his daughter.

"It took me two days before I finally went door to door and found a neighbor who saw you get in a cab that afternoon. That was the first and only time I knew you were even alive."

I flinched.

He dragged his fingers through his hair. "I assumed you'd been abducted from my house, Amelia. *Kidnapped*," he yelled.

I swallowed. Admittedly that had not occurred to me. On the other hand, I gave not one fuck. I was glad he'd been worried. Angry even. I hoped he'd suffered countless hours of ire. None of which would have come close to matching how I'd felt.

"I even went to the police. In another two hours I would have filed a missing person's report." He stared at me again. "Finally my neighbor across the street said she'd just gotten out of her car from returning home when she saw you jog to the taxi in tears. Why, Amelia? What the fuck?"

I cringed, but gave no response.

His chest heaved as he glared at me.

"You should go," I repeated. "I promise to disappear more completely this time. You won't see me again."

He opened his mouth. "Are you fucking kidding me?"

"No."

His tipped his head back to look at the ceiling. "Oh. My. God." He spun around as though disoriented and then came back to face me. "You're the most infuriating woman I've ever met. If my cock weren't rock hard, I'd follow your advice and walk out that door."

I gasped at that remark, and my damn pussy clenched.

Cade leaned his hands on my desk. "But, baby, I'm so fucking hot for you, I can't stop myself. Even though you've clearly lost your fucking mind, I won't leave this room without an explanation."

I whimpered. I couldn't help it. He did that to me. He controlled my physical response to him with his gaze.

"Now we're getting somewhere." He lifted his hands in the air. "The woman shows emotion. She isn't made of stone."

Damn my body. I clenched my knees together tighter, my foot now tapping so hard on the floor I would surely leave a worn spot on the carpet.

"Would you stop yelling," I gritted out. "The entire building can hear you."

"I don't give a fuck if the entire city hears me, Amelia. If you want me to shut up, show me some respect and start talking."

Show him some respect? That did it. I'd never been so enraged. "You want respect?" I yelled.

"Yes, please."

"Like you respected me for ten days?" I stood now. My legs shook, but I held it together and stomped around my desk to face Cade with my hands on my hips. "Was it respect you demonstrated when you lied to me? Was it respect I was supposed to glean from the way you made promises to me you couldn't possibly keep? Was it respect you meant to project when you left me standing at a bar in a room full of people you knew would readily eat me alive and spit out my bones?" Spit flew from my mouth with every few words as I leaned into him.

He looked genuinely shocked.

"What's the matter? Are you out of insults to sling at me?" I pointed at the door. "Go. I need to get out of here. I have a date tonight, and it's going to take a lot of groveling and explanation to even keep that date. He's probably already changed his phone number because of you." Why I chose to add all that, I had no idea, but it was worth it from the look on his face.

He thought for a second and then it dawned. "That guy from Stephen's Engineering?"

"Yep. Not that it's any of your business."

Cade pursed his lips together. If he laughed, I would be furious. Instead he schooled his expression and sighed. "That man is totally wrong for you."

"Not for you to decide."

Cade shook his head, dismayed. "You're lying to yourself if you think that man is capable of making you happy. What was his name? Brad?"

I walked away from him. That he was right was inconsequential. I knew as well as Cade did that I would never have anything significant with Brad. But that was beside the point.

I was done arguing. I grabbed my purse and my phone and

walked right past him. When I stepped into the corridor, I was relieved to find the office almost empty. It was late. Lisa was gone. Most of the staff would be too.

Cade didn't follow me. I wasn't sure if I was relieved or disappointed. And that made me angrier.

I made it to my car on sheer will. I made it to my apartment in a state of shock. I didn't shed a single tear until I was in my bedroom and had collapsed on my mattress, the one that lay on the floor without a frame.

I curled into a ball and let the waterfall begin. I sobbed hard for half an hour, knowing if I didn't, it would just drag out the inevitable.

Damn Cade Alexander.

My perfect life had hit a brick wall, shattering as a physical representation of the fragile existence I'd been living for five months.

I cried harder when I thought about how hard I'd worked to get where I was today. The sacrifices I'd made. The way I'd managed to bury my emotions so deep they were almost unrecognizable. I'd convinced myself I didn't need any of what Cade had offered me. Even though I'd known beyond a shadow of a doubt he'd awakened something I couldn't deny, I wasn't about to risk my heart by letting another man dominate me.

I'd thought for about a half a second about joining a BDSM club or attending a munch, but I'd tamped down the urge and let it go.

There wasn't a Dom alive who would ever make me feel the

way Cade had. Still did. Damn it. Even his presence behind me from the moment he'd stepped into my space had made me want to submit to his will.

I'd put on a fantastic front. I meant every word I'd spoken, but deep inside, he'd proven I was ruined for other men. He owned me. No one else would ever measure up.

Even angry, he owned me. Even though I knew he was married and he was the worst father of all time, he owned me. I hated him for destroying that part of me. Making it so I would never have a normal relationship with another man.

Brad Phelps didn't deserve this. He was too kind. He deserved a woman who would love him back. Not a shadow of a girl who would never be true to herself or him.

I needed to call him and break our date. Hell, if he took the call, it would be a miracle.

I pulled myself to sitting and reached for the box of unending tissues on my nightstand. I'd already replaced it a dozen times since I'd moved to Nashville. How many more boxes would I need in the dead of night before I died?

I padded to my bathroom and washed my face. Pulling off my clothes, I dropped them along the path back to my closet. I even took off my bra, glad for the release of pressure against my chest. My breasts had felt confined and swollen since Cade stepped in the room. I couldn't tolerate another minute of them rubbing against my bra. I grabbed my favorite yoga pants from the floor and tugged them over my legs. Then I reached for my most comfy sweatshirt and pulled it over my head.

Lastly, I tugged my hair up high on my head and fastened it with a discarded hair band from my nightstand.

With a deep breath, I headed for the kitchen to make a few calls. First Brad. Then Cheyenne. Then Meagan. My girls would freak. This was inconceivable. But they needed to know. And I needed to face reality.

Chapter Eighteen

First things first. I needed fortification. I opened my refrigerator and pulled out a bottle of my favorite wine, a Marcassin Chardonnay. I tamped down the part of me that cringed over this indulgence.

It was true, everything I knew about wine I'd learned from Cade. And I'd become a wine snob. My main extravagance, even when things were at their worst, was expensive Chardonnay. I was unapologetic.

I grabbed my second luxury from the drawer in my kitchen, a fantastic corkscrew, and extricated the cork from the bottle with ease.

A few sips of my favorite beverage and I closed my eyes and felt almost human.

And then there was a knock at my door. I stared at it for a moment, which didn't suddenly give me x-ray vision. If Cade had followed me home or gotten my address from human resources, I would personally kill him.

I set my glass on the sorry looking kitchen table and padded to the door with heavy feet. A peek in the peephole told me what I should have realized in the first place.

Shit.

Brad.

I hadn't called him yet. I also hadn't expected him to show up after the scene at the office. I opened the door quick. "Hey." I opened it wider. "Come in."

He walked in, his brow furrowed in confusion. "I thought we were going out?"

He seriously still wanted to go out?

"Am I early?" He glanced at his watch.

"No. I, uh, I just assumed…"

"Ah." He rocked on his feet, his hands tucked in his pockets. And then he shrugged. "Sorry about earlier. I wasn't mad at *you*."

"Of course you were. And you had every right to be. I'm the one who should be sorry."

He looked at me in confusion. "Why? Because some rich guy wants in your pants? I don't give a shit about that. I was just pissed he needed to make that apparent to everyone in the room. You must have wanted to kill that bastard. I don't care if he *is* the owner."

"Yeah." I sure did want to kill him. But Brad didn't know the half of it.

"So, you still want to go out?"

I weighed that possibility for a moment. I could. Would it be wrong of me to ignore my complete lack of sexual attraction for this guy and give it a shot?

Another knock at the door sounded before I could open my mouth.

Brad stepped back and pulled it open before I could stop him.

Cade.

Of course. I mean when would the universe *not* rain on my parade?

Cade rolled his eyes and stomped into my apartment as if he owned the place. "Seriously?" he asked me. He wore the suit and tie he'd worn to the office, which meant he'd probably come straight to my apartment.

"Cade. This isn't a good time."

Brad stood at his full height and faced Cade also. "Dude. I really don't think the lady is interested. Why don't you give it up?"

Cade laughed.

I wanted to punch him. What a dick.

"That's rich." Cade strolled into my apartment, glancing around. He took off his jacket and draped it over the back of the couch. He then proceeded to loosen his tie.

I cringed. *Make yourself at home, why don't you.*

Brad, I wasn't embarrassed about. He'd seen my apartment a few times in the past. He knew I didn't have the money for more furniture.

And why the hell was I silently justifying myself to Cade?

"Cade. Leave." I grabbed the front door and held it open. "You're not welcome here."

Cade ignored me and sat on my couch, stretching out both arms and getting as comfortable as a person could on my ratty, beaten-up, beige sofa.

"You heard the lady. She asked you to leave, Mr. Alexander." Brad stood firm. I admired him for his actions. I even appreciated the way he stood up for me. However, my heart wasn't beating for him. It had started pumping the second Cade walked in.

There was a moment of standoff. Or so it seemed. Though I was sure it wasn't a standoff for Cade at all. He knew exactly who was going to win this battle, and it wasn't going to be Brad. Or me for that matter.

Finally, Cade spoke. "Amelia, unless you want me to air our dirty laundry in front of your friend here, I suggest you tell him good night."

I stopped breathing. He was being an ass, and I was losing my patience. I also knew he would absolutely follow through on that threat, giving me no choice but to dismiss Brad.

I turned to find Brad's shoulders slumped in defeat. "Really? Lillie, you don't have to put up with this. Let's just go. If he won't leave, call the cops."

I wished it were that simple.

I touched Brad's arm and peered into his eyes. "I'm sorry. I truly am. But I need to work out a few things with Cade. Can I have a rain check?"

The hurt on Brad's face made me want to hang my head in shame. But I held steady, trying to convey without words how sorry I was. And not just for breaking our date, but for breaking our future. I knew he was into me. This would burn a little, and I wouldn't break things off with him, things that had never really started, right here in front of Cade. That would have to wait.

Brad sighed and nodded. He walked to the door like the true gentleman he was. His fingers touched my cheek as he turned around. "Call me." He glanced over my shoulder. "Even later tonight if you need."

I nodded.

He dropped his hand and walked away while I watched.

I swallowed what I knew to be true. That was the first time he'd touched my face. And nothing. No sparks. No fireworks. Nothing.

Damn it. It would have been so much easier if Brad were the man of my dreams.

I shut the door finally and turned to face the bane of my existence.

"Have you slept with him?"

I flinched. "None of your business."

Cade narrowed his gaze at me. He sighed and then spoke again. "Come here, Amelia." His voice held less conviction than earlier. His words were still commanding, and I was drawn to him like a puppet, but he wasn't as angry. He'd lost some of the initial edge.

I ignored him and walked to my table to grab my wine.

Cade glanced at the bottle on the counter and smiled. "Good vintage."

I rolled my eyes and then relented. "You want a glass?"

"Thought you'd never ask."

I grabbed another wineglass from the cabinet and poured some of my favorite Chardonnay in it. Of course this required me to stroll across the room and hand it to him, which meant I would need to get within arm's reach, which would be dangerous.

And I wasn't mistaken. Cade took the glass with one hand, but he grabbed my forearm with the other and pulled me down next to him.

Most of his anger had dissipated. I wasn't sure if this was a good thing or a bad thing, but he reached for me tentatively and tucked a lock of my hair behind my ear. "You changed your hairstyle."

"I needed something new." I shrugged. I'd added highlights and shortened it some. My belly tightened at his simple touch. It was impossible for me to ignore what he did to me just by entering a room. This was why I needed to get rid of him. And fast. Before I did something stupid.

"I like it."

"I don't care what you like."

Cade stopped moving, his mouth falling. He took a long drink and then leaned his head back on the couch and stared at the ceiling. "Please, baby. Give me a bone here. If I had any idea what I did to deserve your wrath, I would sleep better at night."

"Really? You think so? So, if I tell you what I'm pissed off about, you'll leave me alone and let me go?"

He lifted his gaze and frowned. He blinked a few times. He had no idea what I could possibly say to make him let me be. "Amelia—"

"No, I'm serious. If I agree to tell you what happened that day, I want you to agree to leave me alone."

"I'm not sure what to say to that."

"Take it or leave it."

Cade took a deep breath and then relented. "Okay."

"It's simple. I can sum it up for you in one word. And you can walk out that door right now."

"Baby..."

"Olivia."

Cade's stance changed in less than a heartbeat. He bolted to an upright position from his slouch and almost dropped his wine. He managed to set the glass precariously on the floor near the couch before he lost it. But he'd also gone noticeably mute.

"Now you know. Please leave me alone."

"What?" His word was nearly screeched. "Are you telling me Olivia came to my house and spoke to you while I was at work that day?"

I narrowed my gaze. "That's what I'm telling you."

He jumped up from the couch and began to pace. "I haven't seen or heard from her in years. That bitch. What the fuck did she say to make you run?" He ran his hands through his hair.

"Oh, you know. Just little details." I raised my voice for the next part. "Like how you're *married* to her and *have a little girl*." I was shouting by the end. I stood and stomped from the room to get more wine. I might as well drink it from the bottle at that point.

"What?" Cade screamed even louder than me. "Are you fucking kidding me?"

I had the bottle of wine hovering over my glass when he asked that question. My blood froze. I stopped breathing.

I set the bottle back on the counter and lifted my face.

Never. Not once in five months had I considered any part of Olivia's tirade to be lies. Hell, the woman had the paperwork to back up her story. I felt a chill as I calmly uttered the damning parts. "She showed me your *marriage* certificate and *Libby's* birth certificate." I held on to the counter with both hands.

Cade's chest rose and fell. His eyes grew huge. His nostrils flared. He clearly wanted to murder Olivia. When he finally moved, it was to spin around in a circle as though looking for something to take his anger out on. I owned nothing worth throwing. I didn't move a muscle. Had I been wrong?

Cade's shoulders slumped finally, and he headed back to the couch. He picked up his glass and downed the rest of the wine in one gulp. He stomped over to where I stood and grabbed the bottle next. After filling both our glasses, he took another long drink.

I took a few steps away.

He ignored me and headed back for the couch where he slumped back and put his head in his hands.

I picked up my wineglass and padded his way. I wasn't scared for my own safety. My furniture maybe, but nothing I had was worth worrying about. The most expensive item in the room had just been swallowed. I didn't think the empty bottle alone was worth much.

Several long, uncomfortable minutes went by.

I waited.

Finally Cade lifted his head and looked at me. For the first time ever, I saw pain in his eyes.

I had been hurting for months. It hadn't occurred to me he'd been hurting also. Perhaps worse.

He leaned back and started talking. "I met Olivia in college. She was a friend of Christine."

"Who's Christine?" I interrupted.

"Riley's ex-fiancée."

"Oh right." I wondered what had happened between those two.

"Olivia was made of sugar for the first few years. She came from more money than me. I was hesitant at first. But she was persistent. I was afraid, for good reason, I wouldn't be able to live up to her expectations. She had expensive tastes.

"She worked hard to get me. I thought she loved me. I never realized the only thing she loved was money, and she'd seen in me the potential to earn more of it. She'd judged me right in that area at least. She'd even submitted for me. When I started dabbling in BDSM and later knew it was a path I wanted to follow, she readily agreed."

I didn't move a muscle.

"After two years, she wore me down. By then I was working my way up the corporate ladder. I was twenty-four. I had a master's degree. I had a fantastic job. And I had big ideas. I was also an idiot. I never saw her for what she truly was—a greedy, conniving bitch."

I flinched. Cade ignored me or didn't notice. He was in his world now. He needed to tell this story in his way, and I needed to hear it.

"I married her. And then she went psycho on me. I tried. I really tried. I gave her four years of dating and four years of marriage before I couldn't take it another minute. I filed for divorce. I thought she would go ballistic when I told her, but she surprised me. She moved out without putting up a fight. I knew she was cheating on me. She probably didn't want to risk that tidbit coming up in mediation.

"Of course she cleaned house in court. Not surprising. It was fast. Really fast. Too fast."

"She was pregnant," I commented.

Cade turned to me. "Baby, I swear to you, if that woman was pregnant, I had no knowledge of it. And there's no way the kid's mine."

"Seriously?"

"I'm telling the truth."

I swallowed. "How do you know for sure?"

He shrugged. "We hadn't had sex in months when I kicked her to the curb, and the divorce was fast, but not that fast. The last time I saw Olivia, it had been months since I'd slept with her. Can't say I looked at her closely, but she never said she was pregnant. Why the hell wouldn't she have told me? She could have milked me for way more money at the time, or even used the baby as leverage to try and blackmail me into staying with her. The father must be whoever the fuck she was sleeping with when I divorced her ass."

I nodded.

Cade gnawed on the inside of his cheek. "Fuck." He set his head in his hands again.

"I'm sorry."

He turned toward me again. His face was hard. "So you just left? Some bitch came to the door claiming to be my wife, and you fucking left?"

"Well, yeah. She had a certificate."

"Of course she had a certificate. They don't fucking disintegrate into thin air when someone gets divorced."

He had a point there.

"She had the kid too."

"With her? She brought a kid to the house?"

I nodded. "She looked just like Olivia. And that woman isn't a fit mother. She was a bitch. I felt horrible for that child. And it made me even angrier with you for abandoning your own daughter."

"Jesus."

"I'm so sorry," I repeated. "I should have had more faith in you."

"You ripped off my necklace and left it lying on the front

steps."

"No. In my defense, Olivia did that."

"That skank touched you?"

"Yes."

Cade picked up his glass from the floor again and drank the last of the wine. "You have more of this?" He lifted the glass into the air.

I nodded.

He stood, mumbling to himself on the way to the kitchen. "My woman has furniture from the dime store and hundred-dollar bottles of wine in her fridge."

I smiled. I especially liked the way he said "my woman."

Was there a chance in hell we could reconcile?

I wrapped my mind around the idea.

Cade returned with the second bottle open, topped off my glass, and sat. I thought perhaps he had my idea from earlier and had decided to just drink from the bottle.

He didn't appear to notice he held it.

"Did she come inside?"

"Yes."

He was piecing together what had happened. His free hand went to his disheveled hair, and he made it sexier. "And the kid?"

"Olivia commanded her to stand near the front door while she pranced to the kitchen like she owned the place."

"That woman touched my stuff?"

"Well, not really. She just set her purse down on the counter and showed me the paperwork."

"Wait. She happened to be carrying an old marriage certificate and a birth certificate in her purse?"

I nodded. That probably was a bit weird.

"And the birth certificate listed me as the father?"

I nodded again.

Cade leaned back and pulled his cell from his pocket. He handed me the bottle of wine while he pressed buttons. Almost immediately he started speaking. "Hey… Yeah, I'm with her now… Yes, she let me in… Okay, right, well that's true. I didn't give her much of a choice… So, get this, Olivia paid her a visit… No, I'm not fucking kidding. If I were, I'd be remarried right now, and the woman of my dreams wouldn't be sitting next to me on a ratty couch nibbling her bottom lip in uncertainty…"

I almost fell off the couch. My belly did a flip flop. He'd be married right now? I was the woman of his dreams? I couldn't move or breathe. My heart pounded.

Cade continued. "Could you? Have Martin handle it, yeah? I don't care what it costs. Find that bitch. I want to know what the fuck she's up to… And, Riley… She has a kid. She told Amelia it was mine." Now his gaze went to me. He took my hand and squeezed it while he finished and hung up.

"That was Riley?"

"Yes."

"You two are in business together?"

"Only from the standpoint that I'm a silent partner of his business. I don't interfere otherwise."

"But both companies are developing the same sort of software for cell phone apps?"

He smiled. "Yep."

I finally caught on. "Is that legal?"

He laughed. "Of course it is."

"But you're creating a competition within the industry."

"Yep."

I rolled my eyes. "No wonder you make the big bucks."

He reached tentatively for a lock of my hair and twirled it around his fingers.

"Did you mean it?" My voice was rough.

"Mean what?"

"What you said to Riley."

His mouth lifted on the corners the slightest amount. "Every word."

My hands started shaking. "I really fucked this up."

He wrapped a hand behind my head and pulled me close to his face. "It wasn't your fault."

"I judged you very fast."

"You'd known me ten days."

"True."

He pulled me closer.

"Can we survive this?" I asked.

"Can we not?"

I took a deep breath and lowered my gaze to his lips. God, I'd missed his lips.

Cade released me and reached down for his wineglass on the floor. He poured another glass from the bottle still in his hand. He held the bottle up for inspection. "When did you become such a wine snob?"

I grinned. "About six months ago."

"I approve. This is one of my favorites." He swirled it around and took another sip. He stood then and wandered around my apartment. There wasn't much to see. But I figured he was antsy. I only had the one bedroom, a bathroom, and the room we stood in. Cade stepped to the entrance to my bedroom and chuckled. "Still a mess, I see."

"Not gonna change," I responded.

He turned to me and leaned on the doorframe. "Is that so?"

"Let's be clear." I took another drink of wine. "I'm not the same woman you met six months ago."

"Really?" He didn't seem to believe me.

"Really." I stood also, strolling in his direction.

"How do you figure?"

"I'm not going to clean my mess no matter what you say." I shrugged. "Tried it for a while. Didn't work. It's not my style. Can't find anything when it's all tucked away somewhere."

"Bet I could change your mind." His smirk wreaked of cockiness.

"And I'm telling you, you can't." I stood firm, a few feet separating us, meeting his gaze.

"I can still picture your pink ass under my palm. You just need a bit of discipline." He took another drink and then let the glass dangle slightly tipped at his side while he held it by the stem.

"If you recall correctly, that only worked once. Then I was immune to that type of corrective action."

"If *you* recall correctly, my next step was time out."

"Yeah, well, I never agreed to that idea. And, though I might have given it a shot at the time, not anymore. I'm a grown woman."

"Grown women sometimes need correction too."

"Grown men sometimes need a good slap in the face." I grinned.

"Dare you."

My eyes went wide. "I was kidding."

"I wasn't."

I inhaled deeply. My body turned to mush. I wanted him to touch me so badly I could almost taste him already. But I forced myself to stay rooted to my spot. Sleeping with him was a very bad idea. Everything was too fresh. My nerves were frayed. His had to be also. We both needed time to think about what had happened.

Cade stepped back a few paces into my bedroom. "It's role play, baby. All we can do is experiment with what gets you off. What works, we keep. What doesn't, we toss." He shrugged and turned to face my room. "Love what you've done with the place," he teased.

"I've been a bit stretched for funds. I was actually looking forward to shopping this weekend with my newfound wealth. Now, I see I'm once again without a job."

He jerked his gaze to meet mine. "Why?"

I rolled my eyes and leaned against the doorframe he'd vacated. "I'm not working for you, Cade. End of discussion."

"You don't work for me. I have no say in the happenings of The Rockwood Group. Silent partner, remember?"

"Oh, like there's such a distinction."

"There is. And if you quit this job, I'll spank your ass until it hurts too bad for you to come." He narrowed his gaze. "You do *not* want to try me on this issue."

I feared he wasn't kidding. Still… "Half the building heard us arguing this afternoon, and the other half must have gotten the details through the rumor mill. I can't go back there."

"Yes you can, baby. And you will. With your chin held high."

I shook my head. "No way."

"So, the going gets tough, and you're just going to quit? Again?"

That stung. I cringed. "Yep."

He stepped toward me. Too close. "Not gonna happen, baby."

"You know you don't own me, right? I can and will make my own choices, Cade."

"What I know is that your face still flushes a gorgeous shade of pink when I make you nervous. You still fidget around me because you can't hold still. And sometimes your choices suck, so you need someone to guide you a bit."

"Guide me?"

"Yes." He grinned.

"Or did you mean, tell me what to do?"

He shrugged. "Semantics."

"Hardly." I crossed my arms.

"Baby, you worked hard for that position at Rockwood. I want you to have it. I'll smooth things over with the staff."

"How? By telling them all you're fucking me and they better do as you say or else?"

"Am I?"

"Are you what?"

"Fucking you."

I shut my mouth. Not yet. But he would be. If my damp panties were any indication, it wouldn't be long before I fell under his spell again. I needed to get him out of my apartment before I turned into mush without the opportunity to consider this turn of events. "You should leave."

"I should. This is true." Cade sank his ass on my mattress. "So, you splurge on wine and mattresses."

"And televisions."

"What?"

"I also bought a nice TV. Needed something to occupy my

mind so I didn't think about Olivia and that poor little girl all the time."

Cade fell back onto the mattress. "I'm trying to imagine what that crazy bitch was up to, how she knew you were there, and why she showed up to run you off and then never came back."

"That is a conundrum. Could it be because she's a crazy bitch?"

"Nope. That was too calculated. It makes no sense at all. If she wanted something, why didn't she come to me? Why just you? What did she gain?"

"Oh I don't know. The satisfaction of knowing she broke us up?"

"Too simple."

"Well, could she get more money out of you?"

"She got plenty of money out of me. And besides, don't know why she would need it."

"Why?"

"Her parents were loaded already."

"Well, she wasn't loaded that day. She had the air of someone with money, but not the clothes or the car."

Cade lifted his head. "You shitting me?"

"No. Honda Accord, several years old. Head held high and mighty. No fancy clothing to back it up."

Cade seemed confused. "Huh. Even weirder. Have you seen her since then?"

"No. Why?"

"I wonder if she's stalking you."

"Well if she was, she probably gave it up when she succeeded in running me off."

"Don't remind me." He flopped back onto my mattress.

"Cade, you can't stay here."

"Why the hell not?"

"Because I need to think."

"About what?"

"Us."

"I've done nothing but think about us for five long fucking months. I'm done thinking."

"Well, I'm not."

Cade lifted onto one elbow. "Come here."

I shook my head and walked past him, heading for my bathroom. I was exhausted. He needed to get out of my apartment so I could sleep on this mess. I hadn't concluded that I would go into the office in the morning, but one way or the other, I had to face my colleagues.

I grabbed my toothbrush and tried to get back to the mundane, ignoring the man on my mattress refusing to leave my apartment. I'd have to strong arm him to get him out.

When I finished rinsing and lifted my face from the faucet, Cade was behind me. I met his gaze in the mirror. He set his hands on my hips and let them slide under my sweatshirt until his palms were spread on my bare skin.

"Cade..." Why was I putty every time he touched me? My belly dipped as I fought the need growing inside me.

Cade spun me around slowly and then lifted me onto the counter. He met my gaze head on and didn't release it while his hands resumed their spot on my waist, roaming up until he cupped my breasts. He inhaled sharply. "No bra," he muttered as he pinched both my nipples at once.

In a flash of material, my sweatshirt was gone, yanked over my head and set aside.

Cades eyes lowered to my breasts. He cupped them again, reverently, stroking his thumbs across my distended nipples while I waged a mental war. I was losing.

It felt so fantastic having him touch me. I'd missed this. I'd missed him. His intensity. His high-handed mannerisms that made me wet between the legs and desperate for release. I moaned.

"That's my girl."

"Cade..." I repeated.

"Just relax, baby. I promise to keep my pants on if you'll let me soak in your beauty for a few minutes."

"And then you'll leave?"

"If you insist."

"I do," I squeaked out as he pinched my nipples again, harder this time. He had my attention. "Looking and touching are two different things."

"Not in my world." He leaned in and sucked one nipple

between his lips. When he released it with a pop, he continued. "What I want to *see* requires me touching you."

A rush of liquid filled my panties. I knew what he meant. I just wasn't sure I was up for it.

Cade lowered one hand to the V between my legs and cupped my sex. "So hot. I can feel the warmth through your strange choice of leggings."

"Yoga pants," I muttered, my eyes rolling back.

"Whatever. You're wet."

"Mmm hmm." No sense denying that point.

"Spread your legs wider, baby. Let me touch you."

I inched my knees out, gripping Cade's shoulders with both hands. Just like that, I was under his hypnosis. Damn it.

Cade spread his palm wider on my pussy and flicked his middle finger over my clit. Two layers of cotton lay between my skin and his hand, and I could barely notice the barrier.

He lowered his face back to my chest and suckled a nipple. He cupped the other one with his free hand.

I stiffened, fighting the need to come. How had I gotten so close to the edge so fast?

"Cade," I whispered, my fingers digging into his shoulders, "this wasn't in the agreement."

He lifted his face to mine. He hadn't kissed me yet. I stared at his lips. "Of course it was. I said I wanted to watch you."

"No. You said you wanted to *see* me. Big difference."

He shrugged. "Again, semantics." His face grew serious as I tightened my thighs and lifted my ass off the vanity.

"That's my girl. Let it go. Remind me what you look like when you come for me."

As soon as he spoke, I hitched my breath and teetered forward. Just for a second. The next second, Cade pushed his palm against my pussy, and I came. Hard. Pulsing against his hand and gripping his arms so tightly I would leave marks from my nails under his dress shirt.

"Baby," he muttered as his hand released my breast to cup my face on one side. He still held my pussy as he leaned in close and took my lips. Finally.

The kiss was urgent, filled with five months of pent-up need. I took as much as he gave, slipping my tongue into his mouth to duel with his.

When Cade finally separated our lips, he was breathing hard. He let go of my pussy and set both hands on my waist. His thumbs continued to stroke my skin. "You never answered my question."

"Which question was that?"

"Did you sleep with Brad?"

I swallowed. "No. There's been no one."

His eyes slid shut, and his mouth curled into a smile. My nipples hardened once again at his pleased expression.

"You're mine, baby," he stated when he met my gaze again.

I didn't move or speak.

He grinned wider, his dimples coming out to tantalize me with their cuteness. "Deny it all you want, baby. But you're mine. Your body knows it. You just need to get it into your head."

I knew he was right. I didn't need to get anything into my head. But, I also didn't want him to get all cocky on me, so I chose to remain still.

Cade lifted one hand to my face. He cupped my jaw again and rubbed my bottom lip with his thumb. "Love when your mouth gets swollen from my kisses." He lifted his eyes to mine. "Love when your eyes glaze over like that with lust."

I melted.

"I don't need you to confirm what I know. It's enough for now that I have you in my arms. I'll never let you go, baby. Not again."

I nodded.

"I'm gonna give you this one night to sleep alone and wrap your mind around us. I'll pick you up at seven and take you to the office. After tonight, you'll be in my bed. Every night. Are we clear?"

I sucked in a breath. My heart pounded.

"Amelia, are we clear?"

"Yes, Sir."

His grin spread again. "Good." Cade lifted me off the counter and set me on my feet. "I'll let myself out. Seven o'clock, baby." He released me and walked toward the bedroom door. I watched him retreat, taking two steps out of my bathroom. He turned at the door, his grip on the frame tense. "Be sure to shave your pussy, Amelia. And don't wear panties."

    I didn't move. My face heated ten degrees. Could he tell through my yoga pants that I'd let my hair grow back? Surely not. Perhaps he didn't care one way or the other. He just wanted to be clear about how it would be from here on out.

    He made himself clear. Crystal clear.

    As usual.

Chapter Nineteen

I tossed for two hours before I fell asleep. I stared at the ceiling in the dark, worrying about every aspect of my life. In less than twelve hours, Cade had turned my world upside down. Again.

I hadn't even called Cheyenne or Meagan. I needed to do that before too long, or they would freak when they heard the news. Hell, they were going to freak in either case.

My body hummed from the orgasm Cade had given me, which had been unbelievably fantastic, while at the same time not nearly enough.

I wore a tank top and loose boxers to bed, knowing this would be the last night for a long time I wouldn't feel every aspect of my sheets against my skin.

And what did Cade mean when he said I wouldn't be sleeping alone? I lived in Nashville. He lived in Atlanta. He didn't even own a place in Nashville as far as I knew.

I had to face Brad. What I'd done to him had been completely uncool.

And Mr. Cross. Fuck. The man probably wanted to throttle me, and rightfully so.

And Lisa. *Shit*.

Finally, I dozed off, awaking to the sound of my alarm a few hours later. As usual, I wormed out one hand and slapped the button on my clock without looking. I moaned. This was not a day I wanted to face.

At seven sharp I was ready to go. Cade's knock was expected, so I took a deep breath and opened the door.

He stood there, looking like a million bucks in his suit, a deep gray with faint pinstripes. His tie was red, which seemed appropriate for a slaughter.

He stepped inside and lifted my chin without a word to place a kiss on my lips, not a peck and not a make-out session that would leave me spinning, but somewhere sweet in between. Nice. I liked it.

His voice was low when he spoke. "Missed you, baby. Ready?"

"Yes." I already had my purse on my arm, so I flipped off the lights and followed him into the hall.

Cade led me down the three flights of stairs to the first floor and across the walkway to the awaiting Mercedes. Arthur stood by the side. He tipped his hat. "Ms. Kensington."

I smiled at him. "Good morning, Arthur."

I swear he smiled as I ducked into the back seat in front of Cade. When we were settled and pulling away, Cade turned toward me. "I'll handle things at the office. You don't need to worry about a thing."

"Like fuck you will," I said back sweetly, my sugary tone not matching my words.

He chuckled. "I forgot how feisty you are."

"No you didn't. You just chose to ignore it. This is my job, Cade. My office. My employees. I'll handle this situation. If I choose to resign, that will be my decision." I leaned forward. At that moment, even in the light of day, I could see no other feasible option. As soon as we entered the building, I would surely feel the buzz of rumors.

Cade grinned. "We'll see."

I humphed as I sat back against the seat, crossing my legs and squeezing my thighs together.

Cade set a hand on top of my leg and gripped, his fingers digging into my flesh hard enough to let me know he was not pleased.

I ignored him.

When he didn't release me, I swatted his hand away. "Cade. Please. I need all my wits this morning. Stop distracting me."

"What did I do?" He chuckled again.

"Thank you." I looked out the window. The world was like a picture frame, a strange one in which a snapshot wouldn't tell the viewer what the temperature was. With no trees around that part of the city to belie the evidence of a warm sunny day, no one would know it was winter. It was cold. Colder than usual for November. But the day looked fresh and sunny, either mocking me for trying to grab onto that warmth or letting me know it would be okay in the end. I didn't know which. But I was nervous.

We pulled up at The Rockwood Group at seven thirty. This gave me plenty of time to make my way to the fourth floor and organize my thoughts before the building flooded with employees.

Cade said nothing as he followed on my heels. The only people we passed were the guards on the ground floor who nodded and greeted us both by name. If they thought it odd I arrived at work with the man who apparently owned the building, they didn't let it show.

Thank goodness for their professionalism.

I was shocked to find Lisa already at her desk, however. The moment we stepped off the elevator and headed toward my office, she stood. "Lillie." She looked nervous. She lifted her gaze to Cade. "Mr. Alexander."

Cade chuckled, probably at the nickname. "Why don't you come into Amelia's office so we can talk, Lisa?" Of course. Cade waltzed into my building and took over.

I swallowed my frustration and continued to enter my office as though the idea had been mutual. In a way it was. But what I hadn't intended was to face Lisa so early, and certainly not with Cade present. I rounded my desk and turned to face my assistant and my...whatever Cade was.

Cade dropped his briefcase on the floor in front of my desk and took a seat in one of the two chairs positioned for guests. He held out a hand to the other leather seat and nodded at Lisa.

Lisa looked like she'd rather scrub toilets, but she inched forward and sat demurely, tucking her skirt under her thighs and crossing her legs at the ankles.

Cade spoke again. "Relax. No one's in trouble."

Lisa nodded, uncertainty written on her face.

I jumped in, hoping to run this conversation my way. "Lisa, what's the damage?"

Lisa jerked her gaze from the intense man next to her to me. "What damage?"

"I know we were loud yesterday afternoon. I'm sure we could be heard for two stories. How bad was it?" I bit my lip and drew my brows together in a way that would hopefully tell Lisa I was asking woman to woman.

She flinched. "I don't think there's any damage, Lillie. Well, except perhaps with Mr. Cross. He called a few times trying to get in to see you, but I put him off. He was curt and a bit miffed, but that's about it."

"What about the staff?"

Lisa shrugged. "I kept the coast clear. Anyone who came by, I told them you were busy and to come back tomorrow. Really, if you're worried about noise, it wasn't that bad. I could hear you myself from outside, but not words, just the occasional sounds of voices."

"Really?" I asked.

Cade laughed. "Guess the insulation is good in this building. See, nothing to worry about."

I shot him a glare.

Lisa's brows rose, and her gaze whipped back and forth

between us. "Is everything okay?"

Cade, in complete disregard for my desire to handle things, continued speaking. "Perfect. Amelia and I had some issues to work out. It's all good now. We had a few misunderstandings, but I convinced her to see things my way." He winked at Lisa.

Winked.

Lisa's mouth hung open.

I seethed. "Pay this asshole no attention, Lisa. He thinks he runs the entire universe. It's easier to let him pretend than to argue."

Lisa closed her mouth and smiled as though a light had flipped on. "Oh God. You two are together."

"Yes," Cade responded.

Lisa beamed. "How did I not know this?" She turned to me, a twinge of hurt on her face. "I mean, of course. It's none of my business. Sorry."

I shook my head. "No worries, Lisa. I didn't know it either until yesterday."

"What?" She leaned forward and then put up a palm. "Never mind. Don't even want to know what that means." She stood abruptly and pointed over her shoulder. "I'm just gonna fire up the computer and get to work. Let me know if you need anything."

Cade stood also. He followed Lisa to the door, shut it behind her, and locked it.

I flinched, my fingers gripping the edge of my desk.

Cade sauntered across the room like a predator and came up

behind me. He set his hands on my hips and leaned his lips in to touch my ear. "See? Not even a blip on most people's radar." He kissed behind my ear, making me shudder.

"Cade... Not here. I have a lot to do. And I still have to face Mr. Cross."

"I'll handle Mr. Cross." He licked my neck.

"No you won't. Stop *handling* everything."

"My mess. I'll fix it." He spun me around and lifted me off the floor to set me on the desk.

I squealed and then bit my lip to keep from making such a noise. I batted at his arms. "Cade. Stop it. I have work to do."

"First you have something to show me."

I flushed. "Cade," I warned.

"Baby, I gave you a directive last night. I want to know that you followed through." He eased his hands to my thighs, urging them wider, and pushed my skirt up so slowly I was panting by the time he reached my center.

I held his biceps, unable to stop him.

When his thumbs reached my core and stroked through my lower lips, I moaned. My toes curled under in my heels.

"Baby... So wet for me..." He slid his eyes shut as he pushed both thumbs into my channel.

I lifted my hips off the desk to give him a better angle. The room around me disappeared as he played me like a finally tuned instrument.

Cade removed one hand and set it at my lower back to ease

me onto the desk. "Lie back, baby."

I let him arrange me, arching my back the second my head hit the hard wood surface. I reached for his forearms and gripped them, trying to convince him to stop. This was completely inappropriate.

Cade had other ideas. "Lift your hands over your head, baby."

"Cade…"

"Now, Amelia. If you argue with me, it won't change anything. It will just take that much longer for me to get what I want and create a long tally of repercussions for later tonight." He lifted a brow.

I hitched my breath, released his arms, and lifted mine over my head to dangle off the edge of my desk. Thank God the surface was enormous.

He was demanding and infuriating. I would speak to him about his high-handed ways later. But for now, he was right. It would behoove me to let him play his game his way. He was going to get what he wanted no matter what. It wouldn't do any good to fight him.

"Good girl. Wise choice." He lowered his gaze and lifted my ankles. "Set your feet on the desk." He showed me where and then pushed my skirt the rest of the way up my torso until I was totally exposed.

I shivered when the air in the room hit my naked skin. It had been a long time since I'd felt that sensation. I'd forgotten how heady it was to have him staring at my pussy, in awe of how incredible he found me.

Cade pressed my knees wide. "Don't move, baby." He released my legs and set his fingers on my thighs, pulling my lower lips apart until I was completely open to his view. He moaned.

Or maybe that was me.

"I missed this." He stroked a finger through my core, barely touching.

I stiffened my legs and clenched my pussy. My head rolled to one side, and I stared at an unseen spot across the room. My vision didn't work. All my attention was on his intense perusal of my open sex.

"So beautiful," he muttered. He flicked his finger over my clit, making me flinch. "And so responsive."

I tucked my lower lip between my teeth to keep from screaming.

And then his mouth was on me.

My breath whooshed from my lungs when he sucked my clit into his mouth and held it. His tongue dipped into my pussy and stroked. He started fucking me with his tongue next.

My office spun in circles as though I were on a tilt-a-whirl. I was dizzy.

When he honed in on my clit again, I gasped. I was so close. His fingers dug into my thighs, holding me wider, letting me know this was his show. I would come when he was ready.

I panted around the need, my hands balling into fists behind my head.

Cade sucked me into his mouth one last hard time, his teeth nipping at my swollen nub. That was it. My orgasm slammed into me, much more forceful than last night. I pulsed forever. He took cues from me and licked and kissed and sucked as I came down. It was heavenly.

I was his. There was no denying reality. I wouldn't even fight him.

Hell, I didn't want to. I lay there gasping to catch my breath while Cade lifted his face and met my gaze with a lazy grin. "Delicious."

My legs shook.

He stroked my inner thighs. "You good? Or you want to come again?"

I widened my gaze. "No, Sir. I'm good. I don't think my heart could take another." *Unless you plan to do it with your cock.* I pushed that thought from my mind fast. This was my office. I needed to pull together some level of professional decorum.

Cade chuckled. "I can read you like an open book, baby. Your face hides nothing." He tapped my clit, making me flinch. "This is mine. You come when I say. You don't argue. You don't defy me. I'm going to let you up now, but not because you want me to. We have things to handle in this office. But make no mistake, if I wanted to fuck you right now on this desk in broad daylight until you screamed my name, I would do so." He narrowed his eyes. "We clear?"

I nodded, swallowing around the lump in my throat.

"We clear, Amelia?" he asked louder.

"Yes, Sir."

Crystal.

Chapter Twenty

Cade made good on his promise and went in search of Mr. Cross. I headed for the ladies' room as soon as he left to pull myself together. The last thing I needed was Mr. Cross taking one look at me and realizing I'd fucked the boss in my office, or at least looked as though I had. When I returned, I busied myself organizing my desk to no avail. I nearly moaned every time I thought about what he'd done to me right where my hands now rested. I'd wiped my come off the edge with a tissue, but that didn't erase the memory.

My papers were a mess, largely because I had straightened them the night before in a mad attempt to ignore Cade Alexander and his presence in my space. Now that my papers were tidy, I had no idea what was what. It was all a jumbled mess.

Twenty minutes after Cade left me to sort through things, I heard his voice in the hall. He was talking to someone, and I found out who when they stepped into my office.

I jumped to my feet. "Mr. Cross. I'm so sorry about yesterday. There's no excuse."

Mr. Cross smiled. "Sounds to me like there are lots of excuses."

I felt the pink as it spread across my cheeks. What had Cade said to him?

Mr. Cross chuckled and took a seat across from me as Cade did the same. "Sit, Lillie. It's all good. I've already called the guys at Stephen's Engineering. Told them we'd come to them this time. I will say, however, Brad Phelps sounded kind of frazzled. You might want to speak with him personally before we head that way."

Shit.

"I told them we'd be there at one."

"Okay. No problem." I was embarrassed that Mr. Cross had seen right through my problems with Brad, but glad about the way he handled it without making me feel like more of a heel than I already did.

Mr. Cross stood. "Well, that's it then." He wiped his hands on his pants and then reached to shake Cade's hand as Cade stood alongside him. "Glad we have that all cleared up. So good to see you again, Mr. Alexander. I suppose we'll be crossing paths frequently from now on. Let me know if you need any help with your move."

Cade nodded. "Thank you. I'm sure it'll all be fine."

Move? What the hell were they talking about?

When Mr. Cross turned toward me and nodded, I schooled my face. The last thing I wanted him to realize was that I wasn't privy to whatever he'd discussed with Cade.

My manipulating, on-again boyfriend needed to share a few details with me. And fast.

Cade shut my door as Mr. Cross exited. This time he didn't

lock it. I wasn't sure if I was relieved or disappointed.

"See? It's all good."

I glared at him. "You can't waltz in here every time I have a problem and clean up my messes, Cade. Of course it's all good to your face. No one's going to piss off the owner. The question is, what are they gonna say behind my back?"

Cade rounded behind me, as he often did, and circled me with both his arms under my breasts. "Relax. You think too hard. I made myself very clear to Mr. Cross. He won't be spreading gossip, and he isn't angry."

I squirmed in his clutches, trying to turn around. "Cade, that's exactly what I don't want you to do."

"Too late." He kissed my neck.

"Stop distracting me." I grabbed at his forearms under my chest and tugged.

Cade chuckled, pushed my hair aside with his chin and nibbled a path up my neck to my ear. "Relax, baby."

Part of me fumed. There was no way for me to relax with him in the building. "Don't you have stuff to do? Like in Atlanta? I need to get back to work. Go play somewhere else."

Cade chuckled again, but released me. He leaned against the floor-to-ceiling window at his back and crossed his legs. "I'm moving to Nashville, baby."

I spun around. "You're doing what?"

He grinned. "Yep. It's a done deal."

"Since when?"

He glanced at his watch and shrugged. "About six hours ago."

"Six hours. That was like three in the morning. What were you doing up at three in the morning? Have you lost your mind?"

"Nope. My mind is clear. I went from your place to Riley's. We talked. We made a plan."

"You made a plan," I deadpanned. "At three in the morning. One that involves you moving to Nashville."

"Among other things, yes."

"Do you ever sleep?"

"Sometimes. Not as often as I should."

"I thought this was Riley's building."

"It was. We switched."

"What?" I was starting to sound like a broken record.

"Don't get your panties in a wad, baby." He chuckled again at his unamusing joke. "Riley and I have been discussing this idea for a few months."

"Why?"

"Well, for one thing, I needed a change of scenery after you left. For another thing, Riley has needed a change of scenery for one day longer than me."

"The day you told him his fiancée was a bitch."

Cade nodded. "That would be the day."

"They broke it off."

"Yes. And Riley has been licking his wounds. He didn't trust easily to begin with. Now he's gotten worse. He's sworn off women. And with Christine living in Nashville, he needs to get far away."

"I see." That did make sense. "So, you've been considering a switch for a long time. This wasn't something you dreamed up at three in the morning."

He stepped closer to me, pushing off the window. "Trust me, baby. I would've done the same thing in the middle of the night last night if Riley and I had never even considered such an option. It just went smoother since the ball was already spinning."

I couldn't breathe. Too many changes in one day.

"Where are you going to live?"

"Your place?" He chuckled. "Just kidding. For now, Riley and I are going to swap condos."

That made sense.

"We'll consider other options later, when you're ready."

When I'm ready...

He held out a hand. "I need your keys, baby."

"What for?"

"So I can send someone over to pack up your stuff."

I widened my eyes. "No fucking way, Cade. First of all, I haven't agreed to this middle of the night plan. And second of all, I can pack my own shit when and if I'm ready."

Cade glared at me. "Keys, Amelia." He shook his open palm.

"Fuck you, Cade."

He closed the gap between us in one stride, wrapping his arm around my middle and pulling me against his front. His other hand went to my thighs and lifted my skirt while he pushed my legs wide with his knee. One split second later, his fingers were at my entrance and three of them were pushing inside. I was so wet, I made it easy.

My knees buckled. He held me upright.

He fucked my pussy hard and fast. "Eyes on me, Amelia."

I met his gaze, unable to do otherwise, and stared at him through the haze.

"That's my girl. Whose pussy is this?"

"Yours, Sir." My voice was a thin thread.

"What do you need, baby?"

I fought hard, but there was no way to deny what he did to me. "To come, Sir."

"When do you come, baby?"

"When you say so, Sir."

He smiled, yanked his fingers free of my pussy and stepped back. His palm, covered in my juices, reached back out. "Keys, Amelia."

I fumbled for my purse on the corner of my desk and grabbed my keys from inside.

Cade didn't move.

I turned and set them in his palm.

As he walked away, switching hands and licking his fingers

clean, I heard him moan. He left my office, shutting the door behind him.

I slumped into my chair, so horny I couldn't do anything else. My pussy pulsed at nothing. I was a wreck. Cade Alexander had swooped in and taken over my life.

I turned my gaze toward the window for several minutes, trying to slow my heart rate. I had so many things to do, and all I could manage was to stare into space.

I attempted to stiffen my resolve.

Cade Alexander had a pile of rules he liked me to follow.

What he didn't realize was I had rules of my own now.

And he was going to hear them if it was the last thing I did.

Chapter Twenty-One

I hung up the phone with Brad as Cade waltzed back into my office. "You okay, baby?"

"Yep." I stood and reached for my purse.

"Where are you going?"

"Lunch."

"Okay. Can I make a few calls first?"

"You can make all the calls you want. You aren't invited."

He paused.

I rounded my desk and faced him head on. "I need to meet with Brad. To do otherwise would be rude. I'm not walking into his office this afternoon without talking to him. You're *not* invited. And you'll trust me to make good choices. Are we clear?"

He nodded. A smirk formed on his lips, but he humored me. "'K, baby. I'll pick you up here at five. Do you mind if I use your office for a while? I need to work through about a hundred messages and e-mails."

"Knock yourself out." I left the room, not glancing back.

Ten minutes later, I stood from my table as Brad spotted me

from across the room and joined me. His face was blank, shocking me with his ability to keep so composed.

We both opened our mouths to speak at the same time, breaking the tension.

"You go first," he said.

"I wanted to tell you how sorry I am. What I did last night was inexcusable and rude. You have every right to be angry with me."

Brad let me finish and then licked his lips. "Are you with him?"

"Yes." There was no way to sugar coat it.

He flinched, as though hoping for another response and unable to control his reaction to what he had to have expected. "How long?"

"Oh. Not like you're thinking. We were together six months ago before I moved here. We had a gigantic misunderstanding, and I left town. When he stepped into the meeting yesterday, it was the first I'd seen of him since then. I was as stunned as the rest of you."

"But he wants you back."

I nodded. "Yes."

"And you agreed."

"Yes."

The pain in his eyes was evident. He exhaled slowly as the waiter brought us some water. We ignored him and he went away silently. "Are you sure about this, Lillie?"

"Very."

His shoulders slumped. "I'm not going to lie. I'm disappointed. I like you. A lot. Have for a long time. You know that. But what I'm more concerned about is *you*. I don't want to see you get hurt."

I smiled in appreciation. "I know, Brad. Please don't worry about me. I'm fine. And, again, I'm sorry for the way I treated you."

He shrugged. "I'll live. It would have been much worse if he'd waited to show up after you and I had really gotten together. No real harm done. It was our first date."

I knew it was more than that for him, and I hated myself for this, but blunt was the best option. Anything else would be cruel. I didn't want to lead him on.

"Shall we order?" Brad asked, picking up the menu. "I'm starving."

I let go of a long shallow breath. "Of course." I wasn't sure what I could swallow with the day I was having, but somehow I needed to manage.

The rest of the lunch hour was awkward, but Brad did his best to make it as seamless as possible. I appreciated his professionalism.

We walked to his office together just before one and joined the others for our previously thwarted meeting. Surprisingly, that too went well. The team from Stephen's Engineering, consisting of several more people than had been in attendance the day before, seemed impressed with our plans. Mr. Cross had completely gotten over his frustrations with me and beamed at my presentation as though I were the best in his office and he was proud of me.

By the time I reached my office once again that afternoon, it was nearly five. I was exhausted. My feet hurt.

Lisa looked up. "You're back. Someone left this on my desk for you while I was at lunch." She held out an envelope.

I took it as she went back to her computer.

I didn't think much of it, stuffing it in my purse as I headed back to my office to plop onto my chair and sigh in relief. The day had gone much better than I'd anticipated. Far better. It seemed I could keep this job. Especially if I could convince Cade to stay out of my hair and let me do it. It would be difficult with him working in the building soon, but I needed to put my foot down. Hard. And soon. Like tonight.

New rules.

Mine.

My cell phone beeped. I bent down to grab it and the envelope from my purse.

Cade: I got tied up, baby. Arthur will meet you downstairs at five.

Me: Aye, aye, Sir.

Cade: Are you sassing me?

Me: Maybe?

I tossed the phone back in my purse before I was tempted to do more damage.

I glanced at my watch. It was almost five. Shit. I had accomplished very little in the office. I would need to come in early tomorrow to get caught up.

Cade would have to get over himself. He wasn't going to dictate what hours I worked. I worked hard for this position. That meant long hours. I earned it. Without his help or knowledge. Just because he'd suddenly resurfaced did not mean I was going to give in to his every whim. At least that's what I told myself.

I sensed someone in the doorway and lifted my gaze to find Riley lounging in the frame. I jumped to stand.

He strolled into my office. "Hey. Sit. I don't bite." He smiled, gesturing to my seat.

I had only spoken to Riley briefly at his farce of an engagement party. Until yesterday, I hadn't known he was CEO of The Rockwood Group.

Now that I stared at him, I could tell he was very similar to Cade in many ways. Including his bossiness. "Amelia. Sit." His voice was gentle. His tone was firm.

I settled into my chair as he sat across from me. "Figured I owed you a bit of an explanation."

I didn't say anything. I was tongue-tied.

"When I saw you in that conference room yesterday, my eyes bugged out. There you were right under my nose, and I hadn't known it."

"Well, I did use a fake name."

He grinned. "A good one too. I'll give you that."

"I didn't want to be found."

"I can understand that too. Cade explained everything to me."

"Sorry about your fiancée." I winced a bit. "I didn't mean to turn your life upside down. I begged Cade to leave it alone."

He shrugged. "You did me a favor. I knew deep down Christine was a bitch. I just didn't realize she would stoop that low. I should thank you."

I waited.

"Anyway, I wanted to make sure you weren't pissed with me for calling Cade yesterday. Maybe that makes us even? He's my best friend. There was no way in hell I could lie about you being in my building while he was living in such pain."

"I understand. You did me a favor too." I smiled.

"Are we even then?"

"Yep. Are you really going to switch cities with Cade?"

He nodded.

"And you aren't doing so under duress?"

"Nope. I'm excited. You did me another favor. Now I owe you one."

I laughed. "I'll let you know when I need to collect."

"I doubt you'll have to. These things seem to fall on my plate." His eyes lit up when he chuckled, the deep blue softening. It occurred to me that Cheyenne would fall hard for such a guy if she ever met him. She had a weak spot for blue eyes and messy blond hair. It matched her own. I needed to make a mental note to ensure they never met. Cheyenne didn't do submissive. The idea made me laugh inside.

And Riley Moreno was undoubtedly a Dom.

"We good?"

"Absolutely," I said, glancing at my watch. "Shit." It was after five. "Arthur's meeting me downstairs." I stood.

Riley stood also. "I'll let you go. Cade hates tardiness." He grinned again. He really was hot when he smiled. I was glad he wasn't with Christine anymore. He deserved better.

"Thanks." I grabbed my purse, my phone, and the still-untouched mystery envelope and hurried from the room. "See you soon."

Riley followed me out, shutting my door. "You can count on it. Maybe next time we can meet under calmer circumstances."

I smiled as I left him.

As soon as I stepped outside, I spotted Arthur by the curb. "Ms. Kensington."

"Amy. Arthur, call me Amy. Or Lillie if you want."

"Lillie, ma'am?"

"My Nashville name," I informed him as he helped me into the back seat. "I have split personalities apparently."

"Well, Amy slash Lillie, let's get going." He shut the door and left me to stare out the window during the drive. I didn't know where we were going, but it didn't shock me when we pulled up to the same hotel where Cade and I had stayed six months ago. Hell, he probably owned the top floor.

Arthur handed me a key card as I stepped out. "Cade said to give this to you. It allows the elevator to go to your floor."

"Right." I took it in my hand. "Thanks, Arthur." I left him

by the curb and entered the hotel.

Two minutes later I stepped into Cade's suite. He was on the phone, as usual, next to the wall of windows. When I entered, he turned toward me and smiled, motioning for me to come to him. His smile was for me, but it was forced and quick. He wasn't enjoying his conversation.

I went to him, dropping my purse and briefcase on the couch. When I reached him, he pulled my front into his side and held me close. His arm was stiff. I set my cheek on his chest and inhaled his scent. His T-shirt was soft against my face. I wrapped my arms around his middle and held him just as close.

"Are you serious...? How long ago...? Damn it... No, keep looking... Yes... Call me if you find out anything new..." He hung up, stuffed the phone in his pocket, and then spun me to his front and kissed me senseless. "Missed you," he mumbled against my lips when he finally pulled back.

My legs wobbled. I worried about the call he'd just had, but I didn't want to upset him by asking. So I left it alone.

"The rest of your day go okay? How did Brad take the news?"

"With grace. And yes, the meeting went fine. Thank you."

"Good. See? What'd I tell you?"

I rolled my eyes. "How much did you pay Mr. Cross to handle me with care?"

He took a step back, feigning hurt, his hand to his chest. "Are you insinuating I would bribe people to respect you?"

"No, I'm flat out saying you would." I swatted at his chest.

"Well, for your information, Ms. Kensington, I did no such thing. Mr. Cross is a reasonable man. He understood where I was coming from."

"Do I even want to know what you told him about us?"

"Probably not. You hungry?" he asked to change the subject.

"Not really. But I'd like to change out of these clothes. My feet hurt from standing so much."

Cade swung me into his arms and carried me from the room, aiming straight for his bedroom. "I would love to get you out of those clothes, baby. No problem."

"Cade," I squirmed in his arms, "put me down. I was going for yoga pants and a T-shirt. Not naked."

Cade shrugged as he tossed me onto his bed. "I like naked better. Besides, I don't have yoga pants and T-shirts for you here."

"I thought you sent someone to get me some clothes?" I leaned up on my elbows while he pulled off my heels.

"I did." That was vague.

I looked around. "I don't see any bags."

"Put everything in the closets, baby." He climbed onto the bed and reached for my waist as he spoke. "Not everyone keeps their clothes on the floor." He smirked at me as he spun me around and unzipped my skirt. Two seconds later it was pulled from my frame.

"Cade..." Already I was wet for him. In a moment he would know.

Cade went to work on my blouse next, unbuttoning it slowly and then pulling it to the sides. "Lift up, baby."

I hoisted myself to sitting, and he removed both my blouse and my bra. When he eased me back onto the bed, he stared at me. "Missed you."

"You said that."

He ran his fingers across my chest and then met my gaze again. "No, I mean, I really missed you. For months."

I swallowed. I understood.

"I need you."

I nodded. The faster the better as far as I was concerned.

Cade pulled his T-shirt over his head and dropped it on the bed. He unbuttoned his jeans. I wondered how long he'd been in the hotel suite, considering he was no longer dressed to kill in the boardroom. He'd switched to dressed to kill in the bedroom. His jeans were hot. Both on him and next to him. He shrugged out of them, taking his underwear with them.

I let my gaze roam to his impressive length. It bobbed in front of him, eager.

"Are you on the pill, baby?"

I shook my head. That wasn't something I'd ever considered.

"Make an appointment. I hate these things." He grabbed a condom from his jeans pocket and rolled it on.

I nodded.

The next thing I knew I was on my belly, Cade having flipped me over so fast I didn't see it coming. He pulled me up to my knees and pushed them wide. His hands landed on my butt to mold it with his fingers.

I moaned into the mattress, my cheek pressed firmly against the bed. My hands came up to fist at the sides of my head.

"You have the sexiest ass, baby. Even better when it's pink."

Was he going to spank me? "Sir?"

He chuckled. "Not going to spank you right now, baby. I don't want you to come yet."

I exhaled and closed my eyes, concentrating on his hands as they moved down to my thighs and spread them wider. He nestled between my legs. His cock teased my butt crack as he reached around my waist and pressed a finger into my heat. I might have moaned again, but Cade's voice drowned me out. He definitely moaned louder. "My sweet girl is so wet. Needy."

I was. Always when he was around.

His thumb landed on my clit, and I rocked forward.

His arm tightened around my waist. "Stay still, baby."

I tried, but sensations were coming at me from every direction. My nipples brushed against the sheets. My pussy grasped at nothing. My clit swelled against Cade's thumb. I thought I might shatter if he didn't let me come soon.

Could a woman have a nervous breakdown from being teased?

Finally, Cade grabbed my hips with both hands and thrust into me. He held himself deep.

I lost my breath. It had been so long, and I'd only had sex

that one weekend in my life. This felt like I'd been reassigned virgin status.

Cade remained steady, his hands holding me tight, his thumbs drawing a pattern on my hips.

I finally found my ability to breathe, my channel accommodating his girth. And then I rocked forward.

"Stay still, baby. Don't move. You okay now?"

"Please…"

Cade pulled almost out and then thrust back into me. "So tight." I could hear the way he gritted his teeth. "God, baby. You're gonna kill me with that pussy of yours."

I pressed into him.

Cade pulled out again and then set a rhythm, plunging in and out until my vision blurred. I was so close. I needed contact with my clit. I would have told Cade, but I couldn't find the words.

He pushed faster. Suddenly he came, his cock buried to the hilt inside me. I could feel the pulsing at the tip. I couldn't find oxygen again. I was on the edge. He didn't take me with him. Did he know?

Cade pulled out just as quickly and flipped me to my back. My legs fell wide. He kneeled between them. I reached with one hand toward my pussy. I never would have imagined masturbating in front of him, but I needed release so badly it hurt.

Cade swatted at my hand. "No, baby. My pussy. My rules."

I almost came from those words alone. So possessive. Demanding.

I thought I might cry if he didn't let me finish.

Cade's face was intense, his gaze narrowed on me, roaming up and down my body. "Set your hands over your head, baby."

I lifted them heavily, doing his bidding. I also lifted my torso off the bed.

"I know you need to come, baby. But I want you to understand how this works." His hands landed on my thighs pushing them wider. He leaned in closer. "You're with *me* now. Got it?"

I nodded. My mouth was dry.

"You don't leave me again without an explanation. Understood?"

I nodded again. "Yes, Sir."

"I can't explain myself if you don't give me a chance. You can't just run from me to a different city and change your name."

"Sorry, Sir."

"It's done. And I understand your side. But I want you to understand how I felt."

I gulped.

"Hurt. Lost. Alone. Pissed even. All the stages of grief. You had all the cards. You knew where I was the entire time. You left me."

I had.

He stroked his thumbs through my pussy. "This is mine. I'm glad you didn't share it with anyone else."

I was too.

"Don't. Ever."

"Okay, Sir." Like I had intentions of sleeping with other men...

Cade set his thumbs on both sides of my clit and pinched.

I yelped. It was too much. And not enough.

Cade leaned in and watched my face. "I love it when you moan for me."

It was easy to fulfill that request.

Cade released my clit, but only to hold the hood back and stroke it with his other hand. "Mine."

I moaned.

Cade pressed his thumb into the space below my clit and continued flicking over the distended nub. "Forever."

I came. Hard. Not as hard as I would have if he'd been inside me, but hard enough to release the tight ball of need. I dug my heels into the mattress and lifted my pussy into his hands.

"That's it, baby. Take what you need." He kept stroking until I lowered my body and collapsed. "That's my girl. So fucking hot when you come, baby."

I didn't move a muscle.

Cade climbed off the bed and padded away. I knew he needed to dispose of the condom, but I hated his absence. A minute later, he was back and a warm cloth landed on my pussy. He wiped me gently and then set the cloth on the nightstand. I rolled to my side as he flattened his front to my back and pulled the covers over us. "Rest, baby. You've had a long few days."

I fell asleep to the brush of his fingers against my cheek.

Chapter Twenty-Two

I awoke a few hours later to the smell of food making my mouth water. I was starving, so it wasn't difficult to drag myself to sitting. I was alone. In Cade's bed. In the hotel. Our hotel.

I swung my legs to the side and stood to pad toward the bathroom. After using the toilet and splashing water on my face, I headed back to find some clothes. The closet I opened contained nothing but Cade's belongings. *Hmm.*

I spun around to search the room. We'd tossed everything we were wearing to the side. None of those clothes were still around. I snorted. Of course.

Easy enough.

I headed back to the closet and grabbed one of Cade's dress shirts. It was huge on me, but it covered my ass and breasts. That's all I needed. I rolled up the sleeves and buttoned the front, leaving the top several undone. No reason I couldn't make the shirt sexy.

When I opened the door to the living area, Cade was standing at the table arranging plates around steaming dishes under metal lids. He lifted his gaze and chuckled. "You'll find anything to wear in a pinch, won't you?"

"Yep." I wandered to his side. "Where're my clothes?" I asked as I wrapped my arms around his middle.

He nodded at the other bedroom. "I wasn't sure how long we'd be here or how much space you might need."

"Ah."

"Sit, baby. You have to be hungry." He pulled out a chair, and I peeled reluctantly from his warm body to sit.

"Smells good."

He pulled off lids to reveal an assortment of meals. "Wasn't sure what you might want."

I laughed. "So you ordered for six?" He'd done that at breakfast too.

He shrugged. "It's just food. Eat what you want."

I had never lived in a wasteful world. It made me cringe thinking about how many people wouldn't have dinner tonight while I indulged in one bite out of six meals.

Cade leaned over me and kissed my forehead before taking his seat. "I know what you're thinking. Stop it. I give significantly to charities. Don't fret over one excessive meal."

I tried not to think about it as I reached for a roll and took a bite. I was hungry.

"How long are we going to stay in this hotel?" I asked.

"Until the weekend. I'll talk to your landlord about your lease sometime this week. We'll move into Riley's condo on Saturday."

I nodded around a bite of ravioli. Fantastic ravioli. "What is this?" I glanced down at the plate.

"Lobster ravioli with a cream sauce."

"God, that's good."

Cade hadn't taken a bite yet, but he reached for the bottle of Sauvignon Blanc in the ice bucket to the side and poured us each a glass. "I hope this one is up to your standards. It's not the 2009, but the 2008 is a darn good substitute."

"Ha ha. I'm hardly a wine snob. I learned everything I know from you."

Cade lifted his glass. "To new beginnings."

I picked up mine and clinked it against his. "To new rules."

Cade chuckled. "What new rules are you going to lay on me, baby?"

"Oh, I have a list." I took a bite of salad, eating everything directly from the containers and ignoring the plate in front of me.

Cade lifted out some chicken from one dish and set it on his plate. "Lay it on me, baby."

At least when he called me *baby*, I knew he wasn't pissed. I set my fork down. "First of all, you can't mess with my job."

He smirked.

"I mean it, Cade. Don't come into my office and order me around. Don't pop into my meetings and take over. Don't do anything that causes me to have to apologize for your behavior or gives the impression that I'm getting preferential treatment."

"You could quit."

I was taken aback. "What? Hell no. Erase that idea from your head right now. I worked hard for this degree, and I earned the respect of my employees. I'm not quitting."

He chuckled. "Relax, baby. I was just giving you shit. I know what your job means to you. Hands off. I hear you. What else?"

He was making this too easy. I wondered when he would lower the gauntlet. "No sex in my office. No making out. No bringing me to orgasm. No touching me inappropriately."

Cade rolled his eyes. "Not sure I can oblige on that one, baby. If you spend too much time there, you might find me popping in for conjugal visits."

"Cade," I warned.

"I'm just sayin'."

"Cade, I'm serious."

"Me too, baby. You come home at night to my bed and leave at an appropriate time in the morning, and I'll do my best."

"Okay." I could do this. Compromise.

"Next."

I took a sip of my wine. "I'm messy, Cade. I leave clothes on the floor and dishes in the sink. It's who I am."

"It's who you *were*."

"It's who I *am*, Cade. And I won't have you bullying me to be someone I'm not. I'll get to my messes. In my time. Not yours. And you'll learn to live with it. I can't have you rolling your eyes every time I leave a sock on the floor."

"You won't be able to see my eyes from your spot in the

corner, baby." He grinned as he stuffed a bite of rice in his mouth.

"Yeah, about that." I waited for him to look at me. "I'm not a child, Cade. You can't put me in time out. I know I let you spank me before. And I won't deny it turned me on. I'll probably let you do it again. It was hot. But standing in a corner doesn't make me warm and fuzzy, Cade. It just makes me feel pissed."

"It's supposed to make you feel pissed, baby. It's to correct behavior."

"And it's reserved for small children, not twenty-four-year-old women. I don't need you to correct my behavior. Are you listening to me?"

He set his fork down. "I'm listening, Amelia. I'm just not sure I agree. Can we come back to this one? Maybe you'd be willing to try it one time? Or maybe you'd be willing to not do anything to earn you a time out in the first place."

I took a deep breath. I could see this was going to be a tough one. "Cade—"

He cut me off. "Leave it, Amelia. Let's come back to that."

"Why?"

He huffed. "Because I'm a Dom, baby. That's why. I dominate. That's what Doms do. And you submit. That's what submissives do. I'm trying to be reasonable, baby. I've agreed, for the most part, to all your other requests, but I feel strongly about this one. When we're at home alone, I want you to bend to my will. It makes me hot, and it makes you horny. That's why we fit together so nicely. If I don't have any means of correcting your behavior, I'm not really a Dom, am I?"

I could see his point. I chewed on my lower lip. "Okay, how about this—I'll let you control me any way you see fit as long as it pertains to our interactions with each other, not my messiness or how the toilet lid is placed, or whether or not my toothbrush makes it to the holder."

"Hmm." He considered my suggestion. "You'll let me put you in time out?"

"I'll consent to one trial time. Use good discretion when choosing it. If I don't like it, I won't do it again."

He paused a moment. "You drive a hard bargain, Ms. Kensington."

"Yep." I resumed eating, stabbing into the same chicken dish he seemed to be enjoying.

"Okay. One time. I choose when and where and for what misdemeanor. Afterward, you don't get to dismiss it so fast. We reopen discussion on this issue."

"Deal."

We finished dinner in companionable silence. The food was good. And surprisingly, we ate more than a reasonable amount.

When we left the table, Cade led me back to the bedroom, stripped his shirt off me, and sat me on the bed. "I need to feel your mouth around me." He slid off his pajama pants and stroked his cock in front of my face.

I wanted that too. My sum total of blow jobs consisted of the one I'd given him months ago. I wanted to taste him again. He spent a lot of time with his mouth pressed to my pussy. It was only fair.

Cade stepped between my legs, and I wrapped my fingers around his hips, drawing him closer. I tentatively stuck my tongue out to taste the come on his slit, feeling the power I wielded when he groaned. The vibrations reverberated through his body, making his cock twitch at my lips. I licked a line down the thick vein along the top of his length and then sucked him into my mouth.

Cade grabbed my shoulders and held me steady.

I leaned closer and sucked him deeper, swirling my tongue around his cock as I thrust on and off. It didn't take long for Cade to stiffen, his entire body rigid beneath my hands and mouth.

When he reached the edge, he grabbed my head and held me to him. He came deep in my mouth while I swallowed him, loving the way he trusted me and seemed to genuinely enjoy my ministrations, experienced or not.

When he pulled out, he leaned my head back, his hand at my neck, and kissed me soundly. "Love that mouth, baby."

I smiled.

"Climb to the center of the bed. I'll be right back." He released me, and I scooted back on my ass.

I was just leaning back when he returned, holding the cuffs he'd bought me—or rather had me run around collecting that first morning of our relationship. I shivered. He'd only used them once, but the memory had kept me up at night. The control he had over me when I lay spread on his bed attached to all corners was heady. I enjoyed giving him that. Immensely. If Cade Alexander needed to tie me down and fuck me to orgasm, I was game.

Cade watched my face as he circled me, attaching first my wrists and then my ankles. "Trust me?" he asked.

"Of course." My voice was hoarse as though I'd been shouting.

Cade opened the drawer on the nightstand and pulled something out. When he held it up for me to see, I flinched. "Have you ever used a vibrator, baby?"

"No, Sir."

He smiled. "I really do get all your firsts, don't I?"

"Apparently, Sir." And this was a huge first.

Cade turned a dial on the side and the dildo came to life, buzzing in his hand. "This won't be like my hands or my mouth, baby. It's much faster to elicit response."

I wasn't sure if that was a good thing or not. I didn't really need faster. I was already horny every time he entered a room.

Cade tapped my nipple with the vibrator, making me buck my chest instantly.

"I think she understands now." He smiled and shifted to the other nipple, making it instantly as hard as its twin. When he applied more pressure, I gritted my teeth. He teased my nipples back and forth, never using the same amount of force.

My knees were wide, my pussy wet. I could feel it dripping down to my ass.

Cade finally left my breasts to lower the dildo to my core. He tapped the hood of my clit first. I moaned, my eyes rolling back in my head. That thing was amazing. He wasn't kidding. I could come a hundred times if he wanted me to. The thought made me roll my head. This was Cade's game. I wouldn't put that idea past him.

When Cade rolled the vibrator lower and pushed it into my pussy, I bucked. "Holy shit, Cade. I can't—"

"You can, baby." He removed the phallus and tapped my nipples again, coating them with my arousal.

The second I had myself under some sort of control, Cade shifted his focus and set the vibrator directly on my clit and held it.

I came so fast, I couldn't stop it. My clit pulsed so many times in rapid succession I wasn't sure I would live through the intensity. And still Cade held the device to my clit until I squirmed to get away.

He released me from his torture, set the vibrator aside, and climbed up my body. His crotch pressed against my sensitive core. He planted his elbows on both sides of my head. "That was gorgeous, baby." He kissed my lips and then nibbled toward my ear. "I love watching you come. Every time it's like you've never experienced it before."

I shivered with his lips pressed to my ear. "Cade, release my arms, honey."

He lifted his face. "Sorry, baby. Wasn't thinking." He reached above me and ripped the Velcro to free my wrists.

I lifted them and wrapped them around his head, burying my fingers in his hair. "Put that thing away. I think I lost brain cells." I giggled.

"No way. I'm gonna use it often."

I rolled my eyes. "Of course you are."

Cade chuckled as he climbed down and released my ankles. I pulled my legs together and rolled to my side. "My limbs forget how to work when you restrain me."

Cade sat beside me and rubbed my arms, shaking them free of the tingles. "I'm gonna go turn off some lights. You need anything?"

"Mmm. Oh, hey, can you grab my phone? I should check my messages."

"Sure. Be right back." Cade padded from the room, his naked ass the best view as his muscles flexed with each step. I was a lucky woman. When he returned moments later, he held my purse. "I assume your phone's in here somewhere. I was afraid to look. If the inside looks anything like your apartment floor, I thought I might get lost."

"Ha ha." I sat up and took my purse from his hands. When I reached inside to rummage for my phone, my hand landed on the envelope Lisa had handed me at the office. I pulled it out. "Forgot about this."

Cade climbed up next to me and settled against the headboard. "What is it, baby?"

"No idea. Lisa said someone left it for me while I was out of the office." I tore it open and pulled out a trifold piece of plain white paper with no company logo. Weird.

I started reading it as Cade set his hand on my thigh. And

then I gasped. "Cade. Shit. What the hell?" I scooted back so he could read it with me.

"What?"

We leaned over the page.

Dear Ms. Kensington,

You don't know me, but I feel the need to reach out to you in hopes you can help me. My name is Luke Milton. I had a brief relationship with a woman you might know, Olivia Grantham, four years ago. We were never married, but I believe she was married at the time to someone you know well, Cade Alexander. Please excuse my interference in your life, but I'm desperately trying to locate Olivia. I've been looking for her for four years. I heard from an acquaintance that she may have paid you a visit some time ago. Perhaps she had a child with her?

I'm confident that child is mine. She disappeared before the birth, and I've never met my daughter. Olivia is a slippery woman. I am not a man with enough means to pay for an ongoing team of private investigators.

If you have any information about her whereabouts, I would really appreciate the help. I have no idea if my source concerning her contact with you is accurate, but I'm running out of options. Hearsay is all I have to go on.

Please contact me any time. And allow me to apologize in advance if I've caused you any anguish.

Thanks in advance for your help,

Luke Milton

Just as I finished reading, Cade grabbed the paper out of my hand and jumped from the bed. "Holy shit."

I was stunned. "Is this the man she was cheating on you with?"

"I assume. I never knew who it was. All I knew was she was fucking some other guy, and I wasn't fucking her anymore. I had her followed and knew she was meeting someone."

"Jesus, Cade. This woman is whacked."

"Don't remind me." He grabbed his flannel pants from the floor and stepped into them. Then he sat back down on the bed and grabbed his phone from the nightstand.

I waited quietly at his side while he made several calls. I assumed he didn't mind me listening in, or he would have left the room. The first call was a heated discussion with Riley. The second was another equally strained conversation with a man I hadn't heard of, Parker. The third must have been to someone he already had looking for Olivia.

Finally, Cade picked up the letter, took a deep breath, and dialed the number at the bottom of the page. I wished I could hear the other end of the line, but I got the gist without, so in the end it didn't matter.

"Hello. Is this Luke Milton?... This is Cade Alexander. I believe you sent a message to my girlfriend earlier today... Yes, she's with me. We just read your letter together... Uh-huh. Right. Oh, trust me, I'm pissed. I'm trying to hold it together, but only by a thread... I understand, Luke, but that doesn't make it okay for you to contact my woman behind my back... Fuck no, I wouldn't have taken a call from you..."

I watched Cade's face closely, holding on to his free arm, hoping my presence would calm him a little. My mind was stuck on him calling me his girlfriend. Cade Alexander, by his own admission, didn't "do girlfriends." My heart beat faster. I wanted to grin, but held it back. Now wasn't the time.

He met my eyes and relaxed his shoulders marginally. "Oh, I get it. I just don't like it... Yes, that's true, that bitch did pay Amelia a visit. Fucked up my life for the last five months too. That crazy slut needs to be locked up... No, I haven't heard from her personally, and Amelia hasn't heard from her since that day either... You're sure the kid is yours...? Fuck no, she isn't mine. My dick was nowhere near that cunt for months before we split... Why? Because I knew she was fucking someone else, that's why. And that someone else was you, asshole... Right... Okay..." Cade rolled his eyes, but his shoulders slumped farther.

I took this as a good sign.

"You're right... Don't I know it... I understand... Of course, if the kid was mine, I'd feel the same way you do... Yes... I already have an investigator looking for her... Yes... Definitely... If I find out anything, I'll let you know..." Cade looked at me. "Yes, I'll tell her...

No, you may not... Good luck with that... Right."

Cade hit the off button and set the phone aside. He ran his fingers through his hair and slumped back against the pillow he'd propped against the headboard. "Jesus that bitch is fucked up." He turned toward me. "Luke sent his apologies for contacting you."

I nodded. Cade could make a rock apologize for being in his path.

Cade scooted down until he was flat.

I settled next to him, setting my cheek on his chest. "You okay?" I whispered.

"Yeah."

A long silence passed. I left Cade alone, knowing he was working things out in his mind. "I just don't get it," he finally said.

"Get what?"

"Why? Why did Olivia show up at my house and con you that day? There has to be a reason. It can't be a coincidence. If she wanted me, why didn't she ever show up after she ran you off? If she wanted money, why didn't she come for it? If she wanted to pawn her kid off on me, again where the fuck did she go?"

I had no answers. I was thinking the same questions.

Suddenly Cade shot upright, causing me to fall off him. He jumped from the bed and began to stomp around the room. "Fuck me. Why didn't I think of this sooner?"

"What, honey?"

"Christine."

"Riley's fiancée?"

"The one and only. It can't be a coincidence that you met Christine the night before *and* managed to ruin her life."

I cringed. I didn't like to think I'd ruined someone's life, but on the other hand, I had saved Riley's, and Christine deserved everything she got. She really was a bitch. "I don't get the connection."

"Christine and Olivia were in the same sorority in college, the same college Riley, Parker, and I attended. That's how we met the girls. Those two girls were thick. I'll bet my last dime they're still in contact."

"And Riley wouldn't know that?"

"Maybe not. I don't pay attention to who you talk to, baby. If you spent two hours talking to your girlfriends, I wouldn't be the wiser."

"True. Do you even know their names?" I grinned, not expecting him to remember.

"Cheyenne and Meagan. Cheyenne's the cute pixie with the blonde hair and deep blue eyes. Meagan is the one with brown curls." He gave me a brief eyebrow lift.

My eyes went wide. "Wow. Impressive."

Cade shrugged. "I pay attention to women. Especially cute ones."

"Hey now..."

"Baby, you're so totally stuck with me. Don't even go there."

I grinned smugly. I knew that. He was equally stuck with me. "Speaking of which, who's Parker?"

"Ah. Parker Darwin. He's another friend of mine and Riley's. We've been friends since we were kids. He works at another technology company in Charlotte, North Carolina, Edgewater Inc."

"I suppose you own that building too," I kidded.

"Yep."

I rolled my eyes. "Of course you do." How the hell had Cade made so much money in ten years?

Cade grabbed his phone again. I knew he was dialing Riley. Who else would he call? "Riley, dude, have you spoken to Christine lately?" Cade held the phone away from his ear.

I could hear Riley shouting at him from my spot on the bed.

When Riley finished his rant, Cade pulled the phone back in close. "Calm the fuck down, man. It was just a question."

I pulled the covers over my chest and piled two pillows on top of each other behind my head to watch the show while Cade explained his theory to Riley that Christine had sent Olivia to make my life miserable.

When they were finished talking, it was clear to me they would be paying a personal visit to Christine early in the morning.

By the time Cade was done shouting back and forth with Riley—most of it in agreement—it was very late. He flipped out the light, climbed into bed, and hauled me against his chest. "Longest day of my life, baby."

"I know. But worth it."

"Totally."

Chapter Twenty-Three

When I woke up the next morning, I was alone again. I could hear the shower running and glanced at the clock. It was early. Way earlier than I would have liked to face the day. I lay back down and waited for Cade to return from the bathroom. No way I would fall back asleep, but I could at least stay warm and covered. The thought of stepping under running water made me burrow deeper.

Ten minutes later, Cade tiptoed quietly into the room.

"I'm awake, honey."

He came to me and sat on the side of the bed. He wore dress pants and was buttoning up a starched white shirt. "I'm sorry if I woke you, baby." He leaned over to kiss me. "Go back to sleep."

"Not gonna happen. Too late." He set my hand on this thigh and squeezed. "Where are you going?"

"Meeting Riley at six to go pay Christine a visit before she can possibly leave her house this morning."

"'K. Be careful."

"I will, baby. I don't think she's dangerous. Just a bitch."

"There's a lot of that going around."

"True enough." He kissed my forehead this time and lifted off the bed. "Arthur will take you to work. I put his number in your phone. Just send him a text when you're ready to go."

"Okay. Call me when you have a chance."

"Will do." Cade left the room, shutting the door behind him with a soft snick.

I closed my eyes for several minutes and then dragged myself out of bed. As long as I was awake, I might as well get the show on the road. I had a ton of work on my desk.

By seven o'clock I called Arthur, apologized for it being so early, and met him downstairs. He smiled warmly when I apologized again. "No worries, Amy slash Lillie," he teased with a wink. "I'm used to weird hours. Seven in the morning is nothing, doll."

I was the first one to arrive on my floor by a longshot and was on my second cup of coffee with a better handle of everything on my desk before Cade showed up. He leaned his handsome self against the doorjamb and grinned from ear to ear.

I smiled. "Talk to me."

He came in and took a seat across from me. "Well, here's what we know. That crazy bitch Christine did in fact call Olivia and send her to fuck with you after Riley broke off their engagement. Even without telling her why he was dumping her ass, she figured you had a hand in it."

"Why did Olivia take the bait?"

"Money." He grinned broader. "Apparently that crazier

bitch, crazier than Christine anyway, ran through every dime she'd squeezed out of me and her entire inheritance in less than four years. She readily took money from Christine in exchange for paying you a visit."

"That's fucked up."

"Oh, it gets worse. Christine bragged about her accomplishment to everyone she knew. And that included a college acquaintance who also knew Luke. Her name is Kim. That woman was slightly less insane and called Luke to tell him what had happened to you. He didn't even know if you were still with me, but he got another call from Kim yesterday, informing him that you were working in this building under an alias."

"Jesus." Talk about being followed.

"Yeah, makes you kinda cringe, right?"

"How did Christine know I was here? Riley didn't even know."

"Christine has been stalking Riley. She follows him everywhere. She saw you coming and going. She was in the process of plotting more shit against you. And she bragged about that to the wrong person again. Kim called Luke. Luke sent you that letter. And we nailed Christine's ass to the ground."

"How did you get her to talk?"

"That was easy. She needed money too. Without Riley, she's also hard up for cash, at least the amount of cash she thinks she must have to live." He rolled his eyes.

"You *paid* her?" I almost screamed that last word.

"Fuck no. But we said we would. We forced her to admit everything she knew and then left her screaming her fucking head off that we didn't hold up to our end of the bargain."

"Is she stupid?"

"Clearly."

"So, any chance you found out where Olivia is from Christine?"

Cade beamed. "The police are arresting her as we speak."

I smiled. "And the kid?"

"Hopefully I can pull some strings and get her to her father as soon as possible. She'll have to go into the system for a few days, but a paternity test will prove Luke the rightful dad. And with the amount of evidence that Olivia intentionally kept her from her father, he'll surely get custody. That's all he wanted."

I blew out a breath and then lifted my gaze as Riley entered the room. "I totally owe you again, don't I?"

"Yep."

"What are you two talking about?" Cade asked.

Riley chuckled. "Private inside joke."

"You have a private inside joke with my woman?"

Now I laughed. "Don't get your panties in a wad, big guy. At the end of the day, you get the prize."

"I better," he grumbled.

Riley slapped him on the back. "You found a good woman, Cade. If only I could be so lucky."

"Now that you're moving to Atlanta, I have connections," I teased.

Cade looked up at Riley. "She does have cute friends. One of them is just your type."

Riley backed off with his hands up. "Do *not* fucking set me up with a woman. I've sworn off women entirely." He turned to face me. "No offense. Maybe it's just rich snooty women. Do you have any regular middle-class friends without a stick up their asses?"

"As a matter of fact, I do."

Riley turned and walked out of the office chuckling. "Not gonna happen, guys, but thanks for the thought."

Chapter Twenty-Four

"You sure that's everything?" I stepped back from the doorway to let Cade pass. He held the last of the many boxes we'd packed up at my apartment that morning.

"Woman, I don't know how on earth you had that much stuff in that little space."

"I like clothes." I shrugged.

He dropped the box and turned to pull me to his front as I let the door shut.

Riley's apartment was spectacular. Downtown Nashville with an awesome view on three sides. I thought we got the better end of the deal in the house swap.

Cade pulled my hair back so I was forced to look up.

"You have too many clothes. Who needs all that?" A smile curved the edges of his mouth.

"Hardly. You have more dress shirts than I have skirts, big guy."

"Then I guess we'll have to go shopping. You have four days off next weekend for Thanksgiving. Did you plan to visit your parents?"

I stared at him, warmth filling my chest. How had I gotten so lucky? "No. I knew it would be too tight after starting a new job. I planned to see them at Christmas. Guess I better warn them to make space for two." I smiled at him.

"Guess you better. And we should plan on spending a few days with my family too. My sisters are gonna kill me for keeping you from them."

"That sounds ominous."

He shrugged. "I'll protect you."

I wasn't sure I liked the sound of that. If I needed protection against his siblings...

Cade glanced around at all the boxes. "You gonna put all this shit away, or is it going to sit next to the front door in boxes for weeks on end?"

I shrugged. "Most of it's wrinkle-free."

Cade narrowed his gaze. "Are you sassing me, baby?" He backed me up until I hit the back of the couch.

"Never."

He reached for the hem of my shirt and pulled it over my head. Next, he popped my bra and dropped it to join my shirt on the couch. Lastly, he grabbed the sides of my yoga pants and wiggled them down my body. "I don't get these pants you women wear. What's the point again?"

"They're comfortable. And you know they're sexy, so don't even try to fool me."

"I don't like pants at all," he grumbled.

"And yet, it would be awkward for me to run around town naked."

Cade met my gaze again, a slow grin spreading wider. "You're sassing me again."

"Never," I repeated. I knew I was pressing his every button, but I couldn't help myself. He clearly wanted to play. Who was I to stop him?

Cade lowered his face to mine and took my lips. We stood there so long in that kiss, I lost track of time. He made my entire body come alive. By the time he broke free, I was panting.

"You wet, baby?"

"Yes, Sir." He knew I was.

Cade reached between my legs and stroked one finger through my folds.

I was more than wet. I was totally ready for him. I hoped he didn't make me wait.

Cade released my pussy and lifted his finger to his mouth. He sucked it clean, moaning around it as though it were a delicacy. And then he took me by the shoulders and walked with me across the spectacular great room until we reached the corner next to the hallway that led to the bedrooms.

I thought he was going to press me into the wall and hopefully fuck me right there. We hadn't had sex against a wall yet.

I was mistaken. Realization dawned fast when he turned me around and pressed me forward into the corner. Heat rose up my body. "Cade," I whispered. I wasn't at all sure I was ready for this game.

"You knew this was coming, baby." He soothed my back as he arranged me the way he wanted. "Spread your legs farther apart."

I stepped out tentatively. "You said you wouldn't punish me for being messy."

"I'm not punishing you for being messy, baby. I'm punishing you for sassing me." He turned my face to the wall and nudged my head gently. "Nose to the corner. Nipples to the walls."

Wetness filled my pussy unexpectedly, making me whimper. This wasn't supposed to happen.

"That's my girl." He stroked my head. "Concentrate on your tits touching the walls and your pussy dripping between your legs while I ignore you." His hand smoothed down my back until he gripped my butt cheek and squeezed. "If you can stand really still and not complain for ten minutes, I'll release you."

I held my breath. Holy mother of God. I was aroused. How was that possible? And did I want him to have that sort of ammunition?

My decision was taken from me when Cade suddenly reached between my legs and stroked two fingers through my folds. "Shit, baby," he whispered as he stepped back. "You leave me with no way to punish you if standing in a corner naked arouses you. I'm going to have to get creative."

I liked the sound of that. Creative was a good thing. At least I thought so...

"I'm going to pour a nice glass of wine. If you can stand still without moving for those ten minutes, you might get to have a sip before it gets warm." He chuckled as he walked away.

I fidgeted, unsure I could actually endure ten minutes of this. It wasn't at all what I had expected. I didn't feel ignored in the slightest as I'd feared. Nope. I knew Cade was behind me somewhere, staring at my naked backside, his cock at least as hard as my pussy was wet.

He may have thought this was a good punishment, but I was sure he suffered right alongside me.

Epilogue

Four months later...

I leaned over the best pork rib I'd ever eaten and took another bite. There was sure to be sauce on my face and running down my chin, but I didn't care.

It was early April, and I was just glad it was warm enough out to have this party outdoors.

Cade sat next to me, straddling the bench seat, one corner of his mouth lifted in an indulgent smile.

"What?" I asked around the bite in my mouth.

"Nothing." He leaned forward and kissed my forehead, the only safe place he could avoid getting barbeque sauce on him. His face remained close. "I love you."

I set my rib down on the plate and wiped my lips with my napkin. "That works out splendidly. I'd hate to think all these people came here to celebrate our engagement and you didn't even love me." I grinned.

"Always so snarky."

A shadow drew my attention to the other side of the picnic table as Riley lifted his leg over the seat and plopped down. "Nice engagement party, Amy." It had taken some convincing, but eventually I'd managed to talk both Riley and Parker into calling me Amy. Cade was stubborn. I doubted he would ever call me anything but Amelia. "So much more relaxed than the wild fiasco my crazy ex arranged."

I laughed. I knew Riley was still getting over Christine. Well, perhaps it wasn't quite accurate to say he was getting over her, but rather the damage she'd left behind. He certainly wasn't mooning after her. He also wasn't ready to jump back in the swing of things, either.

"Any new news about Christine?" Cade asked.

Riley shook his head. "She moved back to Virginia last I heard. Probably needed daddy's money to support her expensive tastes."

Cheyenne walked up to the table next. I watched her as she approached from behind Riley. Her eyes were a bit wider than usual, and her face was bright. "Hey," she said as she took a seat next to Riley. "You must be Riley."

Riley turned to face her. "I am. You must be Cheyenne."

My friend beamed. I was probably the only one who noticed, but she clearly found Riley interesting. In fact, she leaned her chin on her hand and smiled at him. I'd known for months this would be the case as soon as Cheyenne met Riley. However, Cheyenne had very little clue about my submissive relationship with Cade behind closed doors. Nor would she realize Riley had the same tendencies. Cade had confirmed my suspicions in this arena.

His other friend, Parker, also manifested a dominant nature. I'd met him several times by then, and he was due to show up at our party any moment.

My parents were throwing this party in their back yard. I was glad so many of my friends and Cade's had made the trip to LaGrange. It made my mom and dad happy to be a part of our happiness, and Cade had been more than willing to travel the distance for a chance to hang out with my dad.

Ever since the two of them had met at Christmas and Cade had charmed the pants off my parents, Cade and Dad had become friends. They'd bonded over sports and beer, which had shocked me initially since I'd rarely seen Cade drink anything besides wine. Apparently he was also a connoisseur of beer.

I smiled at my man as he took another drink from his bottle. This was a barbeque. There was beer. And everyone seemed to be enjoying it.

Riley turned back to Cade and me. "Heard from Parker?"

Cade shook his head. "Not yet. He'll be here. His flight didn't land until four. It'll take him a while to get down here."

Cheyenne spoke up next. "Ah, the infamous Parker."

Riley chuckled. "Yeah, once he gets his charismatic self here, I'll be chopped liver." He set his hands on the table and pushed to standing. "I'd better grab another drink and find a quiet corner to drown my sorrows in before Parker comes and charms the socks off all the women in attendance."

Cheyenne's eyes went wide. "Seriously? You must be joking? There's no way you'll be able to convince me someone could one-up you in any department."

I was shocked at Cheyenne for being so outgoing and flirty. I was also glad. Riley paused to stare down at her, a grin spreading across his face. "Fantastic. Someone has fallen for my charm. Grab a beer with me, and maybe I'll get you tipsy enough to dance with me later after Parker swoops in."

"I'd love to." Cheyenne stood and grabbed Riley's bicep as they headed toward the coolers.

"Oh Lord. That can't be good," Cade muttered.

"Why not?" I glanced at him. "You don't think they make the perfect couple," I teased. They were so far from similar it was uncanny.

"Not even close." He leaned in and kissed my nose. "But then again, you and I weren't exactly on the same page when we met either, and look at us now." He reached for the necklace I wore and fingered the figure eight at my neck. Cade had replaced the necklace soon after we'd gotten back together. And he often teased me by checking to make sure it was still around my neck and some crazy person hadn't come along and yanked it free.

We could finally joke about Olivia. What else was there to do? The woman's life was a sad disaster of her own making. She'd lost custody of her daughter, who was thriving under her father's care. Not that I figured Olivia gave a fuck about Libby. She'd shown not one ounce of love for the child the only time I'd met her. I still didn't understand why she hadn't given custody to Luke in the first place instead of lying about her parentage for four years. It hadn't done her any good. Neither Luke, whom we were occasionally in communication with, nor anyone else had heard from Olivia in months. It was rumored she was living with Christine in Virginia. Just as well. They deserved each other.

Cade still fingered my infinity necklace as I reached for the beer in his hand and took a drink. "I have fond memories of the day I put this on you."

I shivered. "I have not-so-fond memories of standing in a corner while you teased me mercilessly for way too long, not allowing me to look at what you had planned behind me."

"Yeah, well, I had a fantastic view of your ass during that arrangement."

"And I had a less-than-fantastic view of the wall."

Cade chuckled. "I made it up to you with the ring though, didn't I?" He released my neck and grabbed my hand to finger the giant diamond.

My belly turned to mush. He'd made up for it in spades.

I'd come home from work that day, a month ago, and found three boxes on the kitchen table. A smile had lit my face immediately as I remembered the first three boxes Cade had gotten me. At least this time, he hadn't sent me to pick up my own presents.

It never dawned on me he was about to propose. Cade had made me spend the entire evening earning those gifts. And I'd worked hard for them. My face flushed when I thought about our antics. I kneeled beside him during dinner, dressed in my work clothes. When he was pleased with my obedience, he'd given me the first box, a sheer negligée that made my fingers shake just picking it up out of the box.

After putting it on, I spent some time on my knees in front of Cade, thanking him appropriately for the present.

That had earned me the second box, my first pair of nipple clamps. I cringed thinking about the first time he put them on me. I'd lifted the negligée above my breasts and held it for him while he applied the dainty clamps to each nipple. The sheer material of my sexy new apparel rubbed against the tips of my breasts with every move I made.

My gratitude for that gift was demonstrated by holding my legs open so that Cade could tease my pussy for over half an hour without letting me come.

When he finally took pity on me and let me tip over the edge, I was still panting from exhaustion as he slid the diamond over my finger. I didn't open that last box myself. Cade had been too anxious to wait. He'd torn into the box from the jeweler himself while I caught my breath. Before I knew what was happening, the ring was in place and Cade was between my legs, pushing the negligée up my body and releasing the clamps.

I yelped as each one was removed and the blood flowed freely back to my nipples. And then I lifted my hand to my face. "Cade?"

"Yeah, baby."

"Did you have anything you wanted to ask me?"

"Did you like the clamps?" he teased.

I licked my lips, staring at the giant rock on my left hand. "I did. Anything else?" I peered at him between my fingers.

He grinned. "Will you marry me, Amelia?"

My smile spread wide. That had been the happiest moment of my life.

Cade jerked me back to the present. "What'cha thinking?"

"How lucky I am." I glanced down at the ring that still shocked me every time I saw it.

"I'm pretty sure the luck is all mine," he said as he lifted my fingers to his mouth and kissed them all one at a time.

I figured it was best to let him believe that for as long as possible. "I love you, Cade Alexander."

"I love you too, Amelia Amy Lillie Kingston Kensington."

I laughed. "Is that the closest I'm ever going to get to hearing my name from your lips?"

"Yep. You'll always be Amelia to me." He kissed me soundly, not caring one bit who might be watching as he claimed my lips and let his tongue slip into my mouth. His hand snaked behind my back and pressed me closer.

I knew one thing for sure. I was indeed the luckier party. And I would spend my life making sure Cade thought the luck was all his.

The end

About the Author

Becca Jameson lives in Atlanta, GA, with her husband and two kids. After years of editing, she is now a full-time author. With over 25 best-selling books written, she has dabbled in a variety of genres, ranging from paranormal to contemporary to BDSM. She loves chatting with fans, so feel free to contact her through email, Facebook, or her website.

…where Alphas dominate…

Beccajameson.com
becccajameson4@aol.com
https://www.facebook.com/becca.jameson.18

More Books by Becca Jameson

The Wolf Masters:

Kara's Wolves

Lindsey's Wolves

Jessica's Wolves

Alyssa's Wolves

Tessa's Wolf

The Fight Club:

Come

Perv

Need

Hers (coming February 2015)

Lust (coming April 2015)

Want (coming June 2015)

The Wolf Gatherings:

Tarnished

Dominated

Completed

Redeemed

Abandoned

Betrayed

Durham Wolves:

Rescue in the Smokies

Fire in the Smokies

Freedom in the Smokies

Emergence:

Bound to be Taken

Bound to be Tamed

Bound to be Tested (Coming January 2015)

Bound to be Tempted (Coming April 2015)

Stand-Alone Stories:

Blind with Love

Deceptive Liaison

Out of the Smoke

Awakening Abduction

Three's a Cruise

Wolf Trinity

Frostbitten

Coming Soon:

The Art of Kink written with Paige Michaels:

Pose

Paint

Nude

Sculpt